808 LON
$1

Daborah
you helped me
and taught me
so much!
God Bless you
Samantha
aka
Elaine

Chimpanzee Voices

A Stranger In A Culture of Chimpanzees

M00069174

Sam Struthers Ph.D.

Copyright © 2013 Sam Struthers Ph.D.

All rights reserved.

ISBN-10: 149376988X
ISBN-13: 9781493769889

TABLE OF CONTENTS

Author's Note & Dedication

All of the characters in this novel are entirely the product of my imagination: none of them are meant to bear any resemblance to any persons living or dead or to any of the actual people who currently hold or in the past have held positions at any chimpanzee research facility or oversight agency. The use of chimpanzees in research is a real situation, and of course there really have been sites and programs where chimpanzees were used for biomedical research, space and flight research, and pharmacological research with real toxicologists, virologists, and animal care staff attending them and actual government agencies which provide oversight for the care and use of them. However, all of the characters in *this* novel are entirely the product of my imagination. This book is a creative work of storytelling. The human characters, entities and places in the story and their names are fictional.

I'd like to thank everyone who helped to bring this piece of work to life, and everybody who ever did anything kind, generous, or thoughtful for me. Especially I dedicate this book to my beautiful children: Thea, Jason, Lestat, Magdalena, and Zeppelin, and the rest of my awesome family including my brothers and Dr. & Mrs. Struthers (who are the intellect and the artist who engineered my eccentricities). I also want to gratefully acknowledge the family of Maria Alonso, the Arnold & Baca families, and my friends Malcolm McCollum, Barb Thacker,

Lawrene, and the *many, many* others who helped me along my pilgrimage and also those who have helped captive chimpanzees through small acts of great love. This fictional account is dedicated to chimpanzees who have been held in captive settings and for research at any time or in any place in this world, and to those people who have really tried to care for them.

Frequently Used Acronyms

PRC	Primate Research Center (location of the story)
HIV	Human Immunodeficiency Virus
SIV	Simian Immunodeficiency Virus
NHHS	National Human Health Service
NEPA	National Environmental Protection Act
AWA	Animal Welfare Act (a legislative mandate governing the care and use of animals in retail, commercial, and research endeavors)
CDC	Center for Disease Control
CNS	Central Nervous System
SDB	Self-directed Behavior
SIB	Self-injurious Behavior
USDA	United States Department of Animal Culture

One

From Farm To Monkey House : A Visit That Started An Odyessy Of Ten Years

We came to a small corner of hell carved out of the Chihuahua desert as a sort of retreat from a noiseless and somewhat anti-climactic divorce. Seeking something non-mid-western, not *normal* in the middle class American sense of things, I had chosen to take my daughter and go to graduate school on the border of Mexico. On the border of all my previous experiences and expectations of what my grown up life was supposed to be like. I felt that if I flung myself hard enough against the borders of these two countries I would also be throwing myself against the fences of my own reality, breaking them down to catch a glimpse of something astonishing that lay beyond the known universe. And I did, too.

We lived at first in a rambling adobe farm-house in a quaint Southwestern village. It wasn't much of a farm by most standards, certainly no more than a quarter of an acre, but to my daughter and me it was the globe. We rented our rooms on the farm from the elderly occupants, Martina, and her husband, Sandoval Seville, who was bedridden. All our living arrangements I made with Sandoval, who translated them to Martina, since she spoke no English and I had yet to learn the rudiments of Spanish.

Sandoval used to hide hard candy under his mattress and when children and grandchildren came for a visit, he would throw pieces at them when they weren't looking. If he was accused of throwing the candy he would proclaim it an act of Santo Nino de Atocha, the child saint who succored prisoners and the ill and usually manifested coins. The Sevilles had also peopled the farmhouse with statues of St. Ramon, a particular favorite of Martina's since he protected women and children. Half the descending generations in Sandoval's family were named *Ramon* or *Ramona* after this saint. There were candles continuously burning in the house to honor these saints and I frequently encountered Martina deep in discussion with one or the other of them.

My five-year-old daughter, Nikki (short for Veronica), and I had come to live on the farm because I was attending a nearby University as an anthropology student working on an advanced degree. My research topics were traditional healing practices and midwifery in the Mexican-American border region. I was looking forward to a great adventure and to immersing myself in an unfamiliar culture in true anthropologist style. I was sure I would emerge with a thesis, a degree, and a great offer for a professorship on some collegial, tree-lined campus somewhere. I could envision myself ending my academic career among brownstone and mortar edifices, attending ceremonies in my medieval black robes in between showering illuminating doctrine upon the young and carefully honed intellects of potential scientists that entered through the doors of my classroom. In the mean time all I had to do was take a lot of notes and explain the phenomena I observed in scientifically critical terms that clarified the systemic relations between human behavior and phenomenological outcomes. It was sure to be a snap since I had a gift for gab and had always been a quick study in school.

When we moved to the farm, Nikki defined her own project by immediately taking command of the abandoned rabbit hutches. She demanded breeding stock and started the first in her series of small business ventures with rabbit farming. She was very successful at this, the rabbits being cooperative by nature, and produced quite a nice hybrid from a large English lop-ear buck and a Russian blue dam (Henry and Rebecca).

When the infant rabbits were about 5 weeks old, Nikki would carry them in a box to the village plaza where she set up shop on a park bench. The combination of her crooked-lettered sign, her preternaturally large brown eyes and the toy-like rabbit babies was apparently enough to perpetuate a buying frenzy, because Nikki always returned home with plenty of cash and no rabbits. She made her customers solemnly swear that the rabbits were to be used as pets only and not to be eaten, which they did with every affect of seriousness that belied the steaming soup pot I was sure waited at home. At five dollars per bunny, she covered all her out-of-pocket expenses with plenty left over to squander at the village store. Once, upon returning from a market excursion, Nikki discovered that the highly efficient and reliable Rebecca had produced another litter during her absence. And so, her business prospered.

With Nikki thus preoccupied, and Martina available to care for her at all hours, I was somewhat at leisure to pursue my midwifery research. I was involved in my first semester of coursework during the day but had obtained an apprenticeship with a *partera*, or traditional midwife, during other times. This is when I first learned that the hour an infant finds most convenient to be born is generally the most inconvenient time for everyone else. I answered many a midnight call, and as often as not it was for false labor.

I began attending births regularly. I had worked previously as a medical assistant and I proved useful as an extra pair of hands for the *partera*. As a dutiful anthropologist, I used the long stretches of waiting during each labor to write out my notes. Anthropology dubs this kind of ethnographic work "participant observation." That indicated that although I had a participant role in the birth event, I was also an observer. To be both the participant and the observer I had to discipline myself to watch everything each person did, be responsive to the *partera*, and write it all down as soon as I had a chance. I was usually the busiest person at each birth (except for mom and baby). I little realized at the time how useful this observational practice would be later when I came to work with chimpanzees whose language consisted in such large part of subtle gestures and expressions.

Being a participant observer allowed me a certain invisibility. I was like a piece of furniture. This made people less aware of me as an observer and kept attention focused on the event at hand. Later, when I became enrichment director for several hundred chimps, I often found myself largely ignored while the chimps concentrated on various toy and food items I gave them. This allowed me plenty of uninterrupted and unmolested time to watch them. My learned ability to be invisible and my lack of need to be engaged interactively with others during activities and events made my presence more acceptable to both humans and chimpanzees as they carried out the rituals of importance in their lives.

I diligently wrote out my notes, attended births, and read text after text relevant to my research on parturition. The second semester of my graduate work began. I was supposed to be writing my thesis proposal based on my field notes. While I had produced many fine ethnographic portraits of the home births I was attending, I couldn't bring a relevant thesis statement into focus. I just couldn't envision any practical or beneficial application at the outcome of my project. I wanted to have a mission, to produce something that I deeply felt would benefit someone else. I was wondering how I would illumine my future students when everything I had accomplished seemed rather ordinary and uninspired, and completely without pertinence to a more universal insight to human behavior. I finally decided to express my concerns to my major professor, Dr. Rosedale.

We were engaged in a very circular discussion about my data as it related to the overall body of theory on bipedal evolution. I was feeling increasingly frustrated because I couldn't see any real link between my apprenticeship and something as grandiose as a 'body of theory'. I was beginning to feel like a real intellectual plain-jane (this is a feeling that, in the presence of the many great scientific minds I have met in the intervening years, I have never lost). At approximately the height of our repetitive dialogue, the phone rang. I remember thinking; "thank goodness, saved by the bell!" This proved to be the case, and in retrospect proved how seemingly inconsequential coincidences can have the most profound effect upon the course of our lives.

I sat across the desk from Dr. Rosedale, idly fingering a little stone monkey statue she had picked up on a field trip to Malaysia. Dr. Rosedale was a physical anthropologist and one of her subfields was primatology. I had given little thought to primatology during my anthropology curriculum, except for answering a few questions on my entrance exams about banana box experiments by Menzel, and something about human and ape DNA being less than two percent different. I sat there with a blank mind, toying with the statue, unlike most graduate students who would certainly have used the same opportunity for idle thought to silently recite the theory of relativity forward and backward. While practicing my most intelligent "engaged in serious thought" expression, I eavesdropped on the half of the phone conversation I could hear.

That half actually proved quite interesting. Apparently, Dr. Rosedale's reputation as a primatologist was well known. A Dr. Greenspan had called her in search of a graduate student who might be interested in becoming his research assistant for a breeding project he was developing with great apes. Dr. Greenspan was the director of the Primate Research Center (PRC) situated nearby. Originally PRC had been part of a large military research program. It was now a university-affiliated, non-military remnant colony used for various biomedical research endeavors. My professor ended the conversation by saying that she had absolutely no students with any interest in primatology projects. If I didn't leap out of my chair when she hung up, I certainly felt like I did.

"*I'm* interested in doing that!" I blurted out as soon as the phone hit the cradle.

"*You!* I thought you had a project and an area of specialty, which *isn't* primatology."

"Well, I could at least talk to the guy? Maybe comparing chimp and human births would be a good approach to my thesis. After all, with the very little difference in our genetic make-up, say...about 1.3 %, it might make an interesting comparison. Something that could be used to develop a model about evolutionary trends in birth behaviors." I ad-libbed, trying to look owlish and informed, pulling ideas from titles on the neat line of book spines that filled the wall behind Dr. Rosedale's head. I was hoping to garner some enthusiasm from the usually skeptical Dr. Rosedale so I could take Nikki to go see some monkeys.

"I don't think it's *really* quite what you might think. It's a biomedical research facility and it's located on a military base, miles from everything. The animals aren't in natural settings and they're all used for experimentation." She still sounded skeptical, but I thought she was looking at me in a way that indicated she was trying to gauge how much I *did* actually know about chimpanzees. There is always something so convincing about quoting numbers, I reflected.

"Is the facility near here?" I persisted.

"Oh well, pretty close- at least within a hundred miles. I *don't* think you'd want that drive."

I don't know if was a deliberate ploy on Dr. Rosedale's part, but the more she argued against the idea, the more determined I became to pursue it. I was intrigued that there could be any great apes at all in the sparsely populated Southwestern outback. I found it even more curious that a colony of hundreds of apes could be within a few hours drive, and yet its existence was essentially unknown to the local populace. Captivated, I pled with my professor until I finally wore her down. With a sigh indicating that I was probably following an intellectual tangent that would serve no purpose other than to delay my committee meeting date even further, she caved in to my demands. Reluctantly and with none of the enthusiasm I had hoped for, she called Dr. Greenspan and set up an appointment for me to visit PRC the next week.

At the time of my first visit, PRC housed about 200 common chimpanzees, nearly 800 macaque monkeys of two subspecies (*Macaca mulatta* and *Macaca fascicularis*), more than 100 squirrel monkeys, and a couple of baboons. I longed for just one glimpse of the chimpanzees. I don't think I was even seriously contemplating taking the position;

I was mostly playing tourist. I was so unfamiliar with chimps that I imagined them to be much like Cheetah from the old Tarzan movies. I envisioned them as small and playful, capable of numerous tricks, and, of course, obedient to human command. I took Nikki along with me, hoping she would get to see the little acrobats.

The rules in a biomedical research facility disallow children from almost anywhere but the lobby. This is an excellent practice because of the disease factor and the danger of injury. Most laboratory chimpanzees have been inoculated with variants of hepatitis, many others with HIV. Monkeys carry hazardous and deadly diseases even if they have not been inoculated with anything. Monkeys and apes are often portrayed in the media as cuddly and cute, but in reality they require a lot of personal space and can be quite fierce and dangerous when they are imposed upon.

While I discussed the potential project with Dr. Greenspan, Nikki had to sit in the lobby amusing the receptionist. Dr. Greenspan possessed the natural gentility and telltale accent of a European. I learned later that he was Austrian. After our interview, he offered us lunch in his office. Vienna sausages out of the can, cheese crackers, and orange soda pop.

Before Nikki and I left, Dr. Greenspan took us to a little outdoor viewing window which looked into the chimpanzee nursery. The window had been placed specifically for visitors. The chimpanzee babies were everything one could hope for. They wore frilled baby dresses and little denim overalls, they had toy fire trucks and yellow rubber ducks. A visitor seeing these young chimps sitting on the laps of their human caretakers and hugging them could easily return home with a fond picture of benevolent research and a reaffirmed notion that all chimps were, indeed, like Cheetah. If I had declined Dr. Greenspan's offer to become his research assistant, I might well still hold that happy picture in my mind instead of being plagued with a slew of existential questions.

I accepted the offer. I thought the project very similar to what I was already doing. Perhaps I could compare information from chimpanzees with the notes I had already collected. My assignment was to observe chimpanzee mothers after birth. I was to determine if there were any behavioral differences between mothers that became fertile again immediately after birth and those who did not. I would conduct three observations a day, three days a week until the semester ended. During summer I would be on staff full-time. Each observation session would last two hours with twenty-minute breaks. When I started this schedule in March, I did not realize how long and uncomfortable the days would become by July, when temperatures regularly soared to 105.

During my first summer I often met with Dr. Greenspan to discuss my progress. I learned that he was becoming increasingly interested in social behavior. His original field was endocrinology, but he was pushing his own boundaries and wanted to contribute to a developing body of socioendocrinological research. We also had several long discussions about environmental enrichment, a new area of study that was of increasing concern to animal research organizations. Environmental enrichment was becoming an important issue in the animal industry largely because of modifications in the animal welfare act (AWA), a piece of federal legislation that governed the care and use of captive animals. At the time I first came to PRC the AWA was being modified to include more stringent guidelines to ensure the psychological well-being of non-human primates. The continuing evolution of this legislation to this day is a cultural phenomenon that reflects our constantly changing societal philosophy about our relationship to the animals we use for a variety of commercial and educational enterprises.

Dr. Greenspan had been in the primatology business long enough to realize the new regulations would lead to dramatic changes in chimpanzee husbandry. He knew the time had come to initiate changes at the center. I'm grateful that he pushed his dubious young graduate student to explore environmental enrichment. He said on more than one occasion that primate enrichment could become a lifetime career, given the trends he foresaw. With his guidance, I began to use my extra time to research and develop enrichment approaches for the center. This was and remained a daunting task that often left me feeling overwhelmed and ineffectual.

I agreed to work with Dr. Greenspan with no notion that I would find myself still there ten years later and my destiny inextricably bound up with that of the chimpanzees. I often refer to my years at PRC as my three tours of duty, because I left my position twice, never intending to return. Yet like one of those crazy marbles that I had seen at a toy- shop, constantly wobbling its way toward the magnetic wand, I returned to PRC. During my two hiatuses I was certain I would never again wish to work in a laboratory with captive chimpanzees. Yet both times the pull of the chimpanzee personality and their great need for support to increase the quality of their incarcerated lives drew me back.

My first tour began with the birth project. This project would keep me involved for the next 18 months. I was provided additional support in my project from a professor emeritus who had retired from the department of human biochemistry. Dr. McGuiness was working with Dr. Greenspan to carry out a project related to stress hormones. He had worked in chemical laboratories his entire life and was over seventy. He and his assistant, Imelda, a short chubby lady with hair like a dark cloud and the eyes of a gazelle, would help me place trays under the chimp cages to collect urine. From these samples we would measure hormones related to pregnancy and stress.

In addition to the birth project, Dr. Greenspan wanted me to design various enrichment strategies for both monkeys and chimpanzees, collecting hormone samples to measure stress levels affected by enrichment. Enriching really meant altering the environment in some way that made it more interesting and interactive for the chimps. The result should enhance their well-being, leading to a better quality of life overall. This would be especially so for a number of chimps with psychological problems and related self-directed behaviors including hair pulling, self-biting and scratching, and other kinds of severe self-injury. Presumably, measuring the shifting levels of stress hormone would reflect improvements in psychological well-being.

After the birth project was completed and I had graduated with my Master's degree in biological anthropology, I began seeking a job in the health field, thinking to leave primates behind. I tried various roles, including bereavement counselor at a hospice, forensic archaeologist, and college instructor in a prison. Although I didn't intend to work with chimpanzees in a research setting again, I eventually accepted a position as a research assistant at a primate research center located in the deep South. The facility had an outstanding enrichment department. I decided it was time I settled down and got my Ph.D.

Just as I had gotten used to my new position, Dr. Greenspan contacted me and offered me a doctoral fellowship to return to PRC to extend the birth project and expand enrichment efforts. So Nikki and I packed it up and headed back to the farm, our rented U-haul trailer weaving along behind our orange station wagon as we crossed west Texas with all of our earthly belongings. Nikki spent the trip writing up a magazine quality review of various children's playgrounds along the route and making a list of the new animals we would have to add to the farm once we returned. Topping her list were Polish hens, which she referred to as *chickens with a hairdo*. My mental animal list was filled with the old chimpanzee friends I was going to revisit and all the many new enrichment ideas I was bringing back from the other institute. I believed that this would be a great opportunity to implement all of the new enrichment techniques I had learned. So began my second tour of duty. This tour lasted for three years, saw several administrative upheavals, and finally yielded my Ph.D.

After that, and some political unpleasantness at the center, I again decided to strike out on my own. I worked as a free-lance anthropologist analyzing skeletal remains from archaeology sites. I finally landed a corporate job in environmental engineering and federal compliance under the National Environmental Protection Act (NEPA). I maintained contact with my human acquaintances at PRC and every once in a while they made a job offer to entice me back. Eventually I was pulled back like the unresisting magnetic marble. I found that once enchanted by chimpanzees it was impossible to leave them out of one's calculations about the future. Upon my third return I was promised greater support and supervisory capacity over an independent behavioral sciences division under PRC's new corporate ownership. The AWA had by this time become fully enforceable law, creating a greater need for enrichment activities at all primate facilities. I saw this as the long-awaited chance to implement a strong enrichment program and establish increasingly humane husbandry practices. I returned full of high hopes and confidence to PRC and began my final tour of duty at the center.

I once read that the thirteenth Dalai Lama indicated the place in which his incarnation would be reborn by leaving his boots in a nearby monastery. Taking my cue from the Dalai Lama, each time I left the center, I would leave my boots tucked away neatly. When I returned each time I found my same leather and blue rubber boots waiting for me.

Upon my third incarnation as the enrichment professional at PRC, I actually found my entire office still intact and my shoes waiting in the same attitude I had left them when I last stepped out of them. The chalkboard I had always used as a daily planner remained unerased. The activities I had planned for each day were written in colored chalk exactly as I had left them, and the dates on the board were for the same week of two years prior. I had the uncanny feeling of being caught in a time warp. When I visited the chimps I realized that for them, time essentially had stood still. While I had had two years of diverse and interesting experiences, their lives had remained substantially the same. They greeted me with the same noisy and exuberant enthusiasm I was always accorded, as if I had only been away for the weekend. At the end of my third tour of duty, and before I left PRC for the final time, I fully intended to throw my old cracked and bleach-stained boots in the trash. But, at the last minute, I simply hid them away under a bookshelf where I truly hope they still remain.

My time at PRC was akin to a trek into a landscape as remote and arcane as Tibet must have seemed to most westerners in the early twentieth century. This was due partly to its geographic isolation, embedded as the institute was within a military base, within a missile testing range, within a tractless unrelenting desert scorched and seared much as the high arid shoulders of the Himalayas must be. The other aspect that increased the remoteness of PRC were the many rules, regulations, and procedures that one had to adhere to just to gain access first to the range, then to the base, and then to the institute. Once there, one still had to complete a series of rituals to gain access to the actual animal areas. There was a Herculean quality to the tasks one had to carry out to achieve access to the secret society of chimps contained within the layers of rules and prohibitions. The rules that limited access also formed the foundation blocks of a policy of isolation, which was what had long exempted the research community from accountability for the humane treatment of animals in research. The rules and prohibitions reflected and perpetuated the contrived constructs our culture held about what is human and what is animal. Much the same as any culture devises social constructs and categories to define what is sacred and profane. And much the same as any individual in any cultural milieu the world over, I would discover experientially what I personally held sacred and what profane.

Chimpanzee life in labs and other captive settings didn't have to be arcane and inaccessible. Many fine zoo exhibits permitted public access to chimpanzees without allowing for the possibility of injury or disease transmission. These exhibits allowed chimps to see a more natural array of human social behavior and family life than is possible in the restrictive research setting. They have also allowed humans to be more relational with other great apes. This seemed important because chimpanzees are family, our closest cousins. We have a natural curiosity about one another. Our relatedness draws us together because like speaks to like.

The friendships I made, with both chimps and people, during my first tour of duty would persist and deepen over the next ten years. These years would be filled with a series of wildly unexpected events. I would grow from a student into a professional division director during this time. I would endure the intransigencies of four or five distinct administrations, and two corporate take-overs. Essentially the only thread of continuity over the decade would be my deepening friend-ship with the chimpanzees. Their daily lives would go on much the same as usual, suffering increases and decreases in concert with the political turmoil that ceaselessly plagued the administrative level. I would be drawn deeper into the inner sanctum of chimpanzee friend-ship. I would share in their joys and sorrows to an extent I could not have imagined. Finally, unmistakably, I would learn exactly how *little* difference that 1.3% of genetic material really is.

Two

Lennie: Make New Friends But Keep The Old, One Is Silver, The Other Gold

L ennie was my first and most long-standing chimpanzee friend. He was a handsome fellow with long glossy black hair and a dark face with no light freckles. As he aged, he developed a distinguished looking complement of silver hair around his face. His thick hair curved upward at the ends of his shoulders like epaulets which accentuated his authoritative bearing. I met Lennie during my first Summer at PRC and he was in the prime of his adulthood at about twenty-six years of age.

Because of my project and other "safety concerns" I was restricted to one part of the facility referred to as the 'clean colony'. This area housed chimps not infected with viral diseases and most of these were the breeding stock. Being a chimpanzee in the clean colony meant a reprieve from the rigors of invasive experimental research protocols. These chimps had a relatively benign and relaxed existence. Unfortunately, as soon as an individual was no longer good at producing offspring, they might become a candidate for more invasive research. If a chimp was culled from the clean colony they were sent to 'biocontainment area' where the heavy research was conducted. During my first tour of duty I was never allowed access to biocontainment and I perceived it as an arcane and impregnable place. There was a transitional holding area within the clean colony where culls and others with questionable status could be held before being sent to biocontainment. Some individuals actually stayed in the transitional area for months or years while their future disposition was decided. The transitional housing area was referred to simply as 'the fives'. If I noticed a chimp missing from its regular cage I would sometimes be told;

"They went to the fives."

Lennie was in the fives. I think he had been there for more than a year when I first arrived. The fives was a set-apart building of concrete block with a single central door. The door had a narrow window, but the interior of the fives was too dark to really be seen through the window. There were ten or twelve cages in the fives, all of them faced a blank gray wall except the two in front of the door. The fives was dimly lit and the corridor between the cage fronts and the wall was quite narrow. It had a depressive and claustrophobic feel. The occupants at the ends of the corridor showed severe behavioral disturbances and resented human visitors. They expressed this through throwing feces and spitting big mouthfuls of water. The most even-tempered chimps were found in the cages that faced the door. I was never able to discern if the chimpanzees who showed the greatest hostility were simply innately disturbed, or if the solitary and dank environment of the fives had nurtured their aberrations. I favored the latter theory.

Once I asked one of his care-givers why Lennie was in the fives.

"Oh, well he used to be a good sire, you know, we'd put a female in cycle in there and right away she'd get pregnant."

"Lennie has offspring?" I asked in surprise.

"Sure, several. Only now, he doesn't even like females. Just ignores them or chases them around the cage."

"When is the last time he had a cage mate?" I queried.

"Oh, I guess a few years ago or so."

"Well maybe you could try again, or put a male in for company. Maybe he just didn't like a constantly changing situation. Did he ever stay with the female until the baby was born, or help raise it or anything?"

"No, we never put males together and the babies pretty much all go to the nursery. The female only goes in the cage when she's cycling, like in heat, and then as soon as she conceives she goes back to her own cage."

"Wow, that's interesting." I was learning a lot about laboratory husbandry, but the coming years would see a lot of positive and humane changes for chimpanzees in that regard.

The care-givers often left the door to the fives open on nice days so that sunshine and fresh air could flood inside. According to procedure they were not supposed to do this, but their humanity prevailed. Truly, the life of the laboratory chimpanzee would be incalculably grimmer if it were not for the many compassionate care-givers who are drawn to work with them. There are a special handful of kind-hearted technical staff whom can be found inside all research facilities. While they generally have little input at the policy level, what they contribute to the well-being of chimpanzees at a personal level on a daily basis is beyond measure.

I wasn't authorized to enter the fives during my first summer, but I was never one to view authorization (or lack thereof) as a deterrent. Later in my career, when I was fully authorized to participate in all husbandry policy, I would gratefully see the fives abandoned. I often passed the area as I went about my other observations, but the idea of entering the fives would probably never had occurred to me if the door had always been shut. One sunny and moderately warm day in June, a chimp who was caged by himself in front of the open door began to talk to me. Not in ordinary human speech but in the colorful speech of the chimpanzee. This was the first time any of the chimps had earnestly attempted to initiate a conversation with me. Generally they had affected a cool disdain toward me as I sat taking notes each day.

Suddenly there was Lennie, buzzing at me with pursed lips, nodding his head toward me and gesturing with his hand as if to say;

"You, human girl, come over here."

I looked around timidly to make sure nobody human could see me, and then stepped into the cool darkness of the fives. I walked to within a few feet of Lennie's cage.

"Hello, Mr. Chimp" I said, not knowing his name, "do you want to see me?"

Lennie quietly surveyed me, as if surprised I had the gumption to actually respond to his invitation. He again started buzzing and gesturing, and although he looked me in the eye, he kept averting his gaze to my hands and gesturing;

"Come here, come closer, I want to see your hand, don't be scared, come on, get closer...."

But I was afraid, because I had been warned not to get too close to the cages and to never, under any circumstances, go into a chimp area alone. But Lennie was so charming and obviously sincere that it wouldn't take much of an intellect to see that he meant no harm. Lennie was an astute observer and proved to have a great deal of charisma. I suppose he had been watching me go about the colony for some time, wondering what my role was. I'm sure I was an amusing and novel occurrence in what must have become a series of dull and seemingly endless days, and now he had decided to conduct a personal interview. I inched my way closer to the cage and presented him with my gloved hand. He immediately turned my arm over and began grooming the hairs and freckles there. He continued to buzz enthusiastically the whole while. Lennie was the first chimp to ever groom me. I had seen the other chimps grooming each other, making the same buzzing sound. It reminded me of how ladies talk together while folding clothes at the laundry-mat, a kind of non-profound, convivial conversational drone.

Not knowing quite how to respond, I referred to the motto, "when in Rome...." I returned his gestures and buzzing in my somewhat pale human imitation. Grooming apparently consisted of careful, inch-by-inch combing of hair and skin. Scabs, freckles, and moles required extra intensive investigation, which sometimes resulted in blood-letting. While this seemed ritualistically poignant in an anthropological sense, I knew it was strictly taboo in a laboratory setting. I eventually developed a laboratory grooming technique that was fairly superficial compared to what true chimpanzee custom would mandate. Lennie and I stood there happily content, buzzing and teeth-clacking, investigating each other's forearms for a long while. Our friendship was born, and it would become cemented as these grooming sessions occurred with regularity over the course of the years that followed.

Thereafter, if I passed Lennie's door I would be summoned to a grooming session. If I were on a tight schedule I had to avoid passing his building altogether so I wouldn't insult him by refusing to groom. He became adept at hearing my voice or footfall from a distance and would often call out to me even when he couldn't see me. If I ignored him for too many days in a row, when I did appear he would go into a magnificent display that included bipedal swaggering, charging the cage front, door-pounding, and impressive jumps. After he settled down he might keep his eyes averted from me for a few moments to indicate his disapproval of my methods. However, then all would be forgiven and his usual sunny temper and talkative character would emerge, and our grooming would commence.

I don't know what the specific topics were that we discussed, because my part was mostly imitative, but we both felt the better for these little discussions. I was familiar with the various tomes that had been written on the meaning of chimpanzee vocalization and gesture, especially the works of Jane Goodall. But I still felt there was a deeper intricacy to the communications I found myself surrounded by every day among the approximately one hundred or so chimps of the clean colony. My failure to immediately understand simple commands or innuendos was often met with disdain or frustration by the chimps. This would be expressed by a disgruntled wrist shake towards me, or sometimes by a tiny well-placed spit aimed through the teeth of the offended chimp. I would be left feeling obtuse and shamed. I wondered how I could be so dull if I really had the cerebral advantage.

I have been intrigued by the quantity of high-dollar research that has been conducted over the years generating hot debate over whether or not chimpanzees have the ability to use language. Amazingly, most of this has focused on teaching chimpanzees human language models as opposed to understanding the subtleties and flexibility of their own tongue. I once attended a conference on this very topic and was interested in several papers on the topic of pointing. Apparently several researchers had discovered that chimps in captivity actually use their index fingers to point at objects outside the cage which they would like to have. I have often hoped that my advanced education will enable me to make a discovery of that magnitude. Clearly the chimpanzee has a complex and highly developed communication ability that can adapt itself to various environments and media. If we as human beings can't grasp the intricacies of it, perhaps it is only a sign of our own overwrought cortical activity.

Some of this research has crossed into wider territory, debating whether or not the chimpanzee even has a mind. Maybe it is just easier for us to assume that the chimpanzee has no mind so that we can justify our behavior towards them. It is ironic to think that some of the scientists among us would generate data to prove that the chimpanzee is unable to attribute emotional states to other individuals. Haven't we thereby only proven that we ourselves are unable to attribute emotional states to anything not human? We have spent billions of dollars on the space program in order to create vessels like the Voyager, which we sent out to seek extra-terrestrial intelligence. If we found anyone in the galaxy nearly as intelligent as an ape, we would be thrilled. And yet, because he shares the planet with us, we regard the chimpanzee as being of lesser issue and therefore having little intrinsic individual value. Immersed as I have been in the scientific community, I have often understood how Gulliver felt when visiting the Laputans.

The question of language would be one that plagued me over the years because I never felt I had a complete understanding of what chimpanzees occupied their conversations with. I finally concluded that my severely lateralized, linear and concrete human mind was ill-equipped (by culture, not nature) to fully comprehend the intuitive and gestalt nature of chimpanzee communication. Over the years my friends, including Lennie and others, helped me to learn something of their language. This occurred both through observation and interaction, but my comprehension was much more at a subconscious than a conscious level. Ever after I am prone to have people ask me things like, "why are you making that face, that sound...that gesture...do you always eat like that...." I can only attribute my un-human like behavioral characteristics to a transformation that occurred when I was among the chimps, and they never questioned it.

The long commutes to and from the center gave me plenty of time to ponder our language barrier. While I was working on my first project and getting to know Lennie I would be gone from the farm for as much as 12 to 14 hours a day. Fortunately I didn't always have to drive my own car because the College had a shuttle that went to the military base every day filled with engineering students. We all piled into the shuttle at 5:30 a.m., kept a silent reverie or slept, and arrived on site by 7:00 a.m. Usually we left the site by 3:30 p.m., arriving home around 5:00 p.m. I don't sleep well in a moving vehicle, so during these commutes I would mentally sort out my days' experiences. On these long days, Nikki was attending the village school and being cared for by Martina. I think it would have been a lonely existence for her if it were not for the Seville's grandchildren, of which there were about a dozen. As it was, she was isolated from much of village life because she spoke only English. Everyone else in the village spoke predominantly Spanish. Even the Sevilles only used English when speaking to us directly. One day, as I returned exhausted from a long day at the center, Sandoval summoned me to his bedside.

"I have told my wife to teach Veronica Spanish, this way she can talk to the other children, there will be no extra charge for this."

"Oh, um, well, okay, thank you...." I stammered, having never really given much thought to Nikki's linguistic isolation, although preoccupied with my own.

"She needs to be able to speak with her little friends at la escuela."

"Yes, right, I see what you mean...right...thank you."

"Good, it is settled," he dismissed me with a wave of his hand, "good-night."

This would not be the last time I would be grateful for the Seville's intuitive understanding of how best to raise Nikki. The Sevilles provided the family life that Nikki needed and without which, in later years, our lives would come to feel very solitary. Not many weeks after this incident, I was sitting in Martina's kitchen writing up my day's notes. Martina was at the stove, which is where I remember her most often being, and the delicious smell of caldo con arroz filled the room. Nikki ran in with one of the grandchildren, a shy green-eyed girl with thick braids of curling dark hair, her name was Yvette and she would become Nikki's best friend as they grew up together.

" Mommy! Mommy, yo soy un Mexicana!"

"Good girl, Nikki, that sounds like Spanish, alright!"

The girls ran out giggling. Martina stayed at the stove with her back turned. She was dishing up my dinner along with the house specialty, Sanka with liberal portions of sugar and milk. I could see her shoulders quivering, and then she burst out giggling like a school-girl, too.

"Sandoval," I called into the next room, "why's everyone laughing? What did Nikki say?"

"Oh, uh, she says she wants a pinata for her birthday. I think you better buy one."

"Hmm...well I guess I have time tomorrow."

With that settled, I turned my attention to the bowl of stew and the hot tortilla Martina had placed in front of me. I was thinking how quaint and easily amused the Sevilles were, and vaguely wondering if maybe I should try to learn some Spanish.

Eventually I did learn the fundamentals of Spanish. I developed a large vocabulary mostly by watching Novellas on television with Martina. I learned enough Spanish to follow a conversation and to convey my own thoughts in a minimalist form. While I gained an elementary conversational ability, I still lack the intuitive understanding and art of innuendo found in a native speaker. I never became truly fluent and have since accepted the idea that I am not a person gifted with a talent for languages. When I am in a Spanish-speaking situation, I am still uncertain whether I am laughing along with the crowd, or enjoying a joke at my expense. This lack in my language ability doesn't concern me because it has always been made up for by the sense of convivial camaraderie that arises from the attempt to communicate.

My feeling about attempting to communicate with chimpanzees remains, to this day, very similar. By watching them and being among them I understand much of what is passing. But there are always the subtle gestures, vocalizations and expressions that are lost on me. I never hope to interpret them precisely in terms of my own language. That kind of deep understanding could only come from years of fellowship, and might never come to one who had not acquired it as a first language. The experience of having been included in chimpanzee fellowship has been communication enough to leave me untroubled by the inexactitudes of the translation.

Lennie never tired of our little grooming sessions. He often indicated that he wanted me to remove my latex gloves or my shoes. But it was forbidden to be in an animal area without mask, gloves, and appropriate footwear. Sometimes I let the grooming session run to an hour, but more often it would only be about fifteen minutes before I had other obligations to attend to. I was invariably the one to end each session and that still fills me with regret. Every time I would rise to leave, Lennie would keep buzzing emphatically and start pounding on his cage door until I was out of sight. Just once I would have liked to sit grooming contentedly with Lennie until he tired of it, even if it took twelve straight hours.

I felt such heaviness in my heart when I had to say good-bye to Lennie at the end of my first tour of duty. I knew that it was likely I would never see him again. I had no intentions of returning, and he was in the fives, which meant sooner or later he would be put on a difficult research protocol. I felt that I was abandoning a friend in the most adverse of circumstances. The day we said good-bye he meticulously groomed my hand. I had removed the glove and he seemed amused by the finger nail polish I wore. I stood by in tears. Lennie chose to ignore my tearful state, focusing obliviously on my hand, buzzing and teeth-clacking with vigor. Finally I got up to leave, thinking that Lennie couldn't possibly understand. I walked away, but missing the usual fanfare at my departure I turned and looked back just before I slipped out the door. I saw Lennie sitting slumped against the cage wall, his beautiful head bent forward. His hands lay limp and listless in his lap.

More than a year passed before I returned to the center as a doctoral student. The first day I was back I donned my scrubs (standard apparel in a laboratory) and set out to find my old chum. By some good fortune he had been moved out of the fives back into the clean colony. He still evinced no interest in chimpanzee females, but at least he had a decent indoor-outdoor cage enclosure where he could enjoy sun, rain, moon, and fresh air at his pleasure. He was drowsing in the cool of an early autumn morning when I called out his name. He jumped up and ran to the cage front to verify that it was actually me. He then began an extended and dramatic aggressive display, which ended at a point in the cage that was farthest from me, where he sat pointedly looking away from me.

"Look, Lennie, I'm sorry I had to go away, but I'm back now and we can have a lot of little visits. I'll bring you fruits and stuff, because now they say it will be part of my job. No more sneaking, now everything is on the up and up...come on, Lennie."

He sat ignoring me, staring at the wall. The hair in his epaulets curved upward regally and disdainfully. I think he was angry that I had left and stayed away for so long. His life alone in a cage was unnaturally solitary for a chimpanzee. I doubt that he had been groomed once by human or Pan in the whole time I had been gone. Finally he arose and approached me in a dignified quadrupedal manner. He sat at the cage front, gave me the once over, and began buzzing and nodding his head. He hit the cage door with his bent wrist in the old familiar way;

"You, human girl, come over here...."

From this point onward we had three years of relatively uninterrupted progression in the way of environmental enrichment, and grooming sessions. I was working on a new project for my Ph.D. in addition to being given the responsibility of writing and implementing a center-wide enrichment plan. My project examined mother-infant relationships. This meant that I would often be in the clean colony where I could easily visit Lennie. My enrichment activities opened the rest of the center to me. For the first time, I would enter the fastness of the biocontainment area. I would become closely acquainted with monkeys, although my true interests always centered on chimpanzees. But best of all, I would be able to start a series of progressive steps to improve the quality of life for all of the primates in the center. Some of the initial steps I took included adding a variety of fruits and vegetables to the menu and ordering toy objects for all of the cages. Lennie stayed in the clean colony during this time, and we had many leisurely visits. He was often the first one in the colony to receive an unusual fruit or vegetable.

"Hey Lennie!! Here's an onion, I wonder if you've ever seen that before?"

After smelling and an exploratory bite, the onion was thrown to the floor, "Well, okay, how about a tomato?" His excitement expressed by a series of happy grunts, Lennie put the whole tomato in his mouth. Unfortunately, his demeanor changed to less than enthusiastic when he bit down. He pulled the tomato out of his mouth and looked at it. He looked at me and banged his wrist on the cage front.

"Hey, you human girl, this looks like an apple but isn't, and I don't think I like it either."

"Come on, Lennie. Give it a chance, you need something besides apples, oranges, bananas and biscuits," this was the typical laboratory diet. How had anyone decided on apple and oranges anyway? Were they native to equatorial Africa, I wondered?

"Okay, look, one more new item and that's it for today, I promise," I pulled out a perfectly succulent little kiwi fruit and passed it into the cage. I was amazed when Lennie leapt up with the hair on his neck standing up stiff, and instantly flicked the fruit across the cage with the back of his hand. His expression could only be described as a look of disgust. I had seen a few other chimps behave in exactly the same manner when a mouse accidentally wandered into the cage. I burst out laughing as Lennie shrugged his shoulders and returned to his seat, still keeping one eye on the offending fruit but giving me rueful glances in between.

"Look, Lennie, it isn't a mouse. I'm sorry, sir. Here, I have another one, and I'll cut it open and you'll see its really delicious and...don't be mad...come here." I cut open the fat little kiwi fruit with my pocket-knife while I talked and showed it to him. He watched with interest and when he saw the green meat he came closer. He tentatively touched the offered kiwi with his tongue. Deciding it was good, he took the whole thing, but discarded the skin. When I got up to leave he was casually reapproaching the originally rejected kiwi, making happy little grunts of new discovery.

I was very busy trying to meet the enrichment demands of the center while carrying out my own research. There was a very special group of veterinarians at the center during my second tour of duty, I always think of them as the 'Golden Age of Greece' of veterinary groups. They did all they could to further my efforts, and they had developed an even more ambitious plan to build an entirely new facility with more space for the primates. Dr. Greenspan was constantly busy soliciting funds from various agencies in order to build the new facilities. The administration at this time had a progressive philosophy in regards to trends in chimpanzee husbandry, and in keeping with this, they agreed to hire an assistant for me. This allowed me to expand enrichment efforts.

I hired a girl named Poppy Hadler, her name fit her short and tumultuous crop of auburn hair perfectly. She knew a lot about animals and had worked in a zoo where she had cared for many orphaned and sick infants of varied species. Prior to that, she had been a licensed practical nurse. She had a natural wit, and her boisterous presence added a touch of *Mardi Gras* to the center. She seemed to know instinctively what was required of her, and she had the energy of a steam locomotive. Poppy had all of the qualities I could hope for; compassion, technical ability, and she was funny. She took command of the monkey areas, leaving me more time to invest in the larger needs of the chimps. I was reluctant to let go of my duties in the clean colony but the majority of the population of chimps was in the biocontainment area and they required constant attention. Poppy wasn't allowed to go there, so eventually she took over the care of the clean colony, including Lennie.

When I first introduced the two, Lennie remained very aloof. He groomed my hand as usual, but ignored Poppy's overture. He turned his body so that his shoulder and back cut her out of view, it was as if he resented her intrusion into our private relationship. I was anxious for these two to become friends since I knew I would have less time to spend with Lennie. A few weeks later, Poppy burst radiantly into my office.

" He groomed me! He started buzzing and then I put my hand up there and then there I was twenty minutes later, him still grooming. Look! Here at my hand, see here's where he groomed me!" Poppy was pointing excitedly at a reddened patch on her arm in the middle of which was a freckle that had obviously undergone assault.

"Doesn't that hurt just a little?"

"Oh, well it stings a bit, but you know I hated to interrupt him, I didn't want to be rude, rain on his parade and all that, what if he never tried again? I guess he thought it was dirt or a scab or bug or something. Isn't it great, we're friends!!"

"It is great! I'm really relieved, and not to dampen your enthusiasm, but don't let him get too carried away. The occupational health nurse might order us not to touch the animals if we report an injury."

"Stick-in-the-mud! We're fine and I promise I won't do anything to get our program in hot water with the big-wigs. Lennie is a great guy!"

Worrying over the reaction of the administration to my activities became a necessary habit that governed many of my program decisions. Although the present veterinary group was supportive, later there would be frequent changes in the staff. Not all of the researchers and managers were supportive, and there were a handful of individuals who actively opposed any efforts to improve or alter the environment. Unfortunately, these individuals never thought to seek employment elsewhere, and over the years they not infrequently contrived to create obstacles to the efforts of the enrichment division. Ultimately it was the chimps and monkeys whose quality of life was compromised, so I spent an inordinate amount of time attempting to sell the merits of the program, soothing ruffled feathers, and pacifying opponents.

Among the politics, and concrete and metal of the research milieu, Poppy and Lennie built a thriving and colorful friendship. When I couldn't find Poppy in her office, she was sure to be out talking to Lennie. I began to feel like an outsider. Lennie had always dropped everything as soon as I appeared and sought my attention. But now I had to wait until he and Poppy reached a stopping point in their grooming before I was acknowledged. Lennie had the natural bearing of a leader, so it only seemed appropriate that he direct the interactions in our little group. Poppy and I would often hold our daily planning meetings at Lennie's cage. It almost seems, in looking back, as though our division had three staff members at the time; Lennie, Poppy, and I.

During this second tour of duty there were four administrative upheavals. The board of directors fired Dr. Greenspan. Some of the local populace believed it was because the board wanted to appropriate funds Dr. Greenspan had procured to build new buildings. The remaining scientists ran the center for a short time, but eventually realized that the board would prevail in all decision-making processes, so they quit in a single mass exodus. This exodus of brain power undermined every piece of legitimate research at the center and permanently impaired its reputation. For a short time, the board attempted to manage the center, but being made up of small town entrepreneurs, it failed miserably. The board finally decided to hire a prominent, if controversial, researcher named Dr. Hawker to manage the center. They gave him *carte blanche* to salvage the research programs.

Dr. Hawker was sincere, if overweening, in his efforts. He seemed genuinely interested in the welfare of the chimpanzees and was as determined as Dr. Greenspan had been to build new and better animal enclosures. However, he wanted his personal stamp on everything and his first proposal to the board was that the center should be renamed the Hawker Institute for Procedural Research (HIPR). Purportedly, the association of his name with the center would restore its tarnished reputation. The board rejected this idea, but approved almost every other decision Dr. Hawker made. His next sweeping directive was to dismiss or replace most of the people that had been on staff under Dr. Greenspan's administration. I was one of the chosen, and that is how it came to pass that I said good-bye to Lennie for a second time.

My final day was in late August. Dr. Hawker had already installed my replacements. I was heartened by the fact that it would require three persons with Ph.D.'s in Psychology to run the program that Poppy and I had developed. I was concerned that the salary allotment would rob the chimps of needed enrichment supplies, but had to acquiesce to the notion that it was no longer my affair. Poppy had been spared and would remain on staff to smooth the transition. This was a relief, because I knew she would watch over Lennie. Poppy and I went to see Lennie together on my last day. We all played the finger-chase game together and our staccato human laughter was punctuated by Lennie's more guttural chimp laugh to create a harmonious symphony of humor. The finger-chase game was one Lennie had taught us, in which he poked both index fingers out of the cage and we were supposed to grab them before he withdrew them again. A variation involved sticking his toes out. The trick came when one of us actually caught the offered appendage, because then it was our turn to poke our fingers in the cage for Lennie to grab.

"He'll pull yer fingers right off, you do that much", drawled a care-giver named Redd one day when Lennie and I had been playing alone, and I thought, unobserved.

"Oh, I never thought about that...." I responded lamely.

"One bite and that whole finger'll come clean off, I've seen it happen. Crush yer bones to splinters with them teeth, can't even sew it back together that way. Ask old Henry over in janitorial, he used to work out here, lost his finger same way's yer doing."

"Lennie did that?' I asked in amazement.

"Naw, not Lennie."

"Wow." Well, that figured, I knew Lennie was my friend and would never bite me. Redd drawled on just as if he had read my mind.

"Yer start thinking they're yer friends, but truth is yer can't trust a one of 'em. They watch and when they get a chance they go after yer! No sir, they can't be trusted at all!"

I could easily imagine the same conversation being carried out by two chimpanzees in regards to their human providers.

"Well, I guess I'd better be more careful," about being observed by humans when I was playing with chimps, I meant. "Thanks Redd, appreciate it." I made an exaggerated show of slowly picking up my notebook, pencils, and the five-gallon paint bucket I used for a seat, while Redd walked away. As soon as he was out of sight, Lennie and I returned to our game.

During the decade I spent in a laboratory setting, I would often hear care-givers express this feeling of distrust in almost the exact words Redd had used. Even the kindest and most compassionate provider had extremely conservative boundaries when it came to actual contact with chimpanzees because of this fear and lack of trust. I was never seriously injured by a chimp. Any time one had attempted to grab me or nip at me, they always gave me plenty of warning beforehand. Warnings consisted of facial or hand gestures, specific grunts, showing of teeth or head nodding, depending on the circumstance. I am glad I was never plagued with the distrust evinced by care-givers, but my role was also quite different from theirs. I never had to be adversarial with the chimps or force them to do anything they didn't want to do. I simply watched them and came bearing the gifts of enrichment.

I knew several caring and careful workers who had lost bits of their hands to chimpanzee bites. It was a hazard of our relationship with them. I had always been of the opinion that the hazard was exaggerated by several factors. One was the fact that in the laboratory setting the human-chimp relationship was essentially that of jailor to prisoner. Another fact was that humans often didn't recognize when a chimp was giving them a warning because of the language barrier. Additionally, humans are frail compared to chimps. Our skin, muscle, and bone are fragile in structure compared to theirs. What might pass as a cautionary nip among chimps could decimate a human finger. Finally, humans never viewed a wounding event as an opportunity for trust-building in the way that chimps did. Most wounding events between chimps, I observed, were opportunities for elaborate reconciliation. Reconciliation was very ceremonious and often featured hugs, open-mouth kissing, and tender, solicitous care of the wound itself. Over time, in many cases, the wounding event became a bridge to increasingly intimate and trusting relationships between individuals. Humans, by contrast, viewed wounding (by a chimp) as an insult, an offense, and an extreme violation that became the chasm that could never be bridged.

Probably the most overriding contributory factor that enhanced the risk of being bitten, grabbed, or scratched was the very attitude of suspicion and fear. Chimpanzees are sensitive and reactive to the emotional states of others. I had often seen fear responded to in like, as well as happiness. I encouraged care-givers to spend more time in grooming or playing with their charges because I believed it built trust. I suggested that the care-givers use a toy as an intermediary object in playing with chimps until a more trusting relationship was established. This also allowed both individuals to learn to read one another. Because of the direct contact involved, the finger chase game had some inherent risk, but it also built a bond of trust that would be more difficult for either Lennie or myself to breach. When I put my finger into Lennie's cage and he caught it up in his big leathery hand, he would look me directly in the eyes and we both knew that I was at his mercy. The knowledge that he could harm me, but chose not to, brought us closer than any other interaction that we had. Had I pulled away in fear it would have been a violation of our friendship. Every time he released my finger unharmed, our agreement to reciprocal compassion was increased tenfold.

I left Poppy and Lennie there, playing finger chase in the slanted shadows of an August morning. I was content to have that picture for a farewell. His black coat was gleaming and riffled by a cool breeze, his feet pressed against the cage while Poppy pulled his toes. I could hear them long after I passed from view, Poppy laughing and Lennie buzzing, their mingled voices floating brightly over the still desert. I closed up my office, stepping out of my blue rubber and leather shoes, leaving the colored-chalk scrawls of our daily planning unerased on the board. I had a sense of well-being for the animals even though I was leaving. They had many highly educated people to care for their welfare now, as well as their old friend, Poppy. I felt that Lennie would be secure, and that feeling stayed with me during the next two years of my absence from the center. I am glad it did, because had I known what was really happening to Lennie during my hiatus, I would never have had a single night of peaceful sleep.

A year after my departure I learned that Dr. Hawker's administration was disintegrating. The new division for behavior and enrichment had disbanded, the members all having taken positions elsewhere. Poppy still fought on undaunted. The encouraging news was that new buildings were under construction and nearly finished. I was very tempted to return to the center, but the board seemed unable to resolve its internal inconsistencies, so I opted out of the proffered job. During the course of the next year the board oversaw the completion of the new buildings, sent Dr. Hawker packing, and eventually signed over their interests to a private corporation. The incoming company had its own small group of chimpanzees housed in a warehouse in the nearby town of Fat Gulch. They were full of the enthusiastic zeal of corporate manifest destiny as they added the center to their list of assets. Championed by my colleagues still on staff, I accepted my position back for the third and final round.

There had been various changes in my absence. I was disappointed to find that Dr. McGuiness had retired, but his assistant Imelda was still on board, now in the role of an inventory clerk. My assistant Poppy Hadler had transferred to a research lab position, but readily agreed to return to work for me. I was elated to find that my office and workshop were still relatively intact, as were a number of enrichment routines I had established and the care-givers had continued to implement. I had an additional one hundred chimps to consider, so I rolled up my sleeves and plunged into my work. The first item on my agenda was to locate Lennie. My optimism was curtailed when I learned that shortly after I had left, Lennie had been returned to the fives. The thought of his dark and numerous days there filled me with dismay. Even more depressing was the revelation that Lennie had only recently been moved from the fives and placed on an extremely invasive viral vaccination experiment. This meant that he would spend the rest of his life in a highly controlled biocontainment environment.

I tried to bolster myself as I donned my scrubs and prepared to visit him. After all, I reasoned, he was housed in the new building, not in old biocontainment. Lennie's quarters might be even better than ever before. The new buildings were a bright wonder of modernism and space. The general caging was lofty and filled with fresh air and light. This would be a pleasant place to dwell after the fives, even if it was still short of freedom. It was unfortunate that Lennie wasn't in the general housing, he was in what was importantly referred to as an experimental study room. Here the archaic concepts of experimental housing still reigned unblemished by the innovative trends of enclosure design newly appearing in other facilities and zoos. It was no more than antiquated housing reinterpreted in modern materials.

I found Lennie ensconced deep in the labyrinthine bowels of concrete. There was a small window in the door to his room; it faced into a long, fluorescent-lit corridor. I looked in and saw four separate cages, each with a pale-faced inhabitant sitting listlessly on the barren bars of the cage floor. Lennie sat unaware in a head-hanging reverie. He sat hunched in the tiniest cage in which he had ever yet been housed. It was a gleaming cube of vertical stainless steel bars, 32 square feet in dimension. His gaze was fixed on the concrete underlying the bars, which formed the floor of his cage. Because of his newly-awarded infectious disease status, no one could enter the room unless wearing a white plastic suit that covered the entire body except the head. I had to add a surgical cap, goggles, and a super-filtration mask to this ensemble before being allowed into the inner sanctum. My own mother wouldn't have recognized me, so it came as no surprise that Lennie regarded me with a depressed disinterest.

Not until I spoke his name did he realize it was me. He was suddenly animated, performing a short foot-stomping, cage banging display that ended with a concert of buzzing and teeth-clacking. There was a different and disjointed quality to his gestures that did not speak of the old confidence and self-assurance. A new desperation permeated his performance. There were frequent submissive gestures, which had always been alien to this proud soul. He exhibited bare-teeth grin repetitively and made beseeching whimpers that wounded me to hear. He reached for me through the bars, waving his hands rapidly and erratically, making a series of fragmented gestures, which had they been translated into language would have been stuttering gibberish. I moved forward in response to his frantic and staccato buzzing. My tears began to fill the goggles and leaked out, splashing on the dry gray skin of his fingers as he vainly groomed my plastic suit. The voice he spoke to me in now was one of defeat and humiliation, what was noble in Lennie was being beaten down.

"Hey, hey human girl, hey don't leave yet, nice suit, very nice, look, just let me groom it a bit, pretty plastic, very nice...no don't leave yet, no, nice human girl, please stay longer, please don't go...."

After our initial visit I scheduled regular visits with Lennie, but they were increasingly traumatic. The wide-eyed desperation he showed at my departure and the over-zealous appreciation when I appeared left my breathing constricted and my stomach in a knot. I could only imagine the effect I was having on his vital signs. His skin had a wan and lined look I hadn't noticed before. What, I wondered helplessly, could I possibly do for Lennie? My visits pointed up his less-than-human status and my true powerlessness to aid him. I made sure that he received special fruit and toys from the care-givers, I exhorted the care-givers to play more often with Lennie, spend more time in his room. I tried to avail him of all the privilege that my friendship could provide, but it could never be enough. I felt the way I had imagined the emergency personnel I had seen on television one night must feel. They were trying to rescue a man buried under tons of concrete and twisted metal through which they had lowered a microphone and a straw to give him juice.

"Hold on Mac! We'll get you out, just hold on buddy! Can you tell if you're hurt?" I could just imagine the rescuer turning to his colleague in hushed tones; "Whew, I'm glad I'm not down there! Poor bastard, he doesn't stand a chance!"

I spent another three years at the center before my final resignation. Lennie spent that entire time entombed in the concrete experimental study room like some undying Pharaoh. He waits there still, if he lives at all. On my final day I decided not to go say good-bye. It would seem too final, I preferred that Lennie believe that I might be just down the hall, and liable to drop in for a visit at any time with a toy or fruit in hand. Perhaps even a chimpanzee can know what it is to hope.

Three

Adam: The Forgotten Sibling

A dam sat with his eyes cast down, picking at his fingernails in a studied effort to make me feel invisible. I was beginning to feel like a buffoon, gesturing grandiosely and actually begging him. I was making my best effort at communication and he was simply ignoring me. Either Adam didn't understand me, or he chose not to understand me. Hopefully the former, but I had a growing conviction it was probably the latter. He did not want to communicate with me, he wanted me to go away. I decided to become even more cartoonish and extravagant in my presentation to convey meaning.

"Come on, boy, wouldn't you like a nice piece of blue cardboard?" I pretended to eat the enrichment object I was offering him. For one moment his faraway eyes focused on me with an expression that clearly said, "You're daft." I felt myself blush, until I realized that Adam couldn't possibly have an opinion about my mental state, he was a chimp. I was obviously projecting my own sense of embarrassment and ineffectuality upon the blank screen of his primate psyche.

I thought my clever recycling of the fruit dividers from the produce shipment boxes would be irresistible to any chimp, especially since I had painted the inside of each cup with peanut-butter and sprinkled that with chicken scratch. I was thinking they looked like something from a European patisserie. Clearly Adam hadn't been to Europe. I had the uncomfortable feeling that Adam thought I was uncool. He looked very cool, staring over my head in disdain, not deigning to engage in any social exchange with me at all, not even to indicate to me my subordinate status. It was as if he thought I had gall for trying to elevate my status to that of my betters by approaching him. I remember feeling the same way the first time I was taken to eat at the officer's club. All the brass and flight guys were eating there and it was clear that they existed in a matrix in which we civilians were non-existent points, irrelevancies. Adam would fit well at the officer's club given his demeanor.

As he swaggered up to the cage front where I stood beseeching his attention I thought I was going to get lucky and we would exchange introductions. Instead he looked through me, watching a black pick-up pass on the distant road. He followed the truck's progress deliberately, moving his field of vision across my midsection as if I were invisible, tracking the imminently more important truck as it disappeared into the dust-glazed distance. Then Adam moved back to a corner of his cage majestically and sat down contemplating his little toe. I was given no more notice.

He reminded me of a couple of street tough kids I had had in an archaeology class I taught for the community education program one summer. Like Adam, the gang members I had taught were tough and aloof. They hadn't arrived in my class by free choice either. They had been remanded there by the court for their own edification while they were being rehabilitated. They were provided bed and board in juvenile hall, only being allowed into the outer world if they agreed to take classes at the community college. The boys had always managed to avert their gaze and keep their shoulders positioned in the same stiff and regal way that Adam used when ignoring me. It was an effective strategy with me because I was left feeling ineffectual and irrelevant. However, I recalled that the two boys in my class had become the most enthusiastic researchers by the end of the quarter. They had developed an elaborate project that involved excavating a portion of the yard at the juvenile hall. They cataloged every artifact flawlessly, including some tin soldiers from the turn of the century and several old medicine bottles. They discovered through oral interviews that the site had once been an elementary school yard. During finals week they had given a presentation that would have been worthy of attention at any of the professional academic meetings I had attended. It was this memory that allowed me to be persistent with Adam and not simply give up my overtures in discouragement because he didn't immediately respond.

I met Adam during my second tour of duty in 1989. I had finally been inaugurated into the arcane *biocontainment area*. Chimpanzees used on highly contagious disease protocols were kept there. I chose Adam by chance as my first recruit to the joys of enrichment. He helped me to realize that I had an opportunity to both improve the quality of life for chimpanzees in the most decrepit part of the aging facility, and to atone for some small part of the unhappiness they had suffered at human hands. This revelation was totally overwhelming as I realized the extent of the job that was being given to me. In retrospect I realize the magnitude of confidence the veterinary staff must have had in me to entrust to my responsibility the psychological and emotional well-being of any creature under the physical circumstances we had to work with then. I am still haunted with the notion that no matter how much I did, it could never have been enough to fill the needs or atone for the emotional and physical suffering that these magnificent apes had endured. I was less savvy then, and undaunted.

I rolled up my sleeves and plunged into my work, determined to give it my best shot. Determined to befriend and beguile the chimpanzees in the remote biocontainment section. But there had been difficulty at the beginning; I didn't realize how street wise and jaded these apes had become in order to salvage some sanity and to survive. Most of them had a healthy distrust for anything human, and many of them were just outright hateful and dangerous. I didn't begrudge them that, I am sure the extent of their experience with human beings warranted their behavior.

Adam was certainly not bewitched by my lady bountiful act. I began to experience the dilemma of the oppressor in a way that had never been evident to me from the written page in the sociology course on

Consequences of Social Change that I had once taken. I consoled myself by thinking that it was a trust-building exercise, it would take time, that was all. In the parlance of the behaviorist it was a habituation phase.

"Okay, then, I'll just leave it here and you can get it later." I said, trying not to sound hurt, although I did feel rejected.

Most of Adam's neighbors were studiously ignoring me as well. The next day I found the offering in the same position I had left it, one corner still neatly tucked under Adam's cage door, where I had hoped he would pull it into his cage. It did not improve my temper to note that a small band of rather large cockroaches had enriched themselves at this feast board during the night, and in fact several were still lolling drunkenly about in the peanut butter. I threw the whole mess away in disgust.

"Alright, you smart aleck, I am going to sit right out here with my treats and foods until you can't stand it anymore and you have to pay attention to me!" I announced, glaring down at Adam from my bipedal advantage, my hands on my hips. After all, I *had* read all of the Curious George books, I knew he'd break sooner or later.

He slowly got up, yawning theatrically and ambled in quadruped to the back of his cage where he lay down with his back to me and fell into a peaceful snoring sleep.

"Okay, human girl, live it up out there. I have more important things to do with my time than humor you. Like take a nap."

The hot days proceeded like this. I lounged outside of Adam's cage, waiting. He lounged inside of his squat cage, ignoring. The cage itself was ugly. The yellowish ceramic-block cage was reminiscent of a small dog run. The fence front was rusty, the walls made it impossible for Adam to see the chimps living on either side. The cage top was fencing and sometimes when I arrived I would find Adam hanging from the cage top. His fingers were long enough to stretch through the wire top, across the ceramic block divider and intertwine with the long fingers of a neighbor. Although the neighbors could and did vocalize with one another, these finger twinings were the only mutual physical contact the chimps in the building had had for years.

The staff referred to the building by its number, twelve-twelve, and it was the worst of the old and dilapidated housing, which is why I had chosen to turn my attentions there once I had been allowed into *bio-containment*. Inside twelve-twelve there were two corridors. One gave access to all of the cages for feeding, transfers, and washing. Off of the second corridor I had found a series of dark and abandoned rooms. The electricity had apparently been turned off to this area and it was clearly no longer in use. I had to prop the hallway door open to the outside desert, and then the room doors as well to let even a tiny bit of light into these catacombs. Even then I found myself fumbling by feel among the silhouettes of another era, lifting up a half-round shadow to discover someone's abandoned space helmet, or what looked like a large ladle. There was certainly some interesting old junk inside. Tables, metal bowls, rococo glassware that I thought would look good with bouquets in them. I decided one day to requisition some of the metal bowls for my enrichment use and was hauling them out of the building when a care-giver named Emiliano approached me.

"You really shouldn't take those." He said in a quiet but friendly voice.

"Oh, I'm sorry, I thought no one was using them." I stammered.

"No one does." Emiliano was spare in his words like most of the very pragmatic care-givers were. He pointed to a sign over the door of the abandoned room I had procured the bowls from. It was an engraved gray plastic plaque typical of old military installations. It read *R.L. # 2*.

"R L number two." I said aloud, looking up at the sign.

"Radiation lab." Emiliano said looking at me.

"Huh." I responded quizzically.

"Just a precaution, we don't really go in these rooms or use things that are still in there." He pulled the door to the room open, and knocked on the inside of it in demonstration. "This here's lead."

"Huh." I said again, not really following the gist of his conversation.

"This whole building was a radiation laboratory back then, so we think all of this stuff might be contaminated. We don't ever really come in here or use any of the stuff still here."

"Oh." I placed my little stack of bowls on the floor and using the toe of my boot I pushed them back into the darkened room. Emiliano closed the door. We walked out of twelve-twelve in an agreeable silence. I always wondered afterwards if the radiation were really somehow lodged in the abandoned rooms and artifacts, and if so, what kept it from flowing like an invisible fountain across the corridors and into the animal caging areas of twelve-twelve.

I sat outside Adam's cage each day, offering him various enrichment items. I had the care-givers place a colored plastic ball in each animal's cage, the dull ceramic block cages could now be seen from a distance, the round bright spheres in red and green and blue riveting the eye in the bland desert. Gradually Adam and his neighbors came to accept me. Adam remained aloof for a long time, but after I had visited him several times with proffered foods, he began to loosen up a bit. At first he ignored even the most alluring treats such as apples, turning his head away from me, or staring through the criss-cross mesh out into the middle distance as if I were no more than a passing breath of air. Little by little he began to accept my presence as I made a point to just sit by quietly outside his cage during the long afternoons.

I believe it was just a natural desire for companionship that Pan and human share that brought him out of his shell. He started to enjoy having a visitor. I remember the first day he leaned up to the cage and presented his arm for me to groom, much as Lennie always had. Shortly after this he began to have buzzing conversations with me and occasionally a few satisfied grunts would break forth, he then began accepting food treats. I was glad because I had developed a real admiration and affection for him by this time. I wanted him to like me back. Plus, it is always a disconcerting experience to be snubbed by a chimpanzee. I understood the reasons, but it still hurt my feelings. Couldn't he see I was special and different? How could he stereotype me with those other humans?

I wanted to learn more about each one of the animals I was working with so I searched their medical records for clues about their upbringing and parentage. I discovered that Adam was the son of a special chimpanzee friend of mine from the clean colony and also the relatively unknown sibling of a famous sign language chimp. Adam was the son of Kitty, who I had known for a couple of years. As they say in Spanish, she was *"mi comadre"*, there is no such term in English, and a literal translation might read "co-mother" or "best girlfriend." Adam's father was Paleface. Paleface died in the early 1990's after a long and faithful service to science research. I saw the same self-contained dignity of Paleface reflected in his son, Adam. It must have been some genetic inheritance of character because, though they lived within a few buildings of each other during almost all of Adam's life, they had never actually met.

Adam's mother, Kitty, came to the research business relatively late in life, being approximately ten years old. I had many times attempted to trace Kitty's history, but she was one of the "laundered chimps." Laundered chimps have unknown pasts, they became "laundered" when their owners sold them to or through a so-called animal broker. The animal broker would eradicate all personal history, and present the chimp on the market to any interested buyer, usually a research facility. I had contacted Kitty's broker but he had been vague and evasive about providing information regarding her origins. Presumably this is to protect the original owner, or quite possibly to disguise the fact that an illegal importation of an endangered species has occurred. Through such brokers, many chimpanzees who were previously pets, entertainers, on exhibit, or illegally imported have been railroaded into research over the years. This conveniently alleviated the sense of responsibility and guilt the first owner might experience, and of course avoided all unwanted publicity.

My professional guess about Kitty's origins was that she had been raised by humans, quite probably in a home setting. She was a kind and loving chimpanzee who sought human interaction. She recognized many household items and would openly beg for a cup of coffee. She was exceedingly intelligent, slight of build, and had an odd light colored hair that seemed tinged with an apricot hue. Kitty was a member of the breeding colony at the facility for over two decades, including my entire tenure there. During that time she had many remarkable children, most of whom were removed at birth thus depriving her of exhibiting her wonderful parenting ability. Towards the end of my involvement with PRC, I was able to designate Kitty as a foster mother, and she successfully reared young chimpanzees who (for various health reasons) had spent the first months of their lives in the nursery. Among her own offspring were the two full-blooded brothers, Dar and Adam, sons of Paleface, born several years apart and suffering amazingly contrasting destinies.

It was Adam's destiny to be nursery reared at PRC and assigned to experimental use in hepatitis research from an early age. Adam's keen intelligence and fine social understanding were unrealized attributes in the role he was assigned during his early years. He was isolated and caged alone well into adulthood. When I first met Adam he was already ten or eleven years old. He seemed aloof and unaware of my presence as he sat in a tiny indoor-outdoor cell in the biocontainmnet area of the facility. He kept his gaze fixed on the horizon, his soul seemingly caught in the middle distance. I was determined to win him as a friend. I was especially motivated to win him over because of my friendship with Kitty, and I vowed to work at it until I broke through his cool reserve.

I have often been interested in written and spoken dialogue among the spiritually inclined as they reflect upon what underlies the tiny curvature of destiny that determines within a season who will mourn, and who shall be mourned. I often pondered why Adam, with his cleverness, poise, and complex social awareness ended up locked in that tiny ceramic-block cubicle cage where I first met him. And why his sibling, Dar, became a celebrity. Dar was just a few years older than Adam. He had been sent to the renowned language researchers, Trixie and Allen Gardner, when he was an infant. From Dar's earliest memories he had received human kindness and a material status unrivaled by any laboratory chimpanzee. He was given access to foods, toys, and a freedom that Adam could never hope to know. It was a grimly modern version of the prince and the pauper. Dar eventually joined Washoe, Moja and the other famous sign-language chimps that the scientists, Roger and Debbie Fouts have tended over the years in Ellensburg, Washington.

Why was it, I have often wondered, that Adam was shuffled from one experimental facility to the next as a young child. Why had he ended up warehoused in a boxy cell off of a dark, dank corridor in PRC's bio-containment area? Why did Dar receive love and individual attention, attain safe haven in a bright and spacious enclosure, become a member of a stable chimpanzee family group all while his brother languished? It wasn't that Dar had any more merit than Adam, just better fortune. It wasn't even a new story, it was Dickensian in plot and character, merely being retold in a culture of chimps. I suppose I may as well have asked why one grain of sand fell through the hourglass before another. After I had gathered all of this information about Adam's family, I decided I would make it my business to even up the odds as best I could; beginning with more food and more attention, if he would tolerate it.

At the start of my second tour of duty I hired Poppy Hadler to be my assistant. That was what enabled me to work with Adam and his compatriots in biocontainment. Once Poppy had assumed many of the enrichment duties in the clean colony, I began my foray into the mysterious depths of biocontainment. During the hiatus between my first and second tours of duty, Dr. Greenspan had continued to develop several enrichment ideas. He had also worked diligently on planning for new, spacious animal housing that would allow social groups to be formed and eradicate isolated housing conditions. This had long been Dr. Greenspan's brainchild and he had spent great effort in attracting funding for his idea. Dr. Greenspan had made several communications with Jane Goodall over the years and had developed enrichment ideas based on her suggestions. Though Dr. Greenspan left quite soon after my second tour of duty began, I was determined to maintain his commitment to the projects he had initiated

One such project was to create a strategy to allow chimps in captivity to act out the termite-feeding occupation that Dr. Goodall had observed in wild chimpanzees. The feeder device Dr. Greenspan envisioned would allow a chimp to use a stick to dip into a tube and retrieve a food substance. It would allow simulation of the wild chimpanzee feeding activity that involved dipping termites out of their mounds as a snack. Such a device had already been designed and successfully used at other chimpanzee facilities and we were determined to succeed with our own project. Dr. Greenspan had utilized the efforts of a summer intern who measured the size of chimpanzee fingers, as well as various cage dimensions, and produced a precisely engineered box. The feeder box had removable tubes attached and the whole contraption could easily be affixed to the outside of any cage. Dr. Greenspan's intern was a Ph.D. candidate in the agricultural sciences department. His name was Mbele and he was from Uganda.

Mbele designed the feeder device and worked with the maintenance department welder to build several of the boxes. Mbele told me how he had laboriously attempted to take finger size measurements from the chimpanzees at great risk to himself. He would offer a piece of fruit and then use a cloth tape to attempt measuring the finger length and width. He had lost his tape and spent an afternoon trying to get it back from one of Adam's neighbors. Mbele had tried bargain with the chimp who ignored him but mimicked Mbele by wrapping the tape around his own fingers and toes in a perfect imitation of measuring, and then stuffed the tape carefully through the grate that protected the wash down drain. Later Mbele had gotten a sound dressing down from the care-givers for plugging up the plumbing in twelve-twelve. Mbele told me secretly that he couldn't help but feel that the chimp gloated over him every time he saw it after the incident.

Finally Mbele had decided to take measurements only from chimps who were already anesthetized for other veterinary procedures. Shortly after I came back to work the second time, Mbele was awarded his degree and returned to Uganda. Back at home, Mbele would be the administrative liaison of agriculture for one of the largest farming districts in the country. Before he left he confided in me that it had been nearly impossible for him to resolve the cultural disparity between Ugandan and American attitudes toward human beings and chimpanzees. He explained his perspective to me in his beautifully British-accented English one day shortly before he left.

"When I was a small boy we saw many chimpanzees. My mother and father worked very hard to farm the land there, my job as a boy was to go around the fields with my four brothers and throw rocks at the chimpanzees. They come into the field and eat everything!! Then the rest of us are going hungry, no crops to sell. Now I will have to help solve the problem of this agricultural pest."

"Well, how *are* you going to approach the problem, Mbele? Are there any places for chimpanzees, like a national park or reserve?" I asked him as he cleared out his desk.

"The chimpanzee causes a great deal of mischief! They are very intelligent, they watch the farmers and learn what they do. The farmers are very desperate to make a living, but still I think that it would be bad to just shoot them as some farmers do. More and more the farmers are pushing the chimpanzees to small hilly areas not so good for farming, it is also a problem of growing population and the need for economic growth. I prefer to find a reserve for them, perhaps explore their economic value for the tourist."

My conversation with Mbele made me realize the complexity of chimpanzee welfare and survival issues. Even in their native habitat, the chimpanzee couldn't count on sanctuary and peaceful co-existence. Growing populations and destructive agricultural practices were eating up their natural habitat. They were pushed into smaller and smaller zones with scarce food resources. The predictable result was that they were thrown into direct competition with the other hominoid in the neighborhood (*Homo sapiens*). Crops were simply an accessible food source to a chimpanzee. Chimpanzee couldn't hope to win in the aggressive competition that ensued. They couldn't possibly compete with the technology and firepower of their human cousins. The evolutionary history of our cousin species had favored brawn over brain. It seemed ironic that though we could now outgun them with technology and threaten their existence in the wilds, yet they exhibited an imperviousness to viral agents that were decimating us. In some fundamental physiological sense they were still out-competing us. The longer I worked at PRC, the more I understood how dependent *we* were upon them to provide answers for our own survival.

After Mbele left I often wondered if he ever thought of us back at PRC. I wondered if he would find it as amusing as I did to think that while he would be devoting his energies to devising methods to keep chimpanzees from eating farm crops, I was devoting my energy and efforts to teaching Adam how to eat carefully prepared snacks out of Mbele's box. The world is a funny place.

The feeder box was an unbelievably heavy steel plate contraption. Once it was affixed to the front of the cage, Adam's side of the box sported several drilled holes, large enough for sticks but too small for fingers. On the human side were threaded PVC pipes that could easily be twisted out and filled with various food mixtures. The most successful concoctions were the consistency of baby food. It had been difficult to arrive at that soupy consistency using the meager tools in my lab area. I had smashed, chopped, and crushed all manner of produce only to have it clog up the pipes, or be too lumpy to come easily out of the holes like the little clinging termites in the chimpanzee homeland shows. I was seriously thinking of importing real termites when Adam helped me to find a giant, abandoned industrial-sized Waring blender. Thereafter we could whip up any kind of mousse we thought a chimp might desire with no problem whatsoever.

Adam helped me to acquire the blender, and probably saved my skin into the bargain as well. It happened one day as I was trying to escape the heat and had decided, against all sensible warning, to seek refuge in the cool shade of *R.L.# 4*. Adam, usually calm and often disinterested in my comings and goings around the area, had been particularly against my entering the corridor across the way from his caging that day. Every time I had stood and ventured toward the cool inviting darkness he began to rant and wail in an unusual display that included a lot of long woo-barks and a series of high-pitched yips. Each time I started again toward *R.L. # 4*, he cried out and I returned to his cage front.

Even his corridor-mates had grown uneasy and had all moved to the fronts of their runs to watch this tennis game.

"What is wrong, boy," I queried, squinting my eyes and peering through the mesh at him, was he sick? "Are you okay?" Some animals a few buildings over had come down with *shigella* the previous week and I was worried that Adam might be getting ill. "You are acting like a sick little kid, dear," I told him, gently holding out the back of my wrist. He quieted down. But a few minutes later, when I was once again overcome with the heat and got up to sidle down to the prohibited lead-lined rooms, Adam became almost hysterical. His neighbors joined in with him this time, one shaking a fist at me. I stood puzzled, arms akimbo looking at all of this ape agitation and wondering what I was missing. Just then Emiliano the caregiver strolled carefully around the corner of the mustard block building, he was holding a shovel in both hands and he looked surprised to see me.

"Hey *chica*!" He said before editing himself.

"*Chica*!?" I heard Adam echo from behind me, I turned to look at him, he gave me a level look and shrugged, his epaulets standing on end, "sorry," he murmured.

"Did you hear him!?" I asked Emiliano in awe.

"Yeah, I heard him all the way across the compound. What's going on?"

"You heard him talking just now?"

"I heard him howling for the past ten or twenty minutes. Are you feeling okay, you look hot." It wasn't a compliment.

Maybe I had been out in the sun too long, I looked at Adam again, he was cleaning a fingernail and ignoring us, his building mates were watching Emiliano expectantly.

"Seen anything funny?" Emiliano asked.

"Besides talking chimpanzees?"

"Yeah. What's all the fuss about?" He was being really nosy, I thought, usually Emiliano left me to my own devices unless he thought I was in some kind of danger, like getting irradiated. He was looking around suspiciously and I began to feel irrationally guilty.

"Alright!" I exclaimed, "I *was* going to go into *R.L. # 4* to cool off, okay!?"

"And..."

"Well, and, well Adam didn't want me to leave, that's all. Every time I got up to go down there he started yelling, he's so sensitive today, and then his friends had to join in. Look, I know you don't think I should go in there, but having Adam spy on me and tattle is going a bit far, Emiliano." I had my hands on my hips and was facing Emiliano accusingly.

"*Spy? Tattle?*" Adam echoed from behind me, clicking his tongue against his teeth in a mock outrage. I turned and looked at him again, and then looked back at Emiliano, "You heard him that time, right?" Emiliano laughed.

"Show me where Adam doesn't want you to be, and stay behind me, *chica.*"

Emiliano led the way to the next corridor, shovel held before him like a sword, me trailing behind, and Adam repeating in the background; "Jeez, again with the *chica*?"

When we got to the door of *R.L. # 4*, Adam and his friends had begun their sing-song wailing and barking again, finally I had to ask; "Emiliano what is going on around here, nobody ever tells me a darn thing!" It was at that moment I heard a loud hissing noise, I thought it sounded like a broken high power line, I ducked in an instinctive alarm.

"Stay here and hold still!" Ordered Emiliano tersely as he strode right into the darkened room and shortly after I heard the ringing clang of what could only have been the shovel blade chopping against the concrete floor, my hands were balled up into hard little fists and I was biting my lip when Emiliano reappeared with a very dead rattlesnake carcass hanging across the handle of his shovel. "Snake," he said, the severed head of the creature rested in the cup of the shovel blade.

"Huh." I replied, slowly realizing how close I had come to finding the reptile in the darkened room, alone and unprepared. I had and hadn't understood what Adam was telling me. I knew he did not want me to go to the radiation rooms, but I didn't know why. Amazingly I had unwittingly followed his instructions and thereby avoided a drama I did not want to contemplate. Communication between the species could be very simple and effective if we didn't try to over-analyze it with our outsized neocortex, I reflected.

"That crying you heard them make, that's the snake call, try to remember it, eh *chica*?" Emiliano winked. I was looking at the magnificent snake, whose diamond skin pattern and size I could appreciate now that he was dead. I had been blessed in all my years of living in the desert, which is a haven for rattle-snakes, to have never had to cross paths with one of these fellows in the wilds. The only ones I actually saw close up were safely ensconced in terrariums, or else already dead. Not that I had anything personal against rattlers, nor did I have a reptile phobia. I loved to see a big bullsnake rummaging through the wild grass for field mice. They have beautiful, intricate geometric patterns running up their backs in a brown and russet color scheme. I once saw a four-foot bullsnake wending its way majestically through the remains of a ceremonial kiva at Bandelier National Monument and it was an epiphany. Rattlesnakes, on the other hand, are just too dangerous to have much mystical appeal to a pragmatist such as myself.

"Wow, where was he hiding in there?" I asked, completely entranced by the reptilian corpse.

"Wrapped up around some old blender."

"Blender?" I repeated, looking from the severed head to Emiliano, my eyes narrowing in calculation. "Blender" I said again hopefully, thinking about the tubes in the Mbele box, and forgetting all about the snake.

After Emiliano left and everyone else in twelve-twelve had settled down, I snuck back to *R.L.# 4*, looking around in the dim half-light until I found it. A big red and white box emblazoned with the words *Restaurant Grade Food Processor*. I looked inside and saw it, all shiny and new, seemingly unused for a decade and still sitting in its original box.

"To hell with it!" I said in defiance to myself in the cool tomb-like room I had now braved in spite of both Emiliano and Adam's dire warnings. I decided to appropriate the radiated, snake-hexed culinary machine for enrichment purposes because finding it at all was obviously more in the category of providence than coincidence. And anyway, I rationalized, if there was any irradiating to happen it was probably already too late for Adam and his friends. As for myself, I was studying with a traditional *curandera* on the weekends when I could. I was sure she could use an egg and a prayer to make me *limpiando*, clean. I hoisted the blender box and took it back to my enrichment lab where Poppy cooed over it as if it were a baby. We used inviting edible delights such as pureed squash, peanut butter, honey, mustard, molasses, and fruits to make fillings for the feeder tubes. The really difficult tricks to the whole project turned out to be keeping a ceiling on production time, and teaching the chimpanzees how to use a stick to dip the gooey soup back out through the little holes on their side.

These logistical problems resulted in two caveats that I subsequently appended to my overall philosophy of primate enrichment. First, always strive to develop enrichment strategies that take the other primates longer to undo than they took you to prepare. And, second, carefully consider the implications of the learning curve when it comes to clever devices. I have been reminded many times since that the most enthralling forms of enrichment imaginable can be thwarted by the inability to convey to a chimpanzee the act necessary to carry out an activity. For instance letting a chimp drink Kool-aid from a large bucket using a short piece of clear tubing as a straw. I had not anticipated that the chimps would consider stealing the tubes from me and gnawing them up as a great deal more amusing than sitting and watching me demonstrate the basics of sucking on a straw. I hadn't anticipated the complexities inherent in teaching a chimpanzee how to suck on a straw. Obviously they hadn't had as many strawberry milkshakes at *McDonalds* as Yvette and Nikki had. It took elaborate miming to get even half of the chimps I knew to understand the concept of sucking. I lost a lot of plastic tube straws in the process not to mention the frustration I inspired in my students.

I had blindly assumed the chimps would automatically use the willow sticks I cut for them to dip into Mbele's feeder box tubes. Instead they played with the sticks, chewed them to splinters, and then banged on the feeder box in frustration. Later the care-givers read me the riot act for providing sticks to the chimps which then got washed into and clogged up the drains. So, my first task became demonstrating the use of the feeder box to the chimps in Adam's neighborhood. I did this by placing it in front of myself on the sidewalk outside their cages while they watched, and pretending to dip and eat with gusto. There was a magical aspect of these teaching sessions that I didn't learn about until much later. Once a few chimpanzees caught on to a technique they were more successful than I was at teaching and showing the behavior to the other chimps around them. The trick was to teach a teacher!!

Adam was my very first chimpanzee student in the art of using the Mbele box. I sat patiently in front of his cage with my head bent over the box, my neck getting sunburned, and attempted to teach him the finesse required for tube-dipping. Finally, a few weeks into the whole project, he took an interest in the tube dipping lessons and soon mastered the use of the device. No mother could have been prouder of a child's achievements than I was of Adam's success, although I think he may simply have been indulging me. He seemed to realize that I derived some great happiness from his use of my device and he was being kind. I could easily imagine him telling his building-mates later;

"That girl is kind of a nut, but if we keep her happy she'll keep coming around. She's kind of an interesting thing, isn't she? Isn't it funny how she tries to talk and act like us? I've never seen a human do *that* before! She reminds me of a little chimpling. Well, she seems to have unlimited access to the fruit locker anyway, so let's humor her with the metal box thing".

I knew we had crossed into convivial new territory when Adam could hear me before seeing me and would hoot with anticipation. He began to make soft grunting sounds whenever I presented him with some new and strange concoction for his feeder device, and soon all his neighbors were using it as well. It was an exhilarating moment when one day I arrived on site to see the cage fronts decorated with iron clad Mbele boxes and the whole building started hooting with delight to see me! I had the satisfaction of knowing that the device and my efforts were improving the quality of their lives.

This inspired a renewed sense of purpose in my enrichment activities. I felt it was a worthy goal to alleviate the boredom of the many chimpanzees being used in viral research in order to advance my species. Many of the virally infected chimpanzees that were housed alone in biocontainment weren't merely bored, but had developed obvious behavioral stereotypies, which in some cases resulted in self -directed behaviors (SDB). Some of these behaviors were merely self-stimulatory, such as rocking or repetitive movements and gestures. But in the worst cases some chimpanzees would enact self-injurious behaviors (SIB). In my early days in the biocontainment area I was deeply affected to see the results of this disorder, which I had previously only read about.

Adam wasn't a chimpanzee who responded to his isolation, cramped housing and the sensory-restricted environment through SIB. He instead exhibited symptoms that I frequently saw in singly housed chimpanzees and came to think of as "dreamtime." He seemed to sit in a dream by the hour, staring into the middle distance somewhere between his concrete bunker housing and the jagged lines of the Noche del Muerto Mountains that edged the horizon. It was like he had a listless and insular depression. It was characteristic of many of the chimps in biocontainment. I felt there was an element of stoicism in this behavior. I chose to believe it indicated that a flame of hope was kindled somewhere within the chimpanzee soul, hope for a better time and place to come. There was still something to proceed towards, to wait patiently for, something yet to live out in this life. I saw this state of consciousness as being in direct contrast to that evinced by individuals who enacted SIB. Instead of a physically self-aggressive grappling with their emotional state, dreamtime chimps enacted a kind of self-protective withdrawal.

Adam was a dreamtime chimpanzee in those days when we first met. Those were the days before he was eventually moved to a large new enclosure with five cage-mates drafted from adjacent enclosures in twelve-twelve. He was completely suited to life in a social group, he slipped into it so naturally that it seemed he had never been alone. He did not take the alpha role that was reserved for Zane, Adam's half-brother and another offspring of Paleface.

I first met Zane one afternoon as Adam and I finished a Mbele box session using a new pistachio puree that Poppy had whipped up from a generous donation given by a local pistachio farm. Adam was completely enthusiastic about any kind of nut. It was afternoon wash down time and I wanted to leave before the caregivers came through with their hoses and the accompanying hooting and hollering of the chimps which preceded feeding time. I preferred the long, sedate between-wash down solitudes to the high-decibel ricochet of mass chimp vocalizing in concrete enclosures, it was deafening. I could hear Emiliano beginning his cage cleaning a few buildings over.

"Good-bye, Adam," I waved to him and hoisted my box of empty feeder tubes. As I walked out of twelve-twelve, headed for the decontamination showers, I heard Emiliano stop cleaning and start yelling at the chimps. I detoured around by his area to see what he was making a fuss over. Awkwardly carrying the box I tiptoed past the next building and peered around the corner. I saw Emiliano, his hose was lying on the ground, he gesticulating with aggravation at a big chubby chimp who was hanging upside down from the cage top and obviously refusing to comply with Emiliano's request. He wanted the chimpanzee to pass through a gate to the indoor cage so Emiliano could clean the outdoor run. This was a daily routine, so the chimp knew what he was supposed to do, but even from my spy's nest behind the corner of the adjacent building, I could see that that the chimp was giving Emiliano a hard time.

"Get in there you, Zane, go!" Zane continued to hang upside down like a two hundred pound plum on a high branch, unassailable, he began to leisurely lick his fingers. Emiliano Picked up the hose and shook it at him. "Go!"

For a minute I thought Emiliano was going to open the nozzle and spray Zane. That was a practice that could result in his firing on the spot. There had been a couple of ex-employees who had routinely used the technique of wetting to get the animals moved. It was a demeaning and degrading practice. The animal care supervisor wouldn't tolerate it and anyone caught doing it was summarily fired. I was waiting in disbelief. I hoped Emiliano wouldn't stoop to spraying Zane. I had immense respect for Emiliano's animal sense and I didn't want to be disappointed by finding out he was capable of cruelty. I had never had any indication from the chimpanzees that they had anything but respect and affection for Emiliano. Sure enough, after shaking the hose at Zane with no apparent effect Emiliano dropped it back on the ground unused. I sighed with relief.

"Okay, boy, look, Zane, I've got a little friend for you," Emiliano was saying in a nice friendly tone, at the same time drawing something out of the pocket of his scrub shirt. Suddenly Emiliano held aloft a long wiggling snake and in the blink of an eye, and as quiet as a cat, Zane jumped down and loped inside. Emiliano quickly shut and locked the gate, picked up his hose and began to wash down the cage floor. I was completely indignant about his tactics. I set my work box down and walked up behind him unnoticed. I tapped him fiercely on the shoulder, he jumped.

"*Madre, Dios*!! You scared me, man, thought you were a chimp," he said looking really grumpy, "don't do that to me!"

"*I* scared *you*," I said sarcastically, crossing my arms and narrowing my eyes to mean little slits, or so I hoped. "How dare you say that after what I just saw you do to Zane!" I said hotly. "*You* scared *him*! Let me see that snake." I demanded stretching my hand out.

Emiliano looked sheepish and pulled a brown rubber snake out of his pocket, he handed it over to me. "It's a toy, man! Anyway, Zane wasn't scared.You didn't hear him crying did you?"

"Well, no." I hesitated in my indignation. I couldn't keep up my mean and dangerous act much longer, especially now that I was holding a rubber snake with a silly smile painted on its face. Emiliano sensed this right away.

"It's a game, *chica.*" I noticed he had switched genders on me, I wasn't *man* anymore just *chica,* I would never be an alpha in any group, I lamented to myself with an outward sigh.

"Okay," I acquiesced, "tell me all about it." I began waving the snake around, it *was* kind of a fun toy. I wondered if it would plug up the drains, if I could get a super discount if I bought them by the crateful, and how I could write it into a grant, maybe using wording about *eliciting species specific* behavior. Emiliano sensed all of this and gave me his maddening, lopsided grin.

"Like cards, he bluffs me, I bluff him. In the end I get what I want and he gets what he wants."

"What does he want?" I asked.

"He wants me to dance around with him a little, play it out, shake things up. You know, like going to the market in *Juarez,* you can't pay the first price the vendor asks, it's uncool. Playing" Emiliano winked. "Same thing you do with them, isn't it?"

"It's not fair to terrorize them, Emiliano, they *are* caged!" I said accusingly, but realizing I was losing ground quicker than an *arroyo* in a thunder storm.

"I agree, but it's a game, you saw yourself how he was acting!! Zane's not scared. I gotta get this wash down done in thirty minutes and then feed, Zane could hang out here all night. He knows I'm in a hurry, same as he knows I have a rubber snake in my pocket, so he figures he has a little leverage, maybe I'll give him a fruit bribe, or spend more time just messin' around with him."

I knew everything Emiliano said was true, but somehow it still seemed unfair. "I don't know Emiliano, still..." I mumbled without conviction, twirling the snake toy like a lasso.

"I tell you what, chica, you like experiments, you keep the rubber snake for a day, show it to your ape friends and see if you think anyone is really afraid of it, then tell me what you find out."

"Really!?" I couldn't believe my good fortune, I was going to get to walk away from this exchange with the smiling rubber snake, I guess I had the upper hand after all.

The next day I took the toy snake to surprise Adam, he yawned, and wandered over to his *lixit* spigot for a long cool drink of water.

"I like you because you're a nut," he seemed to say, somersaulting onto his back and spitting some water up like a fountain to rain back down on his face, "But come on, that's a fake."

So next I dropped by Zane's cage. Zane was huge, just as his father Paleface had been. He was as docile as he father had been, too. Zane reminded me of Ferdinand the bull. He spent most of his time sitting quietly, playing with a toy or his feet, or grooming himself contentedly. I pulled out the snake and waved it wildly at him. Zane glanced at me briefly then resumed his manicure. He evinced no other interest in me at all until shortly before leaving I produced a carrot from my other pocket. He dawdled up to the cage front and took the carrot in his immense hand, he nodded toward the pocket with the snake. I held it out to him, he sniffed it and then turning around wandered off to a corner to slowly enjoy his carrot.

A few years in the future I would see Zane become the dominant male in a social group with his half-brother Adam as his second-in-command. He enjoyed a convivial life with his fellows. He hated discord in his group, the moment there was even a small disagreement between anyone, Zane would get up slowly, swagger over, and use his whole body to gently separate the two and make sure they stayed apart until they could be civil. He rarely ever used overt aggression, just quiet assertion and bluff. He was so large and persuasive he didn't have to be violent, and he was a gentle soul. As a social character, Adam blossomed forth in his group to be brotherly personality, able to mediate conflict, and support his younger half-sibling Zane in managing the affairs of the group. As a group member Adam was playful and kindly. I often watched him play tag and wrestle games like a little chimp child, and grooming with tender camaraderie among his fellows. If they had had the rubber snake then I am sure they would have constantly been playing practical jokes on one another.

"I see what you mean, Emiliano," I sighed later as I returned his snake. At the next Christmas dinner when I received my *secret Santa* gift, it was a big green rubber snake. Nobody admitted to being my *Santa*, but Emiliano gave me a crooked and conspiratorial grin over the punch bowl.

It had been a long hot summer but we had turned the corner into September. Adam and I were still relationship building in biocontainment. The new social caging was still years away from being designed or built as Adam and I drowsed in the shade at biocontainment, but in my mind I was already beginning a blueprint for how to form future social groups out of the compatible personalities I was meeting. I was learning more everyday about how the chimpanzees had developed culture and community even given the constraints of the housing. I personally experienced many incidents that demonstrated the social personality of the various individual chimps with whom I was working. I enjoyed the protective and attentive nature they demonstrated towards each other and their caregivers, who were mostly treated as fellow troop members even under the adverse conditions of captivity in biocontainment.

In autumn the shade had a trick of being about fifteen degrees cooler than the sunny areas of the concrete compound, so retreating to the *R.L.* rooms wasn't necessary. Adam sat in his usual posture in the cramped kennel of a cage. His back was leaned against the ceramic brick wall, his knees drawn up and wrapped around with his arms, his chin at rest on one patella. My legs, being absurdly long and disproportionate to my body by comparison to chimp standards, were extended out along the sidewalk. We were both drowsing with eyes half-open, resting from another bout with the feeder box. Adam's stomach was full, and my scrubs artistically spattered with the peanut butter-honey-corn-squash recipe I was perfecting.

The languid afternoon was resolving itself to quitting time, and in a distant hazy kind of reverie I was contemplating what I was going to do when I got home while I practiced focusing on the middle distance through half-lowered lids like Adam. It was then that a gradual awareness of dark movement along the peripheral margin of my vision came to me. Adam, sitting right beside me, even while still on the other side of the fence, hadn't stirred, so I felt no sense of alarm. I straightened up, opened my eyes fully and focused on the movement then instantly jumped to my feet with a shriek. There, limping its way across the pavement to our place of repose was a ragged and pitiful specimen of the arachnid family, specifically a huge brown and gold tarantula. Clearly battle-scarred, he was missing a leg and limped arrhythmically along. He was larger than my hand span.

Adam still hadn't flinched although he was glancing up at my dance-like antics with a cool and bemused expression. I suppose this is exactly how the tarantella was invented. Possibly Adam was wondering if this was yet another phase of my enrichment program.

"Adam!" I exhorted him, "Look at that monster!" I gesticulated wildly toward the horrific visage, which had now stopped and was tentatively waving a paw the size of New York in my direction. Somewhere I had heard that a tarantula can broad jump 15 feet at a go, I was looking furtively for an escape route. Adam glanced briefly at the spider and then returned his gaze to me as if to say;

"This is getting interesting, what are you going to do next, human girl?"

I was fuming and agitated. I couldn't believe the *laissez faire* with which Adam was responding to my crisis. "You can warn me about a snake, but *not* a horrible giant spider about to crawl over me in my sleep?! That's just mean" I exclaimed. Adam yawned.

"What is the big deal, he can't hurt you. Just don't step all over him," Adam seemed to mumble, turning over languorously and falling back asleep in a warm triangle of sun. I gave a deep sigh.

The tarantula, deciding he was under no threat, took a detour around my dance area and continued his journey determinedly and with great speed, given he was one leg short. He appeared to have an appointment to keep, and like the white rabbit, did not want to be late for his very important date. I make no apologies for my stilted view of the swaggering brute of a spider, for I have suffered for many years with acute arachnophobia. The very sight of even the smallest specimen set my teeth in a clamp and sent surges of adrenaline coursing through my system, leaving me with clammy hands and severe jitters.

The deserts of the Southwest are native turf to these absurdly large creatures and I have seen dozens of them over the years, but it didn't lead to desensitization on my part. Every encounter was equally dramatic in my psyche. They simply riveted me with a morbid fascination and horror. The tarantula is basically a harmless fellow though, not nearly the picture of sinister felony that the black widow portrays. Usually they seem awkward and cartoonish, although it is unnerving to see dozens of them moving rapidly and intently across the desert floor at dusk, like an undersized and loosely knit band of Bactrian camels. I have witnessed such migrations in autumn, but have no sane interpretation for it, having confined my powers of observation to the primate family. I imagine them on their way to some huge tarantula congress where next year's insect economics, or the problem with tarantula wasp containment programs is discussed.

In any case, Adam's neighboring chimpanzees appeared to find my fussing and waving antics to be of much greater interest than the object of my agitation. They evinced little interest in the spider. They didn't even ruffle a hair. I have never met a chimpanzee with a case of arachnophobia. Certainly they don't appear to care much for insects, especially cockroaches which abounded in every possible size and form within the confines of PRC. I never noted them to utilize insects as food either. The cockroach problem had increased over the years, especially in the final institutional incarnation, when the private corporate decision making apparatus made the astonishing decision to eradicate not pests, but the pest control program, as it was too expensive.

I have often seen chimps disdainfully sweep insect intruders out of their cage. I have observed them to evince disgust when flicking a cockroach off of their coat, wrinkling up their noses, but never have I known them to raise an alarm over an insect visitor of any sort. They maintained the same condescending attitude toward the all too frequent rodent visitors sadly common in the facility. Any rodent ignorant enough to wander into the chimpanzee's home domain was quickly and unceremoniously dispatched to a happier place, its earthly remains being swept out of the cage. Adam and his neighbor's response to reptile visitors, however, was of an entirely different grade. No chimpanzee I have ever met will countenance the presence of a snake without setting off an immediate alarm throughout the neighborhood.

I think it is safe to say that all chimps hate snakes! The response to snakes appears to go beyond simple dislike and individual preference. Chimpanzee mothers with infants would become especially upset and agitated. The sentiment seems to be primal, ingrained in old and young alike, and my experience in *R.L.# 4* had shown me that the response speaks deeply to something in our human nature as well. The snake call is an unmistakable high-pitched chatter that is immediately recognizable even to human beings after a person has had a few situational exposures.

Sometime after my almost-encounter with a rattler in *R.L. # 4*, and not long after the anticlimactic incident in which I danced the tarantella for Adam and his compatriots, there was another snake incident in one of the adjacent buildings. Unfortunately, it wasn't all that uncommon for rattlers to wander into the buildings in the biocontainment area. The area was isolated in the middle of an undisturbed portion of desert. In the summer and early fall, the hot air made the snakes feel lethargic and dull, the cool wet cement seemed to beckon them in after the evening wash down. Due to the aforementioned pest and rodent problem, the buildings were kind of an air-conditioned version of a rattle- snake smorgasbord.

It is easy to imagine the allure to a snake, if you will. For example, if a person had been driving around in a car with no air-conditioning all day in Phoenix on the tenth of July, they would probably leap at the opportunity to enter a cool, food-filled Luby's Cafeteria. Later on after a night of revelry and chilling, the fat snake would lounge around surrounded by the chattering and banging pandemonium of angry and sleepless chimpanzees. It is a great piece of evidence that rattlers are not especially cued to auditory input, any self-respecting organism with acute auditory processing would leave immediately. The early watch care-givers were the most likely to find the unwanted invaders and would quickly dispatch them, usually by tried and true method of lopping off their heads with a spade. That was a bold act of heroism in my book, but the care-givers made little of it, as though it were but a small deed in the course of things.

The day of the second snake incident I was party to in Adam's neighborhood was a typical blazing hot day in mid-September. Autumn frost wouldn't visit our biozone until December. A team of scientists from "back east" at the NHHS was on site for one of their very infrequent visits, ostensibly to review their research protocols. These protocols were implemented from about 2000 miles away and the scientific investigators actually had no working idea about how their protocols were implemented by the technicians at PRC, people they had never met or talked to in person. These scientists also mostly had no idea what a real chimpanzee looked like.

"Oh, they're so big!" was a frequent comment. Bigger, I assumed, than they looked on all those Jane Goodall television specials. I suppose on a television screen they weren't much larger than a few inches. Aside from an ignorance of the size, the researchers uniformly evinced an ignorance of the daily quality of life of their research subjects; where they lived, how they passed the time of day, what they ate, if they were happy. Mostly the visiting researchers were indulging in a sort of pageantry. Their real fame and fortune came from hovering around the NHHS offices in Washington, D.C. like a bunch of lucre-philic satellites, and interpreting whatever results were air-mailed to them from the facility. The technicians who actually carried out the vital procedures were left unrecognized and generally poorly compensated for the time, effort, and extreme hazards they faced while on the job.

As an anthropologist, I enjoyed these visits because of the pure ritualistic content. There was a preparatory blood-letting ceremony in a lab where tubes of blood were collected from each visitor, and they were also injected with a TB test. After being declared pure of viral and bacterial infection the visitors would be allowed to proceed to the actual site visit. The actual visit required doffing civilian clothing, a shower for purification, and then donning the ritual garb of scrubs, lab coat, booties, bouffant cap, and goggles. Then these great scientific minds, attended by the on-site technician acolytes, were led around the premises (usually accompanied by at least one or two members of the institutional administration). The administrative representatives themselves generally hadn't bothered to stroll around the premises at all since the previous visit.

This procession, which in appearance differed from other local religious proceedings only by lacking the figurine of a saint seated on a platform, predictably elicited a furor of indignation from the caged chimpanzees. Chimpanzees, as has been noted by other more erudite researchers than myself, prefer routine to unpredictability. The presence of unfamiliar interlopers behaving in an incomprehensible and seemingly random manner was really unnerving for the chimps. They screamed and banged and spit, and some of the less civilized among them threw feces.

Adam, like most of the chimpanzees in our facility had developed an understandable prejudice against anyone wearing a white lab coat. White lab coat was part of an algebraic equation, and the other side of the equal sign meant pain and loss of control. Laboratory chimps in general have a sophisticated understanding of economics. I had frequently had to pay exorbitant prices to retrieve a plastic glove or other contraband from an alert chimp. Once, Kitty had extorted two oranges and a quart of strawberries from me in exchange for my stopwatch. I found it amusing recently when I read a research report by a woman who was trying to determine if chimps understood mathematics by inducing them to count out two proportional shares of chocolate candy.

The presence of white coats did not equate with benefit in the mind of the chimpanzees. It did to me because I wanted a larger enrichment budget for the animals and the money would come out of the grant budgets. I had asked today's grantors to double the money amount that last year's grant had allotted to my program. I wanted all of the chimps to look enriched, but still in need so my budget would be improved. Obviously I had failed to explain this to Adam, which might explain why he behaved so rudely to the guests who wandered around the area under the brazen September sun. I had never seen him flinging objects at anyone before, but he now managed to launch a large wad of pasta and molasses I had mixed up for him and had been trying to distract him with. It splattered as neatly as an Ed Pollock painting on the white lab coat of one of the strangers. Aghast and embarrassed for my ape friend, I still had to admire his aim and poise as I watched one of the technical assistants run quickly to procure a new lab coat for the visitor who was waving at us good-naturedly.

"Adam," I said under my breath, "please settle down!"

He looked at me with a barely contained sense of outrage, "White coats!!" he spat out.

"Adam, you can attract more flies with honey than vinegar," I admonished him, still waving and smiling behind my mask at the scientist-victim.

"*What?*"

"Happy white coats mean more grant money, Adam. More grant money means more enrichment. *Capiche?*"

"What language *are* you speaking?" He said sarcastically, but capitulated by retiring to the back of his cage to sit disgruntled but polite until the procession was over, or at least so I hoped.

Besides these processions, virtually the only time chimpanzees would see white lab coats, especially in the highly restricted biocontainment area, was when they were under assault. Care-givers who fed and watered and cleaned never wore white. They wore scrubs of blue or green or purple. I dressed everyone in my division in a rich turquoise, which eventually became immediately identifiable to chimpanzees as being equal to fun, food, and good times. I had once read that the Navajo declared that a man who looked upon turquoise first thing in the morning would have good luck all day, I hoped this would work for the chimps as well. For years after I left (so I learned from my friends who still worked inside) anyone who ventured into the animal areas wearing turquoise scrubs could depend upon a raucously friendly reception from the chimps who would immediately be ready to play, expecting to be fed, groomed, or given a toy. But white was taboo. The only white coats a chimp usually saw would be those worn by the persons performing experimental procedures, blood draws, or inoculations on the chimpanzee.

To understand the unmitigated fury the chimpanzee would heap upon anyone wearing a white coat, you would have to imagine it from the chimpanzee's perspective. White lab coats would generally be perceived when the chimp was lying prone on a gurney, his body immobilized and his perception distorted by the anesthetic Ketamine, a dissociative that still allowed some degree of consciousness. Meanwhile the chimp was poked, prodded, and probed. I tried to imagine what it would be like to see the white blur leaning close, the white glove-clad hands hovering overhead, the far away sensation of a needle prick. The unimaginable fear induced by being unable to fight or flee from the dominating motions of the white blurs. Unable to escape from the irritating and incessant high pitched chatter of the human voices, more akin to the pitch of a monkey than the rich timbre of a true ape voice. This is why, inevitably, the white lab coat became an icon for pain and loss of control, and the perfect target for any materials that could quickly come to hand and be launched as missiles.

However, even during the pandemonium elicited by the processional visit of the out-of-towners, the chimpanzees could occasionally be capable of kindness, amusing antics, and great acts of altruism toward their human kin. For instance, anytime I had the misfortune of being selected to participate in the procession, I always emerged miraculously free of spit or other unmentionables. I am pretty sure this was because the identifying turquoise of my scrub trousers was evident under my white robe.

The current visit in Adam's area was one of the times I saw this capacity for altruism extend even to the strangers, the white-coats. One of the buildings being visited was adjacent to where Adam and I were lounging, observing unobserved. The building where the white-coats were headed contained 16 cages, eight on each side of the barn-like structure facing each other across a wide concrete hall. Each cage held a single chimpanzee. The tour was being met with the usual barking, howling, and tossing events. Although Adam had been sitting quietly while I fiddled his feeding puzzle, he began to get increasingly agitated as the procession approached the barn like structure. He rocked to and fro, the hair on his neck standing on end, and intent on watching the visitors approach the barn building. Still vainly trying to distract Adam with my sweet, brown pasta dish, I finally gave up and turned to watch the procession as well.

About the same time I noted that the over all noise level coming from the barn building seemed higher pitched and more staccato than the measured vocal displays one comes to expect from ordinary expressions of dominance. There was something intangibly different and a bit more hysterical about the general fuss being made. It also seemed somehow familiar. I was just trying to analyze it and remember why, but the only memory that came to mind was from that morning in the enrichment lab. Poppy was happily filling up the *Waring* blender with some windfall apples someone had donated, ice, and water; telling me for the thousandth time; "I'm glad you and Adam found this thing!" She was making smoothies for the clean colony.

Even with that mental postcard I might not have made the connection to the chimpanzee commotion around me if I hadn't suddenly spied Cardenas walking rapidly toward the building that the visitors had just entered. Cardenas was Emiliano's boss, and the overall animal area manager. He always seemed prescient, and to know exactly what was happening with the chimpanzees in any given place or time. He had an uncanny sixth sense for being right on the spot when any problems came up. Cardenas was probably personally responsible for averting any number of disasters and preventing loss of life and limb for a number of chimps and humans. After 25 years among chimpanzees he understood their language better than any psychologist whose research findings I had read. It was exceptionally rare for him to hurry, rush, or walk rapidly. When he did move more quickly than his usual saunter, it was worth paying attention because it was a sure sign of impending drama. By now, Adam was up also, standing on two feet, swaying, and making what sounded like a low wooing noise. Thus cued, I was able to attend to a sight that I shall always cherish.

Suddenly, I saw the five white-coated visitors followed by their administrative guide and technical assistant burst running out of the barn. I finally realized what was happening, and Adam was jumping and hooting with gusto by now. I was trying to be seriously concerned about the welfare of our visitors, but it was too funny to see that parade of prime intellectual composure dispersed so quickly. I burst out laughing and laughed until I cried, thus demonstrating my empathetic insensitivity and comparative lack of altruistic sentiment. Even Adam and the other chimps seemed to be looking askance at my irreverent response to what was clearly a dire situation. I almost felt embarrassed, but not quite. Our erudite visitors looked like little bits of popcorn spewing out of a pan. Adam was in a full display, he clearly did not find the predicament funny and was probably worrying about the fate of the chimps who were still locked in the barn making a terrible cacophony.

Imperturbable, Cardenas made straight for the barn at almost a run and courageously entered, calling to Emiliano in Spanish to follow behind and bring a shovel. Everyone but the white-coats seemed to understand exactly what was happening and work in perfect synchrony. I watched as Emiliano ran into the barn with a shovel. Cardenas and he had recognized the snake call immediately. The visitors had no notion of the meaning of the vocalization or they would never have entered the building from which it was being announced. About five minutes elapsed and Cardenas and Emiliano came out of the building holding a headless rattlesnake carcass across the shovel handle, it was almost three feet long. The whole area fell eerily silent. I looked over at Adam, he was in the shade, sitting in his usual relaxed posture, licking molasses off of his fingers.

A few days later I went to the barn building where the incident had occurred so I could deliver colorful 5 gallon buckets of Kool-ade. This was a favorite hot day treat for the singly-housed chimpanzees because after the Kool-ade was gone, they had the added fun of arguing with me about who was going to get to keep the nice, rubbery 3-foot long tube straw. Two of my friends who lived in the barn building were J.D. and Dash. They were grunting and gesturing back and forth to each other. It was easy for me to imagine that they were recounting the tale of the snake and the visitors, most of which I had already heard from the visitors and Cardenas the day after the whole event had occurred.

"J.D.," I prompted him, "Your cage is right here by the front door, and Dash is across the hall there in the back, I bet all that noise was you guys warning those visitors to get out, just like the time Adam was warning me about the radiation room. And to think they just ignored you."

J.D. gave me a baleful glance and switched his tube straw from the lime bucket to the grape bucket.

"Look, J.D., I know, *nobody* likes lime Kool-ade. Same way when I was little, I wonder why do they even still make it? But J.D. that's what makes it enrichment, just think if life was all just things we liked, it would be wholly monotonous. Including snakes, we don't like them, but it makes life interesting."

He glanced up briefly while continuing to down the grape drink, but I thought I heard him mutter, "Are you for real, human girl? Lime Kool-ade and snakes? Totally *not* the same!!'"

"Admit it, J.D., that grape actually tastes even better after that awful lime!"

The white-coated visitors had said that they thought it strange that in spite of the vocalizing and calling in the building, not one chimp had spit or thrown anything at them. They especially noted that J.D. was gesticulating by shaking his hand at them and running in frantic circles in his small cage. It was easy to imagine J.D. exhorting the scientists;

"Don't go in there, go back! Save yourselves!! Get out, you fools!! Snake! Snake!"

The snake had taken up repose at the end of the building near Dash's cage. Dash had been reduced to a babbling tear-stained picture of himself, his high-pitched screams ending in hoarse noiseless hiccoughs.

The visitors, in curiosity at his obvious stress wandered closer to his cage, they seemed to have no instinct to turn tail and run like any sensible *Pan troglodytes*. It was while they were pondering poor Dash that their guide noticed an odd buzzing sound that he thought might be an electric wire arcing. Glancing around he saw a rattlesnake coiled against the wall, "RUN!" he cried, and run they did. Poor old Dash, to think that for all of his emphasis, the visitors hadn't understood a word he said.

It's right there, *there*! Behind you, for God's sake! No! Don't take another step, run! Are you deaf, run! RUN! Get help!!"

Like tourists the world over, the visitors had seemed oblivious to the tongue of the indigenous. So wrapped up in their own thoughts, they couldn't even read the universal signs of horror and imminent disaster. And, like indigenous populations the world over, in dealing with tourists whom cannot understand their language, the chimpanzees seemed to think that the louder they declared their message, the better it would be understood. As I gave Dash his tube straw and a bucket of fruit punch Kool-ade (his favorite), I told him;

"Dash, that was very heroic, trying to save those tourists like that. You certainly must have been terrified!"

I swear I thought I heard him answer, and J.D. nod in agreement;

"Yeah, I was tryin' to give 'em a simple message. Its too bad about you humans and those extra folds of frontal cortex that occlude your natural good sense."

"Yeah, too bad," J.D. grunted in assent, " don't know how you guys ever made it on your own after you left the homeland."

"Well, in any case they were very impressed with your homespun hospitality. They actually gave our enrichment program *more* money than we had asked for in the new budget, in spite of Adam's target practice. So you can be proud, team!" I encouraged them with enthusiasm, "Well done!!"

"More fruit punch, please," replied Dash.

Later I was retelling all of this to Adam, "Well," he reflected, "I guess that time I warned you off the snake you actually had more sense that I gave you credit for, you didn't just stand and gawk like a some white-coated, camera-toting tourist."

"Thanks for the compliment, I *guess*!!" I retorted. Just then Emiliano came around the corner where I was crouched down talking through the mesh to Adam.

"Another hot one," he said inanely.

"Yeah," I replied.

"You okay?"

"Sure, why?" I asked, looking up and shielding my eyes from the sun with one hand.

"I thought I heard you talking to a chimpanzee," he smiled crookedly down at me and I blushed.

"Don't be ridiculous," I said haughtily, "everyone knows chimps can't talk, they haven't evolved a larynx for that sort of communication. Right Adam?"

"Right," he corroborated, lifting a hand to shield his eyes from the sun and gazing speculatively up at Emiliano who just laughed.

Four

Two Score And Several Years Ago: Clan Matrons And Founding Fathers

Anecdotes related that there scores of chimpanzees airlifted out of Sierra Leone in the late nineteen-fifties, and sent like cargo straight to the military base for use in scientific study. Although I had at various times during my tenure at PRC seen different documentation to support these anecdotes (such as log books, typed lists, medical records, and so on) these documents shuffled around mysteriously, and came and went with numerous self-important people who passed through the management positions at the Center. It was a great loss to our understanding of ourselves as a nation that these documents were never protected and collectively maintained in an archive. Over the intervening decades since the first chimpanzees came to America, the surviving remnant of these early "unwilling ambassadors" (as one famous psychologist would later describe them) became the founder mothers and fathers of subsequent generations of the majority of chimpanzees used in research in the United States today. Numerous of my chimpanzee friends were among these early pioneers.

Mandy was a very easy going old girl approximately 30-years-old at the time we first met in 1987. She was already a seasoned mother with numerous offspring. She had an innate patience and lack of prejudice toward humans that allowed us to build a relationship. I learned that she was a favorite among the care-givers because she was as kindly and cooperative as she appeared. Knowing her harrowing history of capture and research use at the hands of humans, her lack of spite was surprising. Maybe her interest in me was a female-female thing, I reflected. Until the 1980's these chimpanzees had had minimal contact with female humans. Laboratory research and care (especially in military settings) were still mostly a male domain. Perhaps it was only my gender novelty that elicited her initial interest. I like to believe that she saw some special quality in this oddly out-of-place human being that called forth her desire to mentor me into the complex ways of the chimp colony, and that is why she casually reached her huge hand out through the cage bars one hot August afternoon, uncurled her fingers, (easily twice as long and thick as mine) and gently stroked my hand.

Mandy had a sleepy half-lidded look that gave her an affect of wise geniality that really reflected who she was. She had an unusual coloration to her pelage that only a handful of the chimpanzees at the Center exhibited and which I haven't noted to be prevalent in other chimpanzee populations I have visited. Her hair had a silver gray sheen, probably primarily due to age, but also a unique and subtle apricot tone underlay her coat. Her skin was soft and fair. She was not dark-complected like most chimpanzees but neither was she white and freckled as was old Paleface, her skin was light silver-gray in tone, like a smoky pearl.

She was gentle, but her bearing was also confident and regal. While Mandy cooperated with the directives of her care-givers, one could not mistake this with blind obedience or submission. She complied in the speed and fashion that she chose, and with great ceremony and languorous deliberation. The care-givers seemed to implicitly acknowledge her status, not hurrying or intimidating her in any way. Hers was not a personage that would have scurried across a crosswalk she was a traffic-stopper.

When I first met her she had an infant. She was one of only two or three chimpanzee mothers who were allowed to keep their offspring when I first began to work at the Center. The fact that she solicited my interactions under those circumstances was very unusual, but perhaps she was lonely for some adult contact and grooming. Mothering is hard work, and sometimes a little shoulder massage is just the ticket. Not that I was allowed to give chimpanzees shoulder massage of course, but hey, I was a mom and I knew what it was like. Besides, I was already well along the road of rule-bending thanks to Lenny, another chimp who had enticed me into a grooming session. As my landlord Sandoval was fond of saying; "If you're a frog in a well, why care if it is ten feet deep or twenty feet deep?"

Mandy liked to scrunch her back up to the cage, reach over her shoulder with a big groping hand and take my fingers gently in hers, pushing my hand up her shoulders to her neck. Then I was to massage, groom, and scratch, apparently indefinitely. Had Mandy ever been given the opportunity to be part of an extended family, I am sure she would have been the generous but firm matriarch of the band, undoubtedly receiving grooming attention from a multitude. Unfortunately, circumstances conspired to prevent Mandy from ever knowing the joys of extended chimpanzee family life.

Mandy was a member of a breeding colony housed in an older area of the Center. Each morning at seven sharp they would get their breakfast; monkey chow, apples, oranges and bananas. A tall reedy care-giver named Lazaro was telling me his opinion of the diet one morning during the usual raucous food hooting.

"I'm sure its nutritious, you really have to look at all that muscle and tell yourself its a good diet. I don't think it tastes that good, I mean it could get boring. Well, really boring if you know what I mean."

"Why do you think it is a boring diet, Lazaro?"

"Well you know, it seems that it is the same every day, but they are really strong, and all that muscle. You know, I'm in weight training myself."

"Really? What, at a local club or something?"

"Oh yeah, I work out four, five times a week, free weights."

I gave him what I thought was a well-concealed once-over, he looked pretty lanky to be a weight lifter, "Huh", I responded. I guess he caught the once-over and the tone because he reddened and sounded a bit defensive.

"Well, the trick is getting the muscle on and keeping it on, you look at these chimps, now they got a lot a'muscle. Can't be the fruit, so you figure its right there in the monkey chow, some kinda super protein-vitamin formula probably. I'd think."

He gave me a quick sideways glance, so I felt compelled to agree, just to make up for my earlier skepticism about his muscle mass.

"You bet, I totally agree, Lazaro. Definitely think they put something powerful in that monkey chow, well, heck they'd have to." I was over compensating now, wondering where our conversation was headed.

"You see, that's exactly my thinkin' on the whole deal. So I told myself, you gotta try that if you really want to weight train. Yep, I spent a whole month on the chimp diet."

"Huh."

"Well, I mean, whatever is in those biscuits, I figured they can't hurt you, and well they are really bland. It is a boring diet, and, well, I can't see that it really helped my training program either, so, you know... I'm back to regular stuff now."

"Huh. Well, that sounds like a good idea, though. Really." Well, really, I mean it *was* a research Center, after all. I had to admire Lazaro's experiment, I knew I didn't have the kind of scientific zeal that would hold me to a monkey chow diet for an entire month. But our conversation started me thinking about some improvements I could make in the lives of the chimps. Simple substitutions in fruit variety would go a long way to adding interest to their lives.

Breakfast and other feeding times were no secret, because the hooting and drumming could be heard for miles across the still desert. It was a chimp style coffee house chatter. Although the chimps at this early stage of my tenure were still housed only one or two to a cage, and had little or no visual contact with eachother, they were still very effective communicators. They used a variety of vocalizations (Just as Jane Goodall had described in text and on T.V.), and a complex system of drumming.

The cages in the breeding section were all gray. Gray concrete, gray metal, and where there was paint, it was gray too. The cage floors were a kind of expanded metal mesh, and the barred cage fronts were salvaged from an abandoned prison facility. While otherwise uninspiring, these surfaces offered a wide array of percussive opportunities, and the chimps seemed to have developed a highly integrated percussion ensemble and signal system.

Recently I saw a traveling dance show entitled "STOMP". A variety of urban artifacts including hubcaps, metal buckets, basketballs, and lengths of pipe were used as musical percussion instruments. The most amazing and melodious cacophony was orchestrated from these everyday street items. A natural rhythm and music emerged that was hypnotic and calming. As excellent as this repertoire was, it was a mere shadow compared to many of the performances I had attended inside PRC.

One chimp drummer would initiate a slow drumming on his metal wall which would gradually be repeated by several fellows down the row. The drumming would increase in tempo and intensity until reaching a crescendo often accompanied by sonorous wahs and barks. The crescendo would frequently be punctuated by a change in medium from the metal wall to whatever might be even noisier in the way of cage fixtures. Each individual had his own personal flair. Shakey liked to end with a four handed shaking of the cage front, so ferocious that it seemed the door must fly off of its hinges. Sampson preferred to repeatedly slam his tire swing and the suspending chain up against the ceiling with all his might. Fortunately, an enrichment idea that preceded my era was no longer in use, but the indentations of bowling balls once used in drumming could still be seen in mesh and sheet metal walls. The finale, as if on cue, came when the whole concert ended into an abrupt stillness as dramatic as any of the preceding drumming. To my knowledge none of these urban chimp performances has ever been recorded, if so, I am sure album sales would rival that of any other urban industrial band.

Most drummers were male. This was exclusively so in the founder population where most females were separated from the males except for mating purposes. When a female was in with a male during a drumming session, she usually ran for cover immediately upon the initial single drum beat of her mate. It was not uncommon for the non-participating cage mate to become a drumming surface. In later years I would note that second and third generation females had to some extent taken up drumming and it was no longer exclusively a male domain.

Drumming was at the heart of the performance an aggressive display. It also communicated a number of things such as the presence of unknown humans, or humans with a gurney or transfer cage, and other perceived threats or challenges. Within the confines of the caged world, it had taken on the detailed nuances of a primarily auditory, sound performance since vision was occluded and physical contact mostly eliminated. In this regard it was comparable to radio theatre, not as visually stimulating as a play or film, it nonetheless evoked powerful emotion in the listener. Perhaps it was more powerful than a visual display because it left more to the imagination.

The effortless grace and athletic prowess with which individual drumming displays were conducted was astonishing as well. I have only seen the great ballet performances of our time on film. I remember watching Baryshnikov leap from what appeared to be a standstill to a height that seemed at least six to eight feet off the ground. It looked great and I wanted to try it. Despite all of my living room efforts at the farm, I was never able to replicate the feat. I was able to leap high enough to feel just a moment of elation at my midair suspension and sense of weightlessness, and to intuit some small sense of the physical joy of choreographed motion. But no human could ever hope to compare to the amazing agility with which a chimpanzee can hurl itself through space. They perform leaps and twists straight into the air as if their legs were loaded springs. Often as I lounged atop a cage after the new buildings were built during my last tour of duty, a chimp would casually fling himself up eight or twelve feet from the floor to have a little chat with me.

My investigations into chimp anatomy led me to believe that this was due to certain evolutionary differences between us that resulted in a more bowed formation of long bones, a different muscle to bone mass ratio, and different attachment points for a variety of muscle groups including the gluteus muscles of the hip. Chimpanzees have retained anatomical traits that allowed for their lower limbs to swing more nimbly outward, and their upper limbs to heft body weight upward as neccessary for climbing and leaping through a forest environment. My own comparatively weak arms and disproportionately long legs were designed to keep me walking the straight and narrow on *terra firma*. When I compared my fragility to my cousin's agility, it was clear to me which one of us six million years of evolution had nurtured to be physically "fit."

Day after day as I sat out in the sun with the chimps in the founder colony, the old ones, or *viejos* as Sandoval would have said, I pondered the theories of evolution I had been taught. Our predecessors were bright and noble ancestral hominids, who of their own volition set out from the trees to discover the world. But suppose that origin myth weren't really so? What if, when we were all still close family on the original continent, our genetic siblings began to predominate physically. Maybe we were marginalized from the prime territory due to their superior physical prowess. Perhaps there was a different evolutionary scenario than the ego-satisfying one in which a little hominid braves the savannah with a newly enlarged brain and later emerges into Homo erectus leaving behind the homeland in search of adventure. Maybe we were squeezed out of the security of the trees and later into the colder northern latitudes away from the warm and abundant equatorial lands that were home because we were weaklings.

Or worse yet, what if we were forced out by our original family? What if our ancestors were pariahs akin to the character Smeagol in the Tolkien trilogy? A skinny little creature who was shunned by his own family because he was clever enough to invent lies, commit secret murder, and create dissension in the community. Suppose the real reason for our exodus first from safe arboreality and later from the cradle of Africa was that we were undesirable, capable of great harm to the community and therefore unwanted? Thus rejected we turned tail and crept off by shadowed ways, clutching our ring of power, which was our intellectual advantage. Theory of mind research indicates that the very root of what we exalt as intellect must have been born of a sense of self followed by an ability for deceit. The act of keeping information secret, sharing it with only select individuals, and withholding it from others to further our own advantage indicates advanced reasoning and ability for abstract thought. These are the very traits that make us powerful as a species.

Perhaps after our ancestors crept away from home in misery and shame, they holed up in the fastness of the northlands until the time came when we could rule the world. There we nursed our grudge against our siblings until it was pressed into the double helix of our being and we bided our time until we could exact penance from the family that had turned us away. Our superior intellectual capabilities increased, in time we could easily dominate other primates to our own ends. They weren't relatives anymore, they were mere animals, research subjects. Could it be we were like the spindly nerd who grew up and made good in the world, and then returned to the old neighborhood to humiliate the fifth grade bully who was now a day laborer?

During the hot dreamy afternoons, as I conducted my observations under the unrelenting desert sun with my water soaked lab coat wrapped around my over sized cerebral cortex, I wondered if our dominion over the chimpanzee was less noble than science made it appear. Was there a remnant of jealousy left over from our evolutionary childhood, were we still nursing that old grudge? Over the intervening centuries great writs of our intellectual achievements came into existence. Volumes now codified our dominion over the earth and all other animals. Verification by our own hand of not only our superiority, but our divinity. Dominion became a divine right, so that finally we could, with impunity and full justification, incarcerate our own cousins. We could use them to whatever end we chose, assigning them no dignity or elements of personhood. That is how I came to be sitting here in the hot sun watching Mandy groom her baby's head, with a roaring hot furnace belching smoke behind us. The biological incinerator was being used today to dispose of some baboons whose experimental project was now complete. I wondered if Mandy knew that the cloying smell was searing flesh, or if it was just an undifferentiated stimulus in her inferior abstract processes.

Mandy sidled up to the end of the cage, she was holding little Hank right on her lap for me to see. I had never been that close to a baby chimpanzee before. Most babies were in the nursery being raised by humans, and during my first tour of duty I hadn't been cleared to go in there. I stepped a bit closer to see Hank's face, and Mandy reached her fingers out through the cage mesh towards me. I reached out and touched her, she wrapped her big leathery fingers around mine gently and moved Hank closer.

"Human girl, I know you would like to see my baby"

I knew I didn't want to get my fingers bitten off, I couldn't believe this big protective mother would actually be offering her baby for my inspection.

"Go on, human girl, you can touch my little baby. I know you wouldn't hurt him" Mandy looked up at me with her liquid brown eyes.

Gently I laid my finger against the top of Hank's warm, tiny head and stroked the soft wispy black hair that stood up in a little peak. Then Mandy moved off to the back of the cage. Had it really happened? She sat contentedly nursing him in a shaded corner. Maybe I was having sunstroke. But even if I was, I thought Mandy might like a nice orange or an apple. I had learned where the fruit locker was, and using my superior abilities of deceit, had learned how to sneak in and steal contraband for my chimpanzee friends. The few times I was nearly caught by my fellow humans I would put on an official air and make what I thought were erudite comments so it would appear that I had a research-based reason to be rummaging around in the fruit locker. I was happy I had found a way to put my cortex to some use in making amends to my new-found cousins.

One of the first fathers of the PRC population lived a comparatively monkish life in the breeding colony area. Usually housed by himself, Paleface was a large and relatively docile fellow who weighed over 200 pounds at the time of his demise. He was tall and well-proportioned, not obese. He had a partiality for peppermint candies which was legendary at PRC. One of his faithful care-givers, Minda Equus, was there at the very end as Paleface lay dying on the grated metal floor of his cage in the autumn of 1993. Paleface had such deep trust for Minda that he allowed her to hold his head in her lap and feed him a peppermint candy as he rested and then passed from his long and weary life behind bars.

Paleface was an intelligent and gentlemanly chimpanzee. He had been a contemporary of the chimponaut, Ham. He was born in the wilds of equatorial Africa and, in 1957, was flown out of Sierra Leone to begin his career in science. With almost twenty offspring to his credit, Paleface was truly a founding father of chimpanzee research and one of the original unwilling ambassadors. He was unusual in appearance. His skin was pale and covered with freckles, under his pelage he was clearly white-skinned. Paleface loved to sit with his back to the concrete wall of his small compound and luxuriate in the Winter sun. During the hot Summers he could be found in the same position on the shaded side of his cage. He moved with the casual self-assurance of one who had accomplished great things. Like Mandy, he had a meditative air and was not easily ruffled. Had he been human, no doubt he would have been the de facto CEO of some global conglomerate, sitting in a posh club with cognac at his elbow, perusing the *Wall Street Journal*.

I was rummaging through a box of papers that I found stacked in the hall one day ready to removed to the trash receptacle outside. I found several photographs of chimpanzees. One was quite cute because the chimp had on a clear plastic space helmet and was making a play face, it reminded me of *Curious George*. Turning the photo over I noted in writing *Zsa-zsa 1962*. I knew Zsa-zsa, she had emigrated to the United States in 1959, presumably from Sierra Leone. She had an odd way of gazing past you, almost in a cross-eyed trance, her head swayed to and fro as if she had the early beginnings of Parkinsons disease. I had made a few attempts to gain her attention and friendship, but she would have none of it. She had a terrible temper, if you came anywhere near her cage she snaked out a hand as far as she could and took a swipe at you. A number of the care-givers sported long scratches and scars on their arms where Zsa-zsa's nails had connected.

"Whatcha doin'?" It was Festus interrupting my contemplation, He had a wildly unkempt shock of white hair and wore thick glasses that required hefting up the bridge of his nose every five minutes or so, this left finger prints on the central portion of the lens that gave him a bleary-eyed look. Festus swept the halls, did small odd jobs, and generally kept the place in good repair.

"Oh hi, Festus. Well, I just saw these photos here in the trash, and well, I noticed this one is Zsa-zsa."

"Cute little cuss, weren't she? I used to be in caregiving in those days, yup. Wouldn't go near that old girl these days, nope."

I hadn't known Festus had worked around the chimps for such a long time, I looked at him with a new curiosity. "Huh Uh, why are you throwing these away?"

"New director says, get rid of that old stuff, don't need it around anymore, and he doesn't want no one takin' it home neither." He peered at me blearily to emphasize the point. "Their settin' up a new lab or something upstairs there." He pointed behind me and I turned, seeing nothing but a tiled wall.

"Yup," he continued, seeing he had an attentive audience, "brain wave research in those days, dontcha' know. See lookee here..." he fished deeper into the trash bin, producing several more grainy black-and-white photos, "now here's how it was all set up. See there you got yer wires goin' throught the back of the helmet, right on inter the brain."

I looked at the new photo then back at the first photo of Zsa-zsa in the space helmet, but now the playface looked like a fear grimace to me. Festus showed me another photo, this time a close up of Zsa-zsa's head with the wires disappearing into holes in her scalp. I remembered seeing Zsa-zsa getting a physical a few weeks earlier. As she lay anesthetized on the table I had seen two deep and silvery scars on her forehead, just at the hairline. Here she was in a photo with wires entering her young skull at the very same location. Festus continued narrating.

"We musta done a dozen, right in the atmospheric chamber back there," he jerked a thumb upward over his shoulder, again towards the tiled wall behind us, "yessir, she was lucky, alright."

"Was she?" I looked blankly at the tiled wall.

"Yessir, she didn't get infection like a lotta them, had be put away, you know what I mean. Them little wires get infected, infection in the brain's hard to treat, they said. Still it was a sucess they said, got some good information about high pressure conditions and all." Festus was stooped over the box rummaging in earnest, "See, now, here's Paleface, he's cute here, ain't he, all freckled just like a little kid." He held up another black and white photo with a young Paleface strapped into a seat in front of an instrument panel, it looked like a scene from a 1950's science fiction flick. "And a'course Mandy too." He waved another photo while digging through the box with his other hand. "Yep, they're the lucky ones alright. Didn't get the sled ride." He straightened up holding a sheaf of papers.

"Sled ride?"

"See," he held the papers out to me pointing at a column of names followed by a column of numbers, "this here's the list of the ones went on the sled."

I took the list and looked it over. There were at least a hundred names and I only recognized four or five of them. "Huh. Guess most of these chimps aren't here anymore. None of these names rings a bell."

"Course not, now lookee over here," he pointed to a column labeled *DOD*, "date o'death."

I looked more closely at the list and the *DOD* column. "They all died in the same year? Like an epidemic, or what?"

"No sirree!" He exclaimed, as if I were a dull child. "That's the year of the G-force project. See, that's how you can know how fast them jet pilots or astronauts can go nowadays. Yep, lotta them got that sled project. Little train track and sled, lookin' at G-forces, you know, finding the point at which too many G's make you go swish." He illustrated *swish* by drawing a finger across his throat.

"Oh yeah. Huh, so Zsa-zsa never...." I trailed off, she never what? Went *swish*?

"That's right, never went on the sled, that's one of the things as makes her lucky. Don't act none too grateful though, do they? Poor dumb brutes, guess they didn't really have any idea."

"Any idea of what?" I queried, feeling completely lost. My thoughts were swirling like fish dung at the bottom of an aquarium that had just sported some heavy activity.

"How lucky they are."

"Yeah. Huh, um...." I had so many questions I began to stutter, I didn't know where to start. I wanted to get at least one question in before he disappeared down the long corridor with his broom. But I needn't worry, Festus was enjoying having an audience.

"Festus what's an atmospheric chamber?"

"Hate to keep you from your work an' all" he said hopefully.

"Oh heck no, I'd like it if you could show me around a bit, so there's an upstairs, too?"

"Sure, come on now, be happy to give you a tour."

Festus introduced me to a catacomb of hallways and rooms I had never dreamed existed behind the gleaming tile corridors that were the main passages at PRC. He showed me a large metal door with a tiny window of heavy glass. When he opened the door I noted that it was at least ten inches thick. We stepped through into a metal chamber about twelve foot in every dimension.

"Yep this here's a prime atmospheric chamber," he said proudly, "course now I keep cleaning supplies in here." He idly handled a mop where it protruded from a roller bucket as he spoke. Brooms, buckets, and shelves with paper towels lined the walls of the little room. There was an unmistakable stuffiness of dead air in the chamber. Noises from outside the chamber were eerily absent, while our voices seemed magnified.

"Huh" I said, only it came out "HUH-UH-UH" in the confines of the chamber. I was contemplating what kind of *good information* could come from combining high pressure and brains.

"Lead-lined walls, those." Festus commented, tapping the wall with his knuckles. "A lot research done here, radiation, atmosphere, all them things back in the old days," he murmured wistfully, seemingly to himself. The glory days were gone.

"Well, thank you, Festus," I said, breaking into his reverie. "I guess I should be getting back now."

"Oh sure, kin ya find yer way out?"

"No problem, thanks." I was anxious to escape the dreary chamber and get into the pungent creosote-scented desert air again. After extracting myself from the labyrinth of corridors, I settled myself in front of a chimp cage for my afternoon observations. I felt suddenly overcome with a sorrow that seemed to emanate from the concrete walls and floors that converged around me.

After work I passed by Zsa-zsa'a cage. Pausing, I looked closely at her aged and lined face. I could see the lumpy silver scars on her forehead. I stood still too long and she seized the opportunity to fill her mouth with icy water which she then spit all over me. I had been dowsed by chimps in this manner several times, but it was the first time that I actually felt like I deserved it.

It was late August and Hank was turning seven months old. He was beginning to show an interest in adult foods. He would sit on Mandy's lap while she was eating and stare at her mouth. Occasionally Mandy would protrude a nearly prehensile lower lip toward Hank for his investigation. It would be filled with partially chewed food; biscuits, bananas, or other items I had contrived to add to the menu. Hank's little pink tongue would dart out and experimentally sample the food. His first bites of real food came right out of Mandy's mouth. I enjoyed the camaraderie that Hank and Mandy shared. It was a pleasant alternative to the mostly solitary life of the adult chimps during the era of my first tour of duty, before the new family enclosures were built. Many adults spent their days sitting with their heads hanging in a half-drowse, or over-grooming their wrists and arms until their pelts were freckled with spots that had been plucked to bare skin.

While I stood watching Mandy and Hank one afternoon, a dramatic drumming display started a few doors down. I recognized most of the percussive sounds, but there was a new and unusual element to the display. Mandy lifted her head in an attentive manner, indicating that she had heard the unusual bass note as well. I realized the display was coming from Sampson's cage. Intermixed with the usual clashing and clanging of the sheet metal wall, chain, and hanging tire was a hollow *thuk-thuk* noise. Curiously I sidled down to Sampson's cage just in time to see him take a flying leap at a large unopened watermelon. He struck it with his palm-like feet in what appeared to be a practiced martial arts move that involved one foot rapidly succeeding the other, *thuk-thuk*. The watermelon rolled crookedly across the uneven metal flooring and stopped. Sampson began his drumming round again; wall, door, swing, *thuk-thuk*. His hair was flaring upward along his shoulders and neck in a full threat display. I watched with interest, it didn't seem that his kicks were aimed at opening the fruit, he behaved more as if he felt threatened and was attacking an intruder.

"Strange one, old Sampson." Lazaro commented as he approached and stood beside me. Sampson had ceased his display and sat irritably in the front corner of his cage, head averted from the offending watermelon. He licked his wrist a couple of times and then stared past us out across the heat wrinkled desert toward the Noche del Muerto Mountains where they stood in a crooked gray line against the horizon.

"I see the watermelons I ordered came in."

"Oh, yeah. I should of cut it up, but, well, I wanted to see what he'd do with it. I don't think he's seen one before. You know, I guess he's about my favorite."

"Really? So you two are good friends?" I queried, thinking that I had never seen Sampson act particularly friendly toward anyone. He didn't act particularly unfriendly either, just kind of indifferent. He did respond more interactively toward men than women, and as for me, well I must have been invisible for all of the attention I had received from him. I'd tried, but never succeeded in making eye contact with him. He stared past me, around me, beyond me. Sampson was aloof. There was a ritualistic quality to his multitudinous displays. There was a repetitive, practiced and somehow mesmerizing quality to his drumming. During Sampson's many full bristling drumming displays I rarely ever identified an object for his aggression, so I assumed that there was a catharsis in the process of movement, expression, and percussion that somehow helped him to order his universe.

"I wouldn't say friends, exactly," Lazaro's words recalled me from my musing, "well, he likes to be left alone. I just think he's cool." Lazaro gazed at the indifferent chimp with admiration.

"Why?"

"Well, it's in the attitude. Like he doesn't care what we do. Sometimes it's like he's thinking about other stuff, important stuff, like he sees something we don't. My Mom has a cat like that, it chases stuff that isn't there."

"Huh." I made my characteristic non-committal goose honk. I found this noise very useful in eliciting conversation from others. I looked at Sampson staring into the middle distance like a Zen monk. There was a shamanistic quality about him.

"You gotta figure attitude's where it's at. Like when we transfer him. You cannot get this guy into a transfer box if he doesn't want to go. His choice all the way."

Transferring a chimp is probably the single most hazardous task a care-giver has to perform. There is potential for so many things to go wrong during the multi-step process. First, a small transfer cage on wheels is attached to the front of the main cage. The doors of the cages have to match up, but there is always a little gap somewhere around the perimeter that doesn't quite match, leaving a space where the chimp's hand can snake out and make a devastating grab. Next, the transfer cage, which is about three-by-four feet and four foot tall, has to be strapped up tight to the main cage and then a care-giver stands on top of it. Since the portable transfer box is on wheels, another care-giver or two stand behind it to ensure that it stays in place and is pushed up tight against the door of the main cage during the transfer. Finally, the guy on top grabs the handles on the top of the guillotine doors of both the transfer box and the main cage and wrenches them up. Each door can weigh between twenty to thirty pounds. In theory, the chimpanzee should now run into the portable transfer box, the door is then quickly dropped and locked into place.

When everybody is calm and cooperative this works great. The chimp is now ready to be transferred to another site, or can be easily anesthetized with a shot. Unfortunately, the chimp is often scared, angry, or in a full display. The chimps in nearby cages like to contribute to the pandemonium by calling, displaying, spitting or throwing things. If a care-giver is inexperienced or inattentive for even a moment, things can go badly wrong. If a chimpanzee escapes during the process it can mean serious injury to the care-giver because no human is a physical match for a chimp in any mood, and especially a chimp pumped on adrenaline.

During the many years I worked with chimps I was usually barred from being in an area during a transfer. I had witnessed several transfers through windows from an antechamber, but the care-giving staff preferred not to have to concern themselves with my safety if something did go awry. I gladly agreed to this policy, having heard numerous harrowing stories of botched transfers. Cases in which the securing straps gave way, or the transfer cage was flipped up and over, and the chimp escaped underneath. I had seen men's hands with missing bits and fingers lost during transfer events. One warm spring morning I had stood on the curb outside the HIV research unit with several other staff members watching a wailing ambulance cart away an injured care-giver, while his coworkers were still inside rounding up the escapee.

During an escape event the care-giver's duty was to secure the area and induce the chimp back into his cage. This might simply require a banana as a lure if the chimp was relatively calm and willing to return of its own volition. If the chimp was on a rampage, one of the care-givers would have to use a dart gun, shoot the chimp, and wait for several minutes until it fell asleep and could be hoisted back into its cage. Sampson had a reputation as a mean transfer. Lazaro showed me a transfer box with a twisted metal door that Sampson had managed to wrench during a display enacted while the care-givers were trying to transfer him.

"Yeah, we just closed him back in the main cage and decided to wait until he was in a better mood."

"He's pretty rough, huh?"

"Maybe it's because he was in the army."

"Army?"

"Yeah, I saw it in his acquisition letter."

"Acquisition letter?" I prompted, using a practiced echolalia.

"Comes with an animal when they're brought in here from another place."

"I thought Sampson had always been here, like the ones from Africa."

"Nope. He's from Bethesda."

"Bethesda?"

"Well, Africa first, I guess, but then he did a stint in the army in Bethesda, and was sent here."

"You were here when he arrived?"

"Oh hell no! He's older than I am! I wasn't even born when he got here. I saw the letter of acquisition from the Army in his medical file."

"Medical file, huh?"

"Oh, yeah. There's a whole room of medical files on these guys. It's locked up tight, top secret government stuff up there."

"Huh." I'd never been briefed about top secrets, or security measures for that matter. There didn't seem to be any security measures in place at PRC. It was conceivable that there was a room of files I thought, given my previous conversation with Festus. I remembered the strange convoluted corridors and the hidden pressure chamber. I also remembered the photos and papers that Festus had been asked to throw away, they had to come from somewhere, perhaps a hidden file room. It seemed that a lot of historical documents were being left forgotten or being destroyed as though they would hold no interest to anyone.

The personal history of both the people who had devoted themselves to research and the chimpanzees who had contributed so much was quickly and unnoticeably slipping away. I listened to what Lazaro said with greater interest. Several years later (in an effort to close the barn door after the cow had been stolen) I initiated a graduate project with a history student who conducted and recorded oral interviews with many of the care-givers and individuals who had worked with the primates at PRC over the years. My old assistant from the hormone assay days, Imelda, worked in the records office by then but she sadly shook her head when we inquired about the documents and photos that had once been so prevalent. Various administrators and clerks had destroyed much of the documentation in the intervening years, either thoughtlessly or intentionally, as the debate over the use of chimpanzees in research became more heated.

"After I read that letter, I kind of understood Sampson better," Lazaro continued, "like I could see why he had some wires crossed."

"He is a little different isn't he? I notice when you put another chimp with him he just mostly ignores them. He seems to like looking out there at the Noche Mountains."

"Yeah. Sometimes he's real mellow, like he's in a trance or something, then he's just the opposite, like real jumpy."

"Huh. Well, he looks mellow now. That white beard gives him a distinguished look like a professor or a beatnik with a goatee!" We both laughed.

"Kind of like a Timothy O'Leary of chimps." Lazaro commented.

"Definitely, I can see him with shades hanging in Greenwich Village or a smokey coffee house in Berkeley."

"I'm dead serious!"

"About what, Lazaro?"

"In the acquisition letter it said he was in a special Army study in Bethesda between 1958 and 1962. An LSD study."

"An LSD study?"

"Oh, yeah. LSD, and mescaline too. Daily megadoses. Four years, daily. Said it right there in the acquisition letter, I remember we were all amazed when we read it. Thought he'd be fried from that."

"Huh. I'd like to have seen that letter!"

"Well," Lazaro leaned closer and lowered his voice conspiratorially, "You, know, I made a copy and put it at the back of his working file, got it there still."

"Working file?" I wondered how many different sets of files I had yet to learn about, it seemed like everyone found it necessary to keep a personal set.

"Yup, it's a little system I worked out to keep track of everybody, I'll show you." Lazaro led me to the care-givers private lunch room, which was an anteroom attached to their locker room. There was a banged up old metal military filing cabinet in the corner. I'd never really noticed it before since it served as a catch-all, covered with old scrubs and magazines. He produced a copy of the letter as advertised, and on official government letterhead, "Says here Sampson was one of twelve on the study."

"Hey, do you think the rest are here too?"

"Dunno about it if they are. I was talking to a guy last year at that animal handler's conference in Dallas. He'd heard of it, too. Said he had a couple of those chimps where he worked over there in Texas."

"Interesting. You think someone would want to do a follow up study now, I mean all of these years later, what is it, twenty-five years? Maybe there is still something important we could learn about drug exposure." I was often amazed at the many experimental projects that just seemed to dissipate into nothing.

"Yeah, well maybe the government doesn't want the world to know about it. Leave him be, I say. I guess if Sampson's a little different he has good reason. I think he's cool." Lazaro summarized, looking at Sampson as he sat gazing into the middle distance.

"I think he's cool, too." I looked at Sampson and his slightly beat affect with a new appreciation. I wondered if he'd undergone some kind of enlightenment, was there an enhanced awareness and under-standing behind that aloof and energetic facade? I tried to imagine what it would be like to be alone in a little cage for years, taking daily megadoses of LSD, trying to make sense of the macabre and unjust world around me. I was frequently unable to make sense of the world as it was, and I wasn't alone, or caged, or on LSD. I guess that kind of imagining was just beyond my advanced abstract potentialities.

Five

Be It Ever So Humble,
It's No Place Like Home

The Center changed management several times while I remained there. Each change somehow added more chimpanzees to our colony. Chimpanzees came to the Center from everywhere. Aside from the original founders from Africa, there were zoo chimps and ex-performers, including two chimpanzees from a circus who knew how to roller skate. I discovered their photograph in a file years after they had arrived. It was signed on the bottom *Jack and Jill*, and showed the two little chimps at age two in pink and purple satin outfits with puffy sleeves and funny bouffant caps held on with an elastic band. They were standing in tandem, holding hands, and wearing roller skates. Although I suggested it, I was not allowed to provision them with skates.

There were also laboratories that were returning chimpanzees they had requisitioned from us years earlier for research studies that were now completed, and those that sent chimpanzees to our center because their facilities were closing down. During the mid-nineties there was a big rush for many research facilities to get out of the chimpanzee business, either because it was too expensive or too political. Our Center was the only one that was actively expanding and recruiting new chimpanzees, so we took in a lot of refugees from other sites.

In general I believed that the laboratory chimpanzees we received were coming into better conditions, because our cages were larger and newer than those of most facilities I had observed, and I had also developed a very extensive enrichment program. The program included many strategies such as a seasonal fruit menu, which had managed to distribute five hundred donated pumpkins the day after Halloween. A project that allowed the staff of the entire facility to participate in enrichment was *Christmas-in-July*. Everyone would donate their empty cereal boxes, which my assistant and I would fill with dried fruits and nuts, wrap in colorful paper, and distribute to the chimpanzees every couple of months. Despite our best efforts though, there was no getting away from the realities of an experimental biomedical research setting.

The most difficult and heart-rending new conscripts were individuals that had at one time been pets, raised in homes as if they were human children. There was no way to rationalize that they were entering into better circumstances. Their well-meaning owners had condemned them to a life as strangers in a strange land no matter in what setting they ended up. They were unable to adapt to chimpanzee sociality, and couldn't be accepted into human society regardless of their imitative prowess.

Since humans are endowed with an ability to think in abstract spatial and temporal terms, it is hard to comprehend how anyone could imagine a chimpanzee (no matter how adorable as an infant) could possibly grow up to be suited for human home and family life. Clearly logic dictates that there can't be a happy ending to such a scenario. Chimpanzees have incredible strength, quick tempers, and mercurial emotions. They are wild animals. Few of us would consider a lion or bear as a suitable family pet, but many people have initially thought chimpanzees might make a nice pet or companion for their families. If anyone were to ask *me* prior to enacting such madness, I would instead recommend *canis familiaris*.

It was often easy to identify a chimp's origin by certain characteristics they evinced. For example, those who had been actors or circus performers were often toothless, having had all their dentition extracted so they would be less dangerous to work with. As soon as I spotted an adult with a toothless, pink-gummed grin I was certain that they had a theatrical background. Similarly, behavior often suggested rearing circumstances. Laboratory-reared chimps could be the most devious and spiteful. Probably they learned this behavior from their human models, who frequently used trickery to anesthetize, move, or other wise facilitate handling the animals during experimental research protocols. I had more than once been lured cage-side by a playful demeanor, only to have the lab-wise chimp take a swipe at me or attempt to rip off my mask, gloves, or hair. Fortunately I had escaped serious injury by a hairs-breadth on more than one occasion, although I had once had the pocket ripped off of my scrub shirt (two inches west and I would have had a gender dilemma). Usually I was alerted to the ruse by a last minute gaze aversion. I have never had a chimp attempt to cause me harm while looking into my eyes.

Home-raised chimpanzees were always easy to pick out from a crowd, even if they had been in a laboratory setting for years, because they learned and retained so many human behaviors. Many of them eschewed regular chimp vocalizations, which are produced far back in the throat, and attempted garbled noises made more anteriorly along the palate. It took several exposures before I realized that they were attempting to use human speech sounds, an impossibility due to anatomy of the palate. Their labored attempts had a hauntingly human cadence and were a poignant indicator of the twilight zone between species in which they now dwelt.

When PRC had come under the final management take-over governing my tenure there, it added an additional campus, which we referred to as the *in-town* site. Our new managers had established this outlying lab closer to the amenities of the nearest town, Fat Gulch. Amenities included a small regional airport, and a Holiday Inn where the sometimes dubious-looking international pharmaceutical research representatives were lodged. I wasn't involved in the pharmacology aspects of research, confined as I was by training and inclination to behavioral research pursuits, so I rarely met with visiting scientists that contracted work through our facility. However, the new management team made an effort to include me when out-of-town researchers visited, presumably because of the entertainment value provided by my chimp anecdotes. International visitors that I had the pleasure of meeting during this era included some bulky Russians with an appetite for beef and vodka, a couple of pinched-faced Germanic types with no sense of humor (*I* always found it amusing when a caged chimpanzee flung feces at unsuspecting by-passers), and an autumnal Chinese gentleman with a briefcase chained to his wrist.

It was around this time that one could also find correspondents from various media such as the *New York Times* and some Los Angeles newspaper frequenting the local hotel. I didn't suppose they were editors from the travel section, particularly since controversy over the new management team at PRC had begun to brew in the larger world beyond the isolating insulation of our remote desert. With deference to the explicitly stated wishes of the new corporate culture, I attempted to keep my nose to the grindstone and ignore the encroaching publicity. Besides, I had enough on my plate to keep track of the *psychological well-being* (as the Animal Welfare Act so succinctly phrased it) of our rapidly expanding population of chimpanzee immigrants.

One day I was at the in-town site and I saw three care-givers as they stood laughing in front of a cage. None of them was wearing the typical personal protective equipment (PPE) necessary in animal areas. I had already noted that the in-town site operated by its own set of implicitly understood protocols, seemingly unrelated to typical industry standards. I wondered if this *laissez faire* might be at the root of the brewing public controversy. Attracted by the evident fun, I stepped closer to see them feeding a chimp named Toto. Toto was eating yogurt from a cup using a spoon.

"Hey, what's going on?" I queried. Everyone looked nervous. Redd, the general boss of the area turned to the others.

"All right you guys...back to work." When they left he addressed me, "Well, see I was walking by here over lunch hour..."

"You were eating in an animal area?"

"Well, it was kinda mistake, see I heard a noise..." Redd blushed enough to warrant his name, "anyway, Toto here sees me with a spoon and goes ape-shit, pardon me, and I see he wants my lunch, so I give him the spoon."

I looked at Toto who was quite efficiently and hopefully still scraping the bottom of the now-empty yogurt box with the spoon.

"Soon's I give him the spoon he goes over to the water spigot and fills the spoon up and sips outta it like an old maid from a teacup!" Here Redd laughed and winked annoyingly at his double entendre, which was based on the well-known fact that I wasn't married and loved to drink tea. "Well, Toto comes on back over t'me, and I give him the yogurt cup."

"I wonder how he learned to use a spoon." I commented drily, while making a mental note of Redd's transparent techniques to disarm me, including cussing and making personal innuendos.

"Some old lady had him locked up in a trailer's how he learned, kept him just like a little kid, saw it in his record. We like to come out here and give him cups and plates to play with fer fun. He sure ain't in Kansas now, are you, Toto?" Redd laughed at his own Kafka-esque attempt at humor.

Toto was nervously waving his spoon at Redd from under the door of the cage and making excited little hiccupping sounds.

"Wow," I said, watching Toto and thinking that Redd *had* actually hit upon something that was rather interesting, "are there any other chimps out here that lived with people?"

"Well, we kin always get a coffee cup and carry it around until one of 'em asks for it!" Redd gave me a toothless grin (I reflected that he *could* be categorized as something of an actor), and another wink to indicate that he wasn't going to observe any rules against eating and drinking in animal areas, and I was now in collusion. I sighed.

Surprisingly, Redd wasn't far wrong. I learned to spot the chimpanzees who had been reared in human homes by the behaviors that set them apart from the casual self-confidence of wild-born chimps or the jaded disingenuousness of the hardened lab chimps. Their response to the ordinary kinds of objects one might find in a home was most telling. I discovered this when we received a new population of chimpanzees from a lab that was going out of business "back east", as Redd would refer to anyplace east of the clump of cottonwoods that grew on a hill above Fat Gulch.

I had a box of donuts I had swiped from the staff lounge, and thinking I could lure some of the new arrivals into developing a relationship with me based on food bribes. Thelma was an especially beautiful female with a dark shiny face and thick pelt. As I passed in front of her cage she made an intricate hand gesture towards me. I understood immediately that she wanted a large cheese Danish balanced on the top of the box. I realized belatedly, as I handed it to her and she made another gesture, that she was using sign language and had just said "eat" and "thank-you." I was momentarily stunned.

Later I reviewed the history of these recent additions to our colony. They had been transported from a facility in New York (definitely east of the cottonwood clump), which had recently gone defunct. Most of the chimpanzees from New York were sent to various animal sanctuaries throughout the country, but about one hundred came to our center. They had widely mixed backgrounds, almost none had been wild-born or wild-caught. Many were laboratory born and raised. Some had been performers and later sold into laboratories.

Yet others had been used on behavioral research studies whose initiators had lacked the foresight to ensure that they would have funds to maintain the chimpanzees beyond the few years of the project. As a consequence of such oversights, we received several chimpanzees who attempted to communicate their distress using the sign language they had been taught while building the careers of various academics. Thelma was one of these. She often gestured and signed to her human audience, but most of us knew little or no sign language. One of the new veterinarians (who unfortunately had an undergraduate degree in psychology) was convinced that Thelma was displaying psychotic behavior when she signed and suggested administering a dopamine agonist. Thelma eventually resorted to a combination of artful sneers and a well-orchestrated ability to spit in order to express her disdain and frustration toward her human captors.

Not long after the New Yorkers arrived, we received a heart-breaking letter from a young woman who had helped to raise Thelma at home. She wrote telling us how, when she was a teenager, her father had been involved in a research project in Oklahoma, which required that he bring an infant chimpanzee home to live with the family. Over the course of the next year the shy and lonely teenager had a best friend and companion in Thelma. They took bubble baths together. Thelma drove the garden tractor and went horse-back riding with the young girl. A true bond of friendship and understanding developed between them. Inevitably it had to end.

Thelma met the same fate as most home-reared chimpanzees. She grew too big and unruly for a human home, and the architects of the behavioral research project had no financial strategy for her long-term maintenance. Eventually she spent twenty years in a laboratory cage in New York. She left a life of farm living, sunshine, and outdoor play to reside in a sterile laboratory room, in a cage no more than thirty square feet in size. And now she was here with us. As I sat holding the letter from her old friend asking to see her or at least have news of her, I was touched and noted that my hand was trembling. My newly acquired supervisor, Tex Hilton (who was actually from Pennsylvania but had developed both his nickname and a Texas accent after attending Houston City College) informed me we were not to reply, nor provide any information to this inquiry because it might be a clever ploy by some militant animal rights organization to infiltrate our facility!

"Loose lips sink ships." Tex had drawled one afternoon in his office as he gave me his directive. He accentuated the end of his statement with a loud *snick* as he clipped off the end of the fat cigar that was one of his trademarks.

I had wanted to reply to the letter because I was touched by its sincerity. During the many years I had been at the facility no one had ever written or called to inquire about any one of the hundreds of chimpanzees we held. I had often felt a resentment about what I perceived as a convenient eradication of these chimpanzees from the consciousness of the circus owners, zoo personnel, pet owners, and academics who had all benefited from their lives. However, a passage from the young woman's letter, as well as the intervening years which now separate me from the chimpanzees I learned to love, have provided me with deeper compassion for the human side of the story.

The horror of the realization that for the past twenty some years Thelma has been, and may still be existing in a small confined area at the hands of medical research is unthinkable. She awakes every morning, not to freedom, not even to join me on my way to the barn to feed the horses but to the stark emptiness of a concrete and barred cage. There is no warm sun to bask in, no smell of grass and flowers...just concrete and bars. There is nothing to occupy that sharp, mischievous mind...just boredom...hours upon hours of nothing. I have rarely allowed myself to think of Thelma's life after she left me because it is too painful. When I think of Thelma now I am overwhelmed with sadness and guilt... then my defense mechanism clicks on and I return to my busy life and try to forget...for awhile.

The letter went on to ask us to please allow Thelma to be sent to the Bountiful Harvest Ranch, an animal sanctuary in Fort Worth, Texas, established by a famous author from Massachsetts. I stood sadly gazing at Thelma as she sat eating another Danish I had contrived to sneak into the animal area. She would never go to a sanctuary now because she was hepatitis B positive. It would be too risky for other humans and animals who were exposed to her, and her research value was ten-fold greater with this unusual strain of hepatitis.

If I could have written to her old friend, I would have told her that Thelma was loved by her care-givers, who for the most part were tender-hearted animal lovers who kept low-paid highly hazardous jobs so they could be near the chimpanzees. I would have liked to say that now that Thelma was with us she had a large outside play area and several chimpanzee companions. There were no grass or flowers, but there was a view of the distant horizon and plenty of fresh air, not to mention an apparently endless supply of Danish.

Among these easterners was also a diminutive and sweet little chimp named Missy. It was her sweet tooth that led me to discover that she too had been raised in a human home. My assistant, Poppy Hadler, and I were visiting the newcomers with our usual contraband of donuts and danish. We had the box on the floor beside us as we sat on upended paint buckets for chairs, attired in our usual hepatitis containment regalia of scrubs, masks, gloves, goggles and tyvek suits with blue bouffant caps. Missy was housed with two adolescent tyrants named Dolly and Van who were pacing, swaggering, and spitting like some old cartoon of drunken sailors. I held up a chocolate éclair and the two of them shied away from this strange food as if it were a serpent. Born and bred in the lab in New York, they recognized only monkey biscuits and fruit as food.

Missy sat in a corner with her arms folded around her left knee, the other leg was missing below the knee. She sat calmly looking at us as if assessing our intelligence. Dolly and Van stayed well away from her, but continued to harass us until suddenly Missy turned toward them gesturing with her hand and making a garbled barking noise. Dolly and Van instantly ran through the door to the outside play area.

"Good move, Missy!" laughed Poppy as she got up quickly and made sure the kids were locked outside. It was now quiet and peaceful inside. Missy continued to survey us from the corner. "There's something special about her. The look in her eye, I don't know, it's so, well, human."

"Hmmm," I responded, wondering if Missy was another home-raised chimp, "you may be right about that."

Missy moved up to the cage front, gently lifting her legs up and swinging her body between her arms.

"Hi, Missy." I said. She looked into my eyes with such a pure understanding and gentleness of spirit that I felt she must be about to speak. She extended her index finger out of the cage mesh, pointing at the box of donuts. So rare was it that I had actually seen chimps point with an index finger (usually they used the back of one crooked finger or their whole hand to gesture toward an object), and so communicative and human was the gesture, that I took it as an immediate signal that this chimp had had a long and intimate exposure to human beings.

"Give her a Danish!" Poppy chided me.

I offered her the Danish on the top of the pile, but Missy shook her head no. Poppy and I looked at each other in mute astonishment.

"She doesn't want that one," Poppy finally managed, while I sat with the Danish poised in midair, watching Missy in fascination.

She pointed again at the box and I lifted up the chocolate éclair. Another negative, then she rapped on the cage with her knuckle and pointed more emphatically at the box.

"What does she want?" Asked Poppy, peering into the box.

Then I saw what Missy must have seen all along. Under the other rolls at the bottom of the box was a jewel-beautiful jelly-filled cherry donut. I gently lifted it out as Missy extended her hand up through the feeder box and gingerly took the proffered treat. We three continued to sit silently in our private coffee-klatsche. Missy ate daintily for a chimpanzee. Usually there was a lot of food hooting, happy grunts and loud chewing with plenty of lip smacking gusto. Missy was a neat, quiet eater. Upon finishing her donut, she fastidiously wiped her lips, then gestured toward the box again.

"Excuse me, human girl, can you please bring that box over here so I can see what else might be good?" I complied by pushing the box across the floor towards her. "I'd like that one please." Missy pointed at a chocolate frosted cake donut with peanuts. I handed it to her and she carefully chewed it, watching us with a thoughtful expression. "Well, you two may not be so dull after all. I wondered if there were any humans around here who could understand plain English."

"She's really a calm, smart chimp." I commented inanely to Poppy.

"Except when they try and put her in a transfer cage."

"What do you mean?"

"She like, gets hysterical, screams, has stress diarrhea, and fights it. Last time they had to use a dart gun and give her twice the dose. She *never* went in the transfer cage. They had to wait 'til she went down, then go in the cage and carry her to the exam room for her physical," Poppy explained.

I had seen other chimpanzees that had a similar stress response. Their adrenal corticoid level probably shot up so much that the anesthetic, a form of veterinary ketamine, was no longer effective. They would end up getting double or triple dosed. I could only imagine what disturbing memory associated with being anesthetized and transferred would lead to such a profound fear response. I reflected appreciatively upon the technique that the more experienced care-givers used, casually approaching the cage, talking in a calm voice until the chimp would present its arm for an injection and then sit patiently until it took effect. Even when anesthetized the chimp would still be somewhat conscious. I knew from my past experience working in an outpatient surgery clinic that ketamine was a disassociative drug that numbed and rendered the body inert but could leave the mind frantically aware of what was passing, magnify sensory experiences and distort faces and voices into grotesque abstractions.

A few days after we discovered that Missy liked donuts the new managers had arranged a company picnic to elicit a sense of corporate unity among us. The new management group was organized as a private research foundation. A former government researcher named Archibald Cooperston was CEO of the company, and Tex Hilton was his right-hand man. While Tex was tall and pudgy with flaccid cheeks (even when his lips were wrapped around a stogie), Cooperston was short and broad with the craggy keen-eyed look of a bird of prey. Tex drove to work in a turquoise 1957 Ford Thunderbird, while Cooperston preferred to be driven in a limo by a cadaverous old man named Alejandro who doubled as the in-town site gardener. Tex and Cooperston had worked together for years, first as Naval officers associated with various Pentagon projects, and later as business partners. It could easily be said of the pair that the left hand *did* know what the right hand was doing at all times. They made a series of sincere efforts to impart a sense of company solidarity to the employees by sponsoring various picnics and dinners. Most of the workers grumbled that they would rather have a raise. This picnic had been arranged in honor of the merger of Cooperston's foundation with PRC.

I found the location for the picnic rather odd. Tables had been set up for the celebration in a dirt lot next to the new buildings where the New York chimps were housed. The desert winds could be counted on to whip up the dirt into columns of dust that would no doubt inundate the grill and the macaroni and potato salads. I found this perplexing as I considered the fact that when the caregivers cleaned the outdoor portion of the cages, they merely hosed the excrement out onto the sidewalk into a gutter, which often overflowed into the surrounding acreage. The open-air cages, which held the newly acquired chimps, were no more than thirty feet from where the picnic tables had been placed and gaily festooned with billowing red crepe paper ribbons (signifying *biohazard,* I wondered?). The fact that all the newcomers were infected with various strains of hepatitis did nothing to stimulate my appetite, but nobody else seemed to care about this apparently inconsequential bit of information. And, not wanting to be a stick-in-the-mud, I decided to join in the fun (but eat before I arrived).

Conversely, the chimpanzees seemed happy with the arrangements. I could see Missy avidly watching us from her cage. Dolly and Van were running around in the background, food-hooting hopefully at the sight of the plates full of grapes and watermelon slices. It was a rare treat for any laboratory chimp to observe such a gala of unmasked human faces. But especially so for these easterners, many of whom had never lived outside of small cages in sterile white concrete rooms. For the first time in their lives, many of them were experiencing outdoor living with its multiplicity of sights, scents, and sounds. To also be able to view us in our array of colorful everyday clothing, watch our social interactions as we played Frisbee, cooked, chatted, and ate must have been astonishing. Because of their disease status, they were supposed to be kept under a CDC-rated level II biocontainment condition. This meant that during the course of their lives indoors, lab chimps infected with hepatitis would only see humans who were masked, gloved, goggled and shrouded in white tyvek suits with a buffoonish blue surgical bouffant cap completing the ensemble.

While most of the chimpanzees who were now observing us barked and paced nervously, their shoulder hair standing up in the piloerection typical of anxious excitement, I could see that Missy was completely at ease. She was actually enjoying our picnic, looking longingly as if she wanted to join us. Her demeanor was so evident that even one of the secretaries, Greta, took notice when Missy hooted and cat-called, gesturing us to come over to her cage. Greta asked if she could get a bit closer, so I escorted her to within twenty feet of Missy's cage. This was an unusual experience for anyone on the office staff. Many of the staff had worked at PRC or other primate facilities for years without ever having direct contact with the animals. Their experience of the antics and intelligence of our ape cousins was limited to second-hand tales carried from the bowels of the institute by those of us cleared to work in the animal areas. I felt rather sorry for these people because they were so far removed from the best part of the job. Later I learned that they felt sorry for those of us who worked with animals directly because they viewed our jobs, with the close proximity to diseases and animals, as hazardous and under-compensated.

When Missy met someone new she became very vocal. Her vocalizations were pronounced in her forward palate and sounded like garbled human speech. She looked at each human intently, tried to hold eye-contact and made a variety of hand gestures to accompany her tortured speech. Her demeanor was earnest and saddening. She acted as though she were searching for some sign of comprehension, a long-awaited response. Every new person was initially treated with this energetic repertoire of behaviors, which eventually subsided into her typically resigned posture, sitting with arms wrapped forlornly around her one good knee, gazing longingly out of the cage. Still, she seemed to keep some little candle burning brightly inside at a secret altar of hope, as if she were waiting for someone or something that was sure to come.

"My gosh, she sounds like my cousin Harry!" Exclaimed Greta in her lilting east-Texas accent. "Why I swear them two's a pair, if ever.... Why he goes on just like that, just like he's chewing up his words and spittin' 'em out! You wouldn't even know he speaks English half the time, bless his heart, way he drawls out his words. I swear that little girl could be from some holler in east Texas." We both laughed.

I thought Greta demonstrated great acumen in hearing the similarity between Missy's vocalizations and human language formation. Missy seemed to realize that Greta recognized her efforts to communicate and focused her vocalizations and gestures more intently towards her.

"What happened to your leg, Honey?" Greta yelled out to Missy, who responded by jabbering back rapidly. "Where'd that little old girl come from?" She asked turning to me.

"Well, I don't really know, other than she came from the lab in New York." Right then and there I decided I had been remiss not to trace Missy's background and find out what her story was. Maybe someone was trying to locate her, just as had happened with Thelma. "She really likes cherry-jelly donuts," I added, trying to be helpfully informative.

"I do think she tryin' to tell me something, I just wish I could go right on over there and give her a big hug!" Greta turned and looked at me with her heavily made-up blue eyes, which now looked suspiciously tear-filled, and made a pledge, "I can tell you I won't forget about her, neither!"

True to her word, Greta rarely let a week go by without bringing me a box of donuts for the chimpanzees, and there was always a cherry-jelly one in the box. I kept my promise to myself to discover Missy's story. I called the veterinarian in New York to ask her. As I had suspected, she had been raised in a human home. A man in New England and his wife had bought two little infant chimps, a boy and a girl, from an animal park. The result was predictably tragic, and explained both Missy's aversion to the transfer cage as well as the loss of her leg.

For the first fifteen years of Missy's life she lived with her mate, Jake, in a human home where they were initially treated like children. They ate at the table using plates, cups and silverware. They wore clothes, played with toys and had the run of the house. As Jake grew into adolescence he became stronger and more dangerous. I have heard people estimate that the strength of a chimpanzee, compared to that of a human of similar girth, may be as much as seven times greater. Eventually his owners realized he was too agile and strong to be allowed free run of the house. They constructed a large outdoor cage. Missy was more docile and remained indoors, but the owners were feeling overwhelmed and the neighbors had lodged a complaint. The owners looked diligently for a new home, but ultimately they only found the laboratory in New York that would agree to take Missy and Jake together.

An animal transport company was engaged to move the two from New England to New York. One winter evening two men arrived just as it was getting dark, a time Missy and Jake would normally be settling into slumber. The owner had placed both chimps in the garage, Jake in a small cage, and Missy roaming freely. The animals weren't anesthetized because the owner was convinced he could easily lead them into the transfer cage. When the strange men rolled a transfer cage into the garage and the owner tried to lead Missy into it, she bolted. The strange men began to yell and wave their arms at her, she shrieked in fear. Upright posture, arm waving, and loud vocalizations are unmistakable chimpanzee parlance for threatening aggression.

Jake, undoubtedly sizing up the intruders as a dominant male dyad attacking his family and challenging the status of his own male dyad (with his erstwhile owner), broke out of his cage and attacked. He responded as any self-respecting chimpanzee might, charging to the defense of his troop mates, prepared to fight to the death. He managed with one bite of his large male canines to shear off part of the loudest man's hand, flinging him bodily away like a shattered toothpick. Unremitting in his defense, Jake lunged a second time, biting at the man's face and tearing away his ear and half of the scalp.

The stunned owner grabbed a loaded gun and shot Jake dead. It seems unlikely that Jake would have understood this betrayal if he had had time to contemplate it. He fell on the floor next to the strange and terribly injured man. Missy was screaming and running around the garage, pursued by the other stranger still trying to capture her with a long stick and collar apparatus. The injured man was now unconscious and bleeding freely. The agonized owner realized he had to act quickly to what had become a medical emergency. Reluctantly, he shot Missy, aiming for her leg. She fell stunned and was anesthetized and transported to the research facility where she underwent surgery to remove the bullet from her shattered tibia. When she woke up she was in a small cage in a bland laboratory room. Her human parents were missing, her lower right leg had been amputated, and Jake was dead.

The day after hearing this terrible story, I sat in the sun outside Missy's cage while she ate Greta's recent offering. I wondered if I should tell Greta what I had learned. I decided not to. Why share the grief? Missy finished and reached her hand up through the feeder box.

"I don't have any more girl." I told her, and reached over to touch her soft, velvety hand. She gently closed her fingers around mine and looked into my eyes. I felt that she somehow sensed that I had found out about her tragedy and loss.

"I am so sorry," I whispered to her, gazing back into the liquid brown light of her eyes. We continued to hold hands for several minutes. In those minutes Missy became a real friend. The only difference that stood between us was the cage mesh and approximately 1.3% worth of genetic debris. As I thought about her life, I realized how thin the line was becoming for me, the line that defined some banal difference between what my species defined as what was human and what was beast.

It wasn't long after this that I left PRC for the final time. A few months after I resigned, an old coworker called from the Center to let me know that Missy had died. Since Missy was relatively young and in good health (well, except for the hepatitis, of course), I was surprised to hear that she was dead.

"What happened?" I asked with trepidation.

"It's kind of a mystery, really. You know, they knocked her out, had to dart her twice for her quarterly physical, and she never woke up."

"Wow, sounds rough." I would have liked to imagine that Missy's passing had been easy, but I knew her too well for that. I know her last moments on earth were filled with pain and fear. I could easily see her terror-struck eyes, rimmed around with white. I could hear her garbled, human-like screaming echo in my ears. I can imagine her slumping down on the wet concrete in the corner of her cage, where she was driven by the confusion of human yelling, and a water hose. As the light begins to dim for her, she reaches down to what's left of her leg and plucks out the red-feathered anesthetic dart, letting it slip through her fingers to the floor.

"Yeah, they said it was grim. She died right there on the gurney, during the exam. Heart attack or heat exhaustion or something, I guess. Sad."

"Yeah, sad." I agreed. I felt guilty, as if I should have been there and somehow prevented this from happening. Would it have made a difference if I *was* there? Even if I could have heroically saved Missy one time, what about the next quarterly exam, and the one after that? It was an endless corridor of terror for her. When I got off the phone I felt wrung out, and just like Thelma's old friend, I wanted to *return to my busy life and forget*.

That night I dreamed I was in a forest, and I could see Jake and Missy climbing a tree, up through a shaft of sunlight. Gleaming above them in the boughs, I could see the branches laden with a sweet golden fruit. Missy looked back at me for a moment, her large luminous eyes no longer held that searching, unremitting sadness. She looked peaceful and sublime. I reached out toward her, saying her name. She paused, but then Jake called from higher up, and with a last tender glance toward me, she turned and climbed on.

Six

Jornada Del Muerto:
The Long Journey
Of The Dead

Sandoval Seville, my bedridden landlord died in October. His wife Martina was devastated and so was Nikki. It was Nikki's first encounter with death. Nikki and her best friend Yvette Seville, Sandoval's grand daughter, had kept Sandoval company through the hot summer. The three could be observed companionably and raptly watching *novellas* on TV in the cool, cramped adobe room that had come to define Sandoval's world. Sandoval fed the girls from a cache of candies he hoarded under his mattress. After a summer spent inside eating membrillo (a jelly candy made from quince) and cacahuete (a kind of Mexican marzipan made from peanuts), and watching *novellas*, the girls were chubby and pale and girded with a fallacious distortion of social behavior that was surprisingly successful in preparing them for their first year in junior-high school. While Sandoval's death wasn't entirely unanticipated, his absence left a huge void in our lives on the farm. I personally hoped it didn't portend a long and difficult winter. During the weeks that followed Sandoval's death, I caught myself offering pennies to the statue of St. Ramon that stood in the *nicho* in the kitchen surrounded by perpetually burning candles and asking him to restore our lives to normalcy.

The traditional mourning period seemed to last for weeks during which a ritualistic procession of friends and neighbors from our village passed steadily through Martina's kitchen. They brought an amazing array of food offerings that made it impossible for *me* to think about anything but eating. There were little sweet tamales filled with cinnamon, *piloncillo* and pecans, pots of shimmering menudo accompanied by wedges of lime and crushed oregano, pan after pan of red enchiladas, and mounds of steaming rice tinted with tomato and saffron. Dressed in black and draped in a shawl Martina sat stiffly in the corner on a wooden chair. Her face was set and unemotional as the *viejos* passed in front of her taking her hand and murmuring condolences. Every once in a while she would begin to emit a high-pitched keening and burst into a flood of tears wailing *"Mi companero! Ai! mi companero!"* I found this so distressing that I would rush to her side and hug her until she had regained her composure and could continue to sit stoically and receive guests. By the time the *Day of the Dead* arrived on November second, most of the mourning had subsided. Nikki and I sat in the kitchen surrounded by the Seville clan making extravagantly colored tissue flowers for Sandoval's grave to celebrate the day. The little room filled with laughter. The wound caused by Sandoval's passing had begun to mend and we were going on about the business of living.

Perhaps St. Ramon couldn't respond to the entreaties of someone from a different faith, or maybe it was just going to be a long and difficult winter. If Shiloh had been a human boy instead of a chimpanzee he probably would have been about the same age as Nikki and Yvette. Shiloh died at five in the afternoon one day late in November. He lay on the bottom of his cage staring at a darkened stain on the aluminum wall. The shape of the stain reminded me of the African continent. I hoped that Shiloh was dreaming of tangled treetops with fig-laden boughs. The pitiful mound of colorful toys I had managed to sneak in under my white plastic space suit during his dying days sat in a pile on the floor next to him. He had never touched one of them. His biscuit box was full, and a slice of watermelon wept into a puddle on the aluminum perch.

Shiloh spent his last four or five days in the same position. He lay on his side, one arm crooked like a pillow under his head, the other reaching around over his back and cupping his anus. He refused food and drank little water. He urinated where he lay and defecated into his hand, laying the feces neatly in a row by his feet. During the last few weeks of his life he exhibited no will to live. Despite our efforts to engage him, feed him, and heroic veterinary measures to provide IV nutrients, he had chosen to die. That much was clear to me.

Shiloh was housed in the biocontainment quarantine area, where incoming chimps were processed and monitored for disease before joining the larger populace. During my second tour of duty I was first cleared to work in the severely restricted biocontainment areas. It was here that I became intimately acquainted with the deeply complex emotional lives of chimpanzees. I learned that they could feel loss, loneliness, and grief. Some of them cried tears (I had never read about *that* in any Jane Goodall book). Dash sobbed and cried buckets when he was scared. Rebecca's tears came in a slow trickle as she lay exhausted and wan upon her perch after her baby was stillborn, ignoring my efforts to comfort her, turning her face away tiredly. Other chimps experienced emotions so profound that they resorted to self-inflicted wounding (SIB, or *self-injurious behaviors*) to alleviate their own suffering. Some among the population would give up their will to live or injure themselves so grievously as to end their own lives.

During this epoch of my career at PRC I frequently commuted the sixty miles to work with the new biostatistician, Bart Milchausen. Bart had a Ph.D. in research biometrics, but he held undergraduate degrees in both art and philosophy from a prestigious liberal arts college in Colorado. Bart's life had been marked by a series of poignant tragedies including two tours as a medic in Viet Nam. He was married to a willowy anorexic. She later took her own life, but at this juncture was working as a comptroller for the university that had management oversight of PRC. Bart was helping me to analyze the final data I was using to complete my Ph.D. Bart's analytical skills were visionary, and with his artistic sensitivity and the fact that he drove a Porsche our two-hour daily commutes were fascinating and thought-provoking. One day we debated the sentience of apes as it related to a recent incident in which a chimp had died from self-inflicted wounds.

"In my opinion that chimp took his own life."

"Of course it did," agreed Bart. "The evidence is clear."

"I mean I think he *intended* to take his own life because he was miserable and saw no hope."

"How can you ascribe a state of hope to an ape? You imply that he had a grasp of temporal reality related to abstract ideations around self-determination," said Bart in his level, logical voice.

"Well, they *do* have a neocortex," I offered hopefully.

"But a sense of self?" Bart prodded, "Or a sense of personal future? How do you support *that* with empirical evidence?"

"Well, what about my mirror toys?" I was inordinately proud of this invention, in which I had glued plexiglass mirror discs into the flat bottom of a dog dish.

"What about them?"

"Well, the monkeys make threat faces at their reflection, but the chimps look in at their own reflection and use the mirror to pick their teeth, or clean out their eyes. They know the reflection isn't some other chimp. That shows that they recognize themselves, and therefore have a *sense* of self! " I proclaimed triumphantly, congratulating myself on my abstract reasoning.

"Personal future?" Bart insisted.

"Well-" I hesitated- "let's say a chimp is so miserable for so long that he acquires a knowledge of self as painful, uncomfortable. He has to use some means to alleviate the discomfort. He decides to change his condition through the only means available. By harming or killing himself, he alters his state. That implies comprehension of the *possibility* for a change in state. And isn't it the understanding of *possibility* or potential that constitutes future-consciousness?" I thought this reasoning was clever, if a bit contorted, but with his background in philosophy I thought Bart might buy it. I hoped I might at least win his tacit agreement on the subject since he seemed distracted now that a racy-looking red Saab had pulled up next to us and was trying to out-gun him. Bart shifted up and pressed the accelerator. The turbo drive kicked in and we reached warp speed. The Saab became a red gumdrop in the rearview mirror.

"Conditioned response."

"What?" I muttered distractedly, watching the shrinking red dot in the mirror.

"Pay attention. It's merely conditioned response. The internal state reaches some critical mass, which produces an automatic response that discharges the mass. Call the mass misery, discomfort, angst, whatever. The point is, that it is akin to a Pavlovian response. You're trying to anchor it to consciousness, value judgment, a sense of self-determination; all of the abstractions that *you* have," Bart turned and looked at me coolly with his clearly superior intellect. I couldn't see his eyes behind the dark polarized sunglasses lens- only a reflection of my own anxious face; it reminded me of a nervous macaque.

"I'm not saying I don't buy your version," he continued, "even if it *is* simplistic anthropomorphizing. I'll allow that the relatedness of our species warrants it, and I actually *prefer* your interpretation. Somehow it's comforting. Maybe we humans aren't alone in being burdened with consciousness; the regrets of the past, the weight of the future...." Bart mused on, "I'm just saying that your intuitive pseudo-hypothesis isn't demonstrable with quantitative empirical data."

"Hmmph." I snorted. I was stung by his comment about my simplistic anthropomorphizing, and irritated by the linguistic coup he had delivered with *intuitive pseudo-hypothesis*. I clicked my tongue against my teeth in disgust and reached over to the console to turn up the radio.

In my practical experience over a decade, cases of self-injurious behavior (SIB) occurred consistently in 5-10 % of the population. Rather than viewing this phenomenon as a deviant behavior innate to the individual, I came to understand it as a predominantly behavioral response to environmental conditions. Initially I thought it was a kind of ritualistic sacrament to frustration, powerlessness and defeat. But as I witnessed the high frequency of SIB in the most noxious enclosure areas at PRC, I came to think of it as having a function that must somehow organize the individual. As I studied self-stimulatory and self-injurious kinds of behavior in chimpanzees over the years, I came to believe that it was a dysfunctional adaptation (where *dys-* carries its true meaning, *painful,* as a prefix). That is to say that the behavior functioned, albeit in a painful way, to adapt an individual to distressing environmental or internal circumstances. In this capacity, SIB operated to re-establish homeostasis and an associated sense of well-being in an individual whose internal equilibrium had become disrupted.

As an anthropologist, I had been fortunate to have many opportunities to attend Native American rituals and ceremonial events. At one such event I was invited to attend a Lakota Sioux woman who was mourning the loss of her lover in a tragic farm accident involving a grain combine. After a carefully proscribed series of prayers, which included wrapping bundles of tobacco with red and black cloth, she used a sharp knife with an elkhorn handle to cut a long deep wound in one forearm. My role was to help her wrap the wound after she completed what was to my mind a long (since she was bleeding quite freely) rondeau of prayers and songs related to the depth of her grief, loss and longing.

This experience expanded my understanding of self-injurious behavior. I began to view it as a self-modulating act. Self-injurious behavior seemed to provide a sense of relief and a release from tension. Goaded by my need to find a functional explanation for SIB, and with the added impetus of wanting to prove to Bart that I was a worthy intellectual opponent (not merely a pseudo-hypothetist), I dug through reams of psychological research. I learned that SIB stimulated endogenous mechanisms to modulate pain input. Pain impulses were conducted along the phylogenetically oldest nerve fiber pathways to the brain. Input on this tract eventually stimulated the release of opioid-like neurotransmitters (e.g. enkephalins and endorphins) both systemically through the central nervous system (CNS) and locally along the fiber pathway. This class of neurotransmitter acted to decrease the release of pain and inflammation-producing substances. The result was a body-wide analgesic effect. I reasoned that the radical and immediate release of neurotransmitters brought on by wounding must act to *dispel* anxiety and despair (at least in some individuals). If SIB functioned in this way, then it persisted because it had an adaptive value to the individual as a proximal survival strategy. Although it seemed counterintuitive, I wondered if SIB might be a life supportive rather than destructive pattern of behavior.

I knew that the human and primate CNS was designed to be functional by means of a system of input-throughput-output. Input was largely provided by sensory experiences an individual had when interacting with the environment. Throughput referred to the integrative functions of the CNS as it processed input. Output was the resultant motor planning and purposeful behavior enacted by the individual. It was the activity of processing throughput that kept the organism balanced and functional. Disruption in any component of the integrative input-throughput-output cycle would result in systemic disorganization and a concomitant drive by the individual towards balance or homeostasis.

The literature I read was rife with examples of the disrupted cycle and related symptomatology. Generally when input was eliminated throughput became disorganized. When throughput was scrambled, output was disorganized, dysfunctional, or maladaptive. Some conditions involved a normal capacity for input and throughput, but resultant output was impaired. Conditions of impaired output included lower motor neuron disorders like Lou Gehrig's Disease, where output simply could not be enacted because of muscle death. Conditions of skewed throughput were demonstrated in diseases like Alzheimer's dementia, where neurological changes impacted the brain's capacity for integrative functions and output became dysfunctional, even nonsensical. There were other innate conditions that disrupted throughput including Schizophrenia and autism spectrum disorders, which presented with acute symptoms of integrative dysfunction. Disruptions in input could result from multiple causes, both intrinsic and extrinsic, and adversely impacted the important integrative throughput cycle.

Sensory deprivation and over-stimulation were two of the circumstances that disrupted the ability of the CNS to perform basic integrative functions. Sensory deprivation eliminated necessary input resulting in disorganization of throughput processes and overall CNS function. This had been established by deprivation studies such as Harlow had conducted with monkeys, and by cave-living studies examining circadian rhythms, POW research, and studies related to chronic institutionalization. The antithesis of deprivation (over-stimulation) could also produce CNS disorganization. The results of over-stimulation could be demonstrated by spinning in circles for too long, trying to eat in a loud, smoky restaurant against the background noise of a nearby jack-hammer, or attending strange carnivals in unfamiliar cities in February while drunk. Over-stimulating sensory conditions could result in fatigue, disorientation, self-endangerment and other symptoms and complaints associated with an inability to regulate input. Adding to the complexity of the whole input-throughput-output process was the vast individual variation in humans and chimpanzees. This individual variation was reflected in a personal ability or inability to modulate and respond to the natural and continual fluctuations in the sensory environment.

The drive toward homeostasis elicited by disorganization initiated volitional processes in each individual to seek a change in state. Self-directed behaviors (SDB) that I observed, including wounding and non-wounding, probably provided a venue of controllable input that over-rode disorganizing sensations. When SIB successfully produced a different, ostensibly more modulated and homeostatic state, it was reinforced by the release of pleasurable opioid neurotransmitters. The drive toward homeostasis was an innate life-preserving mechanism and probably triggered by autonomic nervous system sequelae of the fight-fright-or-flight response (FFF). I had discovered volumes of research indicating that deprivation and over-stimulation would trigger the adrenal corticosteroid stress cycle related to FFF. It seemed self-evident that chronic states of stress were being induced in the barren, fume laden, and noisome experimental research units where chimps lived out their lives and where I observed the most severe cases of SIB.

The most dramatic cases of SIB seemed to constitute a unique population of individuals. As I learned more about the hormonal stress response, I began to think that within the life cycle of these unique individuals SIB had value as a distal as well as a proximal survival strategy. Irregularities in the chemical communication between the adrenal and pituitary axis during stress crises could result in localized and systemic inflammatory conditions. Chronic and acute inflammatory responses adversely impacted the heart muscle and other organs. Inflammation would also increase the permeability of the blood brain barrier. Once the blood brain barrier was weakened, unhealthy protein debris would float across and result in neurotoxicity. Then a physiological *Catch-22* was set up. The adverse effects of the neurotoxins served to heighten the endocrine stress response, which impacted the system in some individuals in a way that could further increase neurotoxic effects and stress! I believed that in these individuals the drive toward homeostasis triggered events of SIB. The immediate response to the opioid neurotransmitter release was alleviation of stress and decreased inflammation. It seemed plausible that this interruption of adverse stress effects brought about by SIB must increase the distal survival potential of the individual.

My deeper understanding of SIB as a life-preserving strategy rather than a destructive and pathological aberration helped me to support the needs of the chimpanzees. As I worked to ameliorate SIB, it was helpful for me realize the value of SIB to the individual, and to honor it. To merely seek to eradicate such behavior could plunge the individual back into a frightening world of sensory inundation or insufficiency, or an unregulated and life-threatening FFF cycle. My goal became to extend my efforts to provide environmental enrichment that alleviated stress and provided measured input through novel diversion, entertainment, and old-fashioned food fests. I enriched the most restrictive housing areas with strange new foods like spinach, ginger root, and corn-on-the-cob. I also managed to enlist the maintenance crew to install closed circuit television in the HIV research modules so my friends Yogi, Peter, Courtney, Nick-El and the others could watch (what else?) *Jane Goodall* movies.

With my new perspective on SIB I began to take note that in our own culture there were multiple examples of socially sanctioned self-injury and mutilation. We had social contexts for ear-piercing, tattooing, body piercing, and optional plastic surgery as acceptable acts of self-injury. The increasing popularity of tattooing and body piercing was especially intriguing to me. Clinical reasoning suggested that the increase in prevalence and severity of such practices was correlated to something in the cultural milieu. Perhaps the behavior was in response to a cultural over-inundation of sensory systems that left the internal state of the individual disorganized. Maybe it was even possible to quantitatively correlate the number of tattoos or piercings a person had with dysregulation of the adrenal response (I couldn't wait to tackle Bart with this idea).

I thought more about this while I was attending a national conference on primate research being held in the confusing interurban jungle of Seattle. I had become inured to the cold intermittent drizzle as I wove my way along the sidewalk holding my briefcase like a shield and being jostled every few minutes by strangers. I felt disoriented by the layers of city noise, and the dizzyingly reflective vertical edifices that appeared to teeter crookedly toward the waterfront. The acrid fumes of the city had initiated a histamine response and my nose and eyes were beginning to swell up. I also began to experience a mild hypervigilance and irritability, which I knew to be the initial stages of the adrenal stress cycle. I gawked at the multiple tattoos and piercings that the people of the city displayed. The culturally sanctioned mutilations filing past me suddenly took on a new appeal as a potentially modulating form of adaptation. The next tattoo and piercing parlor looked almost irresistibly inviting, with its cushioned salon chairs and warm light. It promised an immediate and electrifyingly concrete definition of self that was appealing as I struggled to map the boundaries of my physicality against a ceaseless stream of sensory intrusions.

I shivered and walked along on the wet sidewalk looking for a coffee shop to escape into. I tried to imagine the opposite extreme of sensory overload. Maybe it was something that a spouse might experience

upon losing a mate after years of marriage and companionship. Or perhaps what a chimpanzee in an isolated research module might endure,
I reflected, missing my shaggy friends. The sudden or sustained cessation of sensory input must be even *more* disorganizing than the overload
I was experiencing, because there would be no available sensory means
to modulate the internal state. Input couldn't be invented from an environment *devoid* of stimuli. Unless, I realized, one were to use one's own
body as a modulating instrument through acts of self-directed behavior. I settled myself in a coffee bar booth overlooking the waterfront.
All of these thoughts were jamming themselves into my head along
with dozens of new enrichment strategies I planned to enact as soon
as I returned from my trip. As I sipped my latte, I savored the glowing
sense of well-being that seemed to emanate in tingling waves from the
blue tattoo of Taweret, the Egyptian hippopotamus goddess, who now
resided on my left shoulder.

Until the time of my second tour of duty, I had only seen the milder
cases of SIB. The severity of SIB I encountered in captive chimpanzees
varied widely. There were cases of a mere repetitive plucking of the
same scabby spot on an arm or a leg, leaving an open lesion about the
size of a quarter. Then there were the more dramatic cases- self-gnashings and pickings that were life-threatening, and sometimes fatal. In
one case a chimp who had been housed for years in an isolated cage
in the most remote level III HIV biocontainment module severed his
femoral artery with a canine tooth in a fit of self-gnashing. The drama
was enacted within view of five other animals all housed singly in their
isolette cages, but no humans were present. His corpse was found by
an incredulous care-giver during evening feeding, sprawled across the
bars that formed the floor of his cage which was suspended about eighteen inches above a yellow concrete floor rich with dark clots of his
blood. Another similar case resulted in severing of a tibial artery, but in
that incident the chimp was found and treated. He survived but continued to enact self-wounding.

It was clear that the more sensorily restricted the environment became, the more dramatic were the cases of SIB. I responded by developing a sensory-based enrichment protocol. I felt it was imperative that every sensory modality be addressed by enrichment. Sometimes a researcher only allowed one enrichment object in a highly controlled experimental setting. It then became my mission to use that object as an enrichment vector. Many researchers preferred an innocuous object such as a large hard plastic ball or a piece of PVC pipe. I used sanders and drills to alter the texture and put holes in the shiny plastic surface. Sometimes I attached chains so it could be hung in space for dimensional visual stimulation. At one time I found and ordered red apple-shaped balls from a manufacturer who had developed a process of imbuing the plastic with an apple smell. Using a stopwatch, I determined that these seemingly minor alterations resulted in longer periods of engagement and greater variation of activity with the toys.

During my second tour of duty PRC had two very compassionate veterinarians overseeing animal care: Fran Perette, a Midwestern farm girl who loved to go to the horse races, and Joe Echevarria, an Idaho native whose sheep-ranching family were all tough-minded Basque descendants. They agreed that they wanted me to institute a comprehensive enrichment program to document and prioritize the needs of animals with repeated history of SIB. My responsibility was to visit every one of these individuals and observe them carefully, designing personally tailored plans of remediation.

Joe initiated me to his plan by asking me to help him with a little five-year old chimp named Shiloh. Shiloh was a contract chimp, which meant that he had been used at another lab under a kind of rental contract with PRC. When he was eighteen months old Shiloh had been shipped from our nursery to a research lab in New Jersey where he was inoculated and used to study respiratory synctitial virus (RSV). It was a small study with only four chimps, which allowed each baby to be handled by the care-givers everyday in a personal and playful manner. Each of the four had recently returned to PRC with little flowered blankets, and several lovingly worn stuffed toys, which were immediately thrown into the trash. Fabric was not an acceptable enrichment material given the scale of our husbandry practices. In the context of our industrial scale laboratory, such debris became simmering petrie dishes at the bottom of the small barred cages, spawning dangerous virus and bacteria.

Each of the four chimps was kept alone in a cage in quarantine until it was determined that they could join the larger populace without communicating some kind of plague from New Jersey. Shiloh's lab-mates had more or less adapted to the new circumstances, learning to play with their new plastic toys and interacting with the care-givers who fed them and washed their room twice a day. Shiloh didn't seem to be thriving under the new circumstances. He was listless, not interested in food, and growing thin. Joe had given Shiloh several physical exams and a complete blood work-up. Physically, Shiloh was in good shape, but Joe was worried because he seemed to be wasting away. Joe asked me to accompany him to visit the little chimp, and bring some toys and food to see if we could spark up his interest.

What I saw when I peered in the tiny rectangular window of the room was four small cages crowded together, but not close enough to allow the little chimps to touch one another. The door was festooned with a large red *biohazard* sign and additionally stenciled in black with the word *quarantine*. There was a care-giver outside, leaning against the wall smoking a cigarette. Inside the room we could see another man in a white tyvek suit washing the floors under the cages with a steaming hose. Three of the young chimps could be seen jumping and rocking, barking and showing their square little teeth at the care-giver as he methodically worked. They avidly watched him, making various vain attempts to grab his hose, and reaching out to him for attention.

The fourth chimp was obscured by the steam, but could be seen as a dark unmoving lump at the bottom of his cage. The care-giver turned off his hose and reached out toward Shiloh where he lay, but still the little chimp didn't move. Not even when the man scratched his back and neck did we see Shiloh make any response. I was nervously clutching my sack full of fruit and the toys I had hand crafted out of PVC pipe. PVC pipe was inexplicably one of the few things the research scientists at PRC seemed to universally approve of as a toy item. After reading the material safety and data sheets (MSDS) related to poly vinyl chloride (PVC), I wondered if the erudite scientists thought it was an appropriate medium mostly because it was a sterile-looking white. As I peered in at the unmoving dark lump on the cage bottom I began to wonder if I had come too late and Shiloh was actually dead.

"C'mon in, let's take a look," Joe said wistfully, "I'd hate to lose this little bugger."

Shiloh clearly liked Joe, and as soon as we entered he sat up and slowly reached a small brown hand out between the bars. Joe took a plump strawberry from my grocery sack and put it in Shiloh's hand. Joe had to curl the little ape's fingers around it and give his hand a slight push before Shiloh retracted it and gave the strawberry a cursory examination. He simply placed it on the bars that made up the floor of his cage, idly wiggling the berry with his foot thumb and reaching out to Joe again. Joe held the limp little hand in his own big rancherman's paw, sheathed as it was in a latex glove.

We were both wearing clear plastic face shields, which were now sprinkled with the condensed steam that was dripping from the tiled roof. The tiny quarantine room reminded me of my favorite lunch hour hang out, the gym on the military base. There was a steam room there that made the cool dry days of the desert winter more tolerable. In our suits in the confines of Shiloh's room it was over-poweringly humid and uncomfortable. I looked at Joe and wondered if I was imagining that he looked distinctly teary-eyed, in any case his face shield was fogging up. A large drop fell from the ceiling onto Shiloh's nose. He hung his head but made no effort to wipe it off. The drop rolled down over his lip and fell onto the strawberry, which lay forgotten now and wedged between two bars in the cage floor.

"Well," I said cheerily, trying to break up the scene of pathos that was unfolding before me, "how about a nice new toy?" Shiloh looked up at me with a lighted interest. I wondered if it was because the timbre of my voice was feminine, recalling that the New Jersey team had female care-givers. I produced a PVC pipe with holes drilled in one side and peanut butter smeared on it.

"What the heck is that thing!" Exclaimed Joe

"A termite feeder, Joe. You see, it emulates the kind of species-specific behavior and activities one might find in nature." I was reciting some new language I had found in a trade journal article about monkey enrichment.

"Huh," he said as though I were trying to sell him a used Buick. I noticed that he had stolen my favorite word sound. His eyes were on Shiloh, and I could see that he was impressed with the little ape's increased enthusiasm. I think that was a turning point for Joe, from then on he gave me *carte blanche* to visit any area in the facility with my toys and treats, and ran constant interference for me with the rigidly resistant research teams.

"You go on ahead then and do whatever you need to," Joe conceded, "I just want to make sure we keep this little guy going." Joe reached in the cage and ruffled up the hair on top of Shiloh's head in the same affectionate way that I had seen my landlord, Sandoval, ruffle up the hair of his six-year-old grandson on more than a dozen occasions.

Joe left me with Shiloh, and I spent the next hour showing him my PVC toy collection. I tried to lure him into eating some of the fruit I brought, but he remained reticent. He finally accepted some dried pineapple and ate four or five pieces before I left. He sat up alert and relaxed as I went out the door, watching my every move. He clutched my termite feeder offering in one foot. I smiled, though behind the shield and filter mask it was lost on Shiloh. I wondered if a human smile meant anything to him anyway, many chimpanzees interpreted our tooth-flashing friendliness as an imminent threat to battle.

"I'll be back, you sweetheart!" I told him. He looked like he didn't believe me. "I'll be back tomorrow morning, and every morning after that," I promised. I kept my promise and returned everyday for several weeks. During that time, Shiloh showed great enthusiasm for all my tricks and treats. He would wait for me to arrive and make a play face. He began to vocalize excitedly and greedily take the offered fruits and vegetables. One of the care-givers, Emiliano, started to visit the little chimp with me. Since Shiloh seemed so much improved, I asked

Emiliano to take over my efforts so I could turn my attention to some other projects. He agreed, chuckling about the fact that his new job duties included playing with a chimpanzee.

I got busy with some other problems and projects. I was trying to balance the enrichment needs of fifteen hundred macaque monkeys and three hundred chimps, and I didn't have an assistant at that time. It was difficult to prioritize where the greatest need was. I often felt I was wandering from one crisis to the next. A monkey named Tequila was biting his hind leg, a monkey mother with twins wouldn't nurse, it was time to wean a baby chimp named Spock, the USDA inspector was coming and all of the toys had to be cleaned and repaired. It seemed endless. It was as if I were the only psychotherapist for the whole city of New York. These were the excuses I gave myself when Joe called to say that Shiloh had experienced a sudden and dramatic reversal in his condition. I told Joe I would stop by the very next morning.

"Good. Hope you can do something for him, he seems worse this time."

"Is he sick?"

"Naw, seems in good shape, but he refuses food. He won't even get up from the floor to say hello to me."

When I heard this I felt a knot of panic in my gut. Shiloh adored Joe. That much was clear to even the uninitiated observer. If Shiloh had lost interest in his dear friend, it must be serious. A human being in an emotional state like the one Shiloh displayed might be labeled as disassociated or dysphoric, with a concomitant withdrawal from all meaningful and pleasurable activity.

"First thing tomorrow," I promised again.

That evening I sat in the kitchen with Martina, sipping our usual syrupy and cream laden Sanka, trying to come up with a plan for Shiloh. I was gazing out of the window at the high colorful streaks of the desert sunset when my thoughts were interrupted by heart stopping howls that emanated from the backyard. The cacophony seemed to consist of a combination of high-pitched wailing and strains from *swing low sweet chariot*. Martina and I hurried outside where we found Nikki and Yvette sitting in folding chairs around a mound of dirt strewn with dandelion flowers. They were rocking on the edges of their chairs, alternately singing and moaning. They had obviously been in Martina's closet and were both swathed in black lace *mantillas*. At a sharp command from Martina, the girls ceased their strange concert.

"Nikki! What in the heck do you think your doing?" I barked in relief. "You scared us to death!"

"We're having a funeral." She answered, sighing soulfully. Yvette nodded her curly, dark head in solemn confirmation.

I looked more closely at the suspicious mound of dirt to which they had been addressing their mournful duet. "And who died?" I asked somewhat sarcastically.

"A little lizard that Tigger caught." Yvette hiccupped, bursting into tears.

Tigger was the farm cat. I was pretty sure the premises were littered with a variety of Tigger's cast off carcasses. If every one of the pitiful creatures were to receive a similar funeral, it really *was* going to be a long and difficult winter. Yvette's tears set Nikki off again and both girls began keening and wailing with renewed sincerity. Martina looked at me and shrugged, heading back to the predictable serenity of the kitchen table.

The next morning when I arrived at work there was an unscheduled last-minute meeting and I was unable to get over to the biocontainment area to see Shiloh. The next day there was a big monkey fight in one of the outdoor social cages. Three days later I got over to see Shiloh. I talked to Emiliano while I was suiting up in my unusually bulky tyvek outfit and taping the latex gloves to the sleeves to eliminate the little space that might leave my wrist open to RSV exposure.

"How's the little guy?" I asked brightly. Emiliano just shook his head and twitched his mouth to the left. I didn't think that was a positive sign.

I had arrived so early it was before the seven a.m. feeding. The four young apes were just getting up from their slumber. I had brought a mixed fruit breakfast with orange and grapefruit quarters. Shiloh's three roommates greeted me with raucous enthusiasm, and I had to give them all their portions to quiet them down. Shiloh lay in a corner of his cage, the same way he had the first time I met him. Under my tyvek suit, I had snuck in a bright green and red rubber dog toy that squeaked and was shaped like a parrot. I tried to pique his interest, but he remained immobile. With some difficulty, I forced the toy into his cage through the feeder box. It bounced on the bars in front of his face, rolled over once and came to a halt against the wall of the cage. Shiloh didn't even blink. He seemed completely oblivious to me. I squatted down next to his cage and reached through the bars to pet him.

I was revolted to see that his plush dark coat of hair had a layer of mice feces stuck all over it. Gritting my teeth I flicked as much of the feces off of him as I could reach by stretching my fingers into the cage, but my tape-bulky wrists wouldn't fit between the bars. The rodents must have been running over him all night, and yet he hadn't moved to avoid them or clean his coat of their excrement. I was battling tears now and fighting down a sense of acute nausea. I tried to mitigate my physiological response to the horrific scene I was witnessing and the overpowering stench of a night's worth of chimp feces by thinking of something outside of the tiled cell where I stood.

My thoughts turned to the pest control team. I wondered if they had even bothered to monitor the biocontainment intake rooms where Shiloh and his companions resided. It was certainly no secret that PRC had epidemic cockroach and rodent problems. One winter evening I had stayed late and thought it might be fun to go into one of the chimp areas and wake them up for a late night snack. I filled my arms with green bananas, which they preferred to the ripe kind, opened the door and turned on the lights. My screams mingled with their food hoots as I scattered bananas all over the corridor when I saw what appeared to be a river of dark mice flowing out from every feeder box and down into the walls and floors through every impossible crack that formed part of the fifty-year old edifice. I had known that various traps and poisons could be found behind doors, in corners, and under shelves all over the facility, but I had never before considered what this implied. The administration must have had some notion because they had eventually created a permanent staff position to oversee pest control. A gregarious woman named Nancy Griffith had previously been the facility shipping clerk and now occupied the position.

Nancy drove a pink Harley-Davidson motorcycle to work and had a pink leather outfit to match it. Her pink jacket and chaps hung on a clothes tree behind her office door. Her office had an assortment of aquariums in it. They had various unusual pest specimens she had found in the live traps. There was a pig-nosed rattlesnake, a white tarantula, and a mouse with five legs from under the loading dock where the chemical trailer had been parked for over two decades. One night several years later a military transport vehicle came and quietly removed the trailer.

Her collection also sported two stinking vinegaroons, which explained why Nancy insisted on burning sweet cherry incense. She also insisted on wearing pink scrubs at work. After a professional pest-control consultant had been hired to develop a control plan for the facility, the administration gave Nancy the go-ahead to hire an additional staff member. She hired an ex-military conscript named Dave. She made him wear pink scrubs, too.

"Pink is the color of our department," she had announced proudly in a staff meeting one day. "When you see pink I want you to know we are working on the pest control problem." Dave was blushing and scooting down in his folding chair at the back of the staff meeting room. She made one concession to him in the matter of the pink scrubs, she let him have his name monogrammed over the pocket in gleaming black thread.

I was in her office admiring the rattlesnake through the greenish aquarium glass one day shortly after she hired Dave.

"So how's Dave working out," I asked, tapping on the glass at the snake with the eraser end of a pencil I had been chewing on. The snake slithered to the other side of his box.

"He really likes the work, puts his heart and soul into it."

"Oh yeah?" I responded idly, shifting the pencil to tap at the snake again. I thought I could see its little nostrils flare open.

"Oh yeah, he's invented a humane way to euthanize the rats from the live traps."

"Huh," I said tapping harder. The snake started to wrap itself up into a circle. "Was that a recommendation from that high-powered consultant they hired?"

"No, uh-uh, just personal interest, you know. Something we could tell animal rights guys- even our pest program is humane."

"Oh," I replied, turning the pencil around so I could make a louder tapping with the pointed lead end. A buzzing like the sound of an arc welder began to fill the room. "What's the method?"

"Stop teasing Henry," Nancy ordered.

"Okay," I sighed, I was hoping to see Henry strike at me like he had at Dave the last time I'd been in their office, it was interesting to watch the cloudy drops of venom slide harmlessly down the glass.

"Dry ice."

"Dry ice?"

"Yeah, Dave puts the dry ice on top of the live trap, then covers the whole thing with a cardboard box, and the little varmints go to sleep, real peaceful," Nancy sounded proud of her departmental innovation. She clearly felt the same sense of accomplishment I had when I developed the mirrored dog bowl.

"Huh," I pondered, trying to imagine I was a rodent. Would I want my neck broken immediately, or would I prefer to be transported in a box from place to place, locked in a dark cubicle and gassed? "Why not just use a kill trap?" I asked, perhaps illogically.

"Too messy."

"Oh, so what *did* the consultant guy say to do?" I queried.

"Basically he said the only way to eradicate the rodent population at this point is to dig a trench around the facility and fill it with liquid rodenticide formula, and starve them out. When they run out to the desert looking for food, they'll fall in the trench and drown."

"That's a joke, right?" I asked, looking at Nancy's very serious face.

"Nope." She hefted a thick report off of her bookshelf onto the desk. "It's all in here if you want to read it yourself, I think the trench has to be...." She thumbed through the pages as she spoke, "oh yeah, here it is, four foot deep and ten foot wide," She looked up at me with her wide, guileless blue eyes.

"No, thanks," I said, looking at the bulky report as she pushed it across her desk, "But how in the heck are you going to do *that*?" I wondered aloud, unconsciously starting to tap at Henry again. I was recalling my conversation with the USDA inspector a few weeks earlier. He had informed me that based on fecal sample tests from rodent dens throughout the state, the USDA office estimated that approximately ten percent of all wild rodent populations had endemic *Hanta* virus. This had been a parenthetical aside during our lunch at the officer's club after his inspection tour. He had discovered a six-inch layer of rodent droppings under the dock where the five-footed mouse had been living. I glanced at the five-footed mouse in his cage clumsily trying to negotiate his exercise wheel.

"Oh, we're *not* gonna do *that*, its only a suggestion, anyway. Now I have Dave on staff, we should be able to manage things all right."

"Huh."

There was a sudden loud *thunk* as Henry struck, his turned-up pig nose knocking against the glass opposite my hand. I shrieked and jumped, my pencil skittered across the tops of the aquariums, serendipitously falling through the mesh and coming to rest in a bed of cedar chips at the bottom of the five-legged mouse's cage. He stopped struggling with the wheel to investigate his new acquisition. I could see his nose quivering over an indent made earlier by one of my own premolars. Henry looked suddenly bored, and stretched himself out for a *siesta*.

Nancy was looking at me with a smirk that seemed to indicate that I would never be among the steel-nerved elite that rode Harleys. She was right, of course. I was terrified of motorcycles. They were dangerous.

"I told you not to tease Henry."

"Sorry," I mumbled, red-faced.

"I'll get your pencil." She said, rising from her desk.

"Hey no big deal, let him keep it," I blurted. "I've gotta run." I looked theatrically at my wrist where a watch would be if I owned one.

I was in full motion now, bolting for the door, "you know, all these dang meetings...."

I contemplated the appalling ineffectuality of the pest control program as I stood next to Shiloh, vainly swiping at the dung. I took his limp hand in mine and even through my protective latex gloving I could feel that his little fingers were like ice. I came every day after that, morning and evening, but Shiloh never stirred from his spot again. Even when the care-giver opened the door of his cage and tried to prop him up, Shiloh would simply reposition himself as he had been. There was no resistance and no engagement. Within four days he was dead. Joe came personally to collect his little body for necropsy. He wept openly as he lifted Shiloh out of the tiny metal cage. Necropsy results indicated *no apparent cause of death.*

"He just gave up the will to live," I concluded, after explaining the events to Bart that evening when we drove home through the purple twilight.

"There's *always* an *apparent* cause of death," Bart commented dryly, "even if its respiratory failure, or cardiac arrest. Biologic function ceases, death follows."

"He died slowly of a broken heart, *Bart.*" I insisted.

"Cardiac arrest, then." He summarized.

"Fine!" I said hotly, "Have it your way, you...." I paused looking for the appropriate epithet, " you scientist!" I spat out. "I'm *just* saying that maybe it's what *isn't* apparent that's the most important. Maybe we should be trying to *intuit* what that is, instead of intellectualizing about empirical data which can only come *post ipso facto!*"

Bart gave a derisive snort and reached irritably over to the console to turn up the radio.

Benjy's case was the next one Joe put me on, his faith in my skills apparently not diminished by my futile attempts to save Shiloh. Benjy was an adult, well into his teens when I met him. Benjy had picked the entire top of his head clean of flesh, and it was a bloody pulp. He looked as though he had been scalped. His medical records indicated that he had sporadically been administered valium, but the ameliorating effects were minor and temporary. His condition had to be painful, and as I watched him pick at himself I could see he was wincing. This did not deter him, and in fact strengthened my theory that a release of pleasurable and analgesic neurotransmitters must also be occurring. Every two or three days Benjy would burst into a fit with bare-teeth screaming and hyper-ventilation which sometimes led to fainting. Afterwards he would sit quietly in the corner of his tiny solitary cage, slowly and methodically picking at his scalp. The picking had a calming effect on him. He had been enacting and reinforcing this behavior cycle for years. I was pessimistic about my ability to interrupt the internal chemistry loop that governed this pattern, but I agreed to try.

Sometimes the veterinarians chose to medicate a chimpanzee to alleviate SIB, thus allowing some intervention time to break the behavioral cycle. As a general rule I didn't agree with this approach except as a temporary measure. This was one point on which the administration and I were in agreement, although their interest was purely fiscal. During the final corporate phase at PRC, when the golden age of veterinarians had long passed and Fran and Joe gone on to new endeavors, there was a period during which young, inexperienced veterinarians blew through the Center like leaves through an open door. Almost without exception these inexperienced practitioners heavily medicated chimpanzees with SIB, using anti-psychotics in preference to enrichment and changes in husbandry practices. This seemed to be an illogical excision of the personhood of the chimp from the qualitative matrix of its daily existence. How could this irony be lost on anyone? We had induced SIB through environmental stress, and instead of alleviating the problem we were medicating the symptom! The general response to antipsychotic drugs was that the chimpanzee would temporarily reduce SIB, but the behavior would reassert itself and the antipsychotic would be increased until the dosage was inordinately high.

I put Benjy on an enrichment schedule. He received feeding puzzles, special meals, and extra interaction time with human care-givers. He seemed mildly interested in these goings-on, but his behavior persisted. I was pleased that sometimes a few weeks would pass and the scabs on his head would be dry and healing. Inevitably, though, I would arrive in the cramped wardroom where his cage sat alone, only to find a fresh wound on his head, face, or neck. This usually signaled the start of yet another cycle of picking. I tried to convince myself that the cessation periods indicated that he was making progress away from SIB, but he never ceased the pattern altogether. When I left PRC after my second tour of duty, I admonished my assistant, Poppy Hadler, to keep him busy with toys and attention. I was anxious for news of Benjy when I returned for my third and final tour of duty a few years later. The news I received was that he had fallen into an increasingly destructive cycle. When one morning he was discovered to have peeled all of the skin from his head, neck, arms and thighs a dreadful but humane decision was made to euthanize him.

Earl was another chimp referred to my care. He was easily identifiable by the ropy scars that criss-crossed his forearms. Earl was an early conscript to the colony, and cut something of a grandfather figure among the second and third generation chimps. He was housed by himself in a small indoor-outdoor cage reminiscent of a dog run with concrete walls. For years of his solitary confinement he had been denuding his arms of flesh, which accounted for the shiny ropes of scar tissue. I spent hours of observation time characterizing his pattern of self-mutilation. It always began with itching and slapping at his arms as if they were irritating him. I wondered if he had a peripheral neuropathy, or an itchy skin disease. Eventually Earl would itch harder and harder, and then begin to peel away bits of skin and scab until his arms were red with blood. Then he would sit and suck or lick at the wounds. Aside from these oddities he was a friendly and outgoing chimp who gladly tried all of the treats and toys I offered him, peering out at me from under his shaggy gray brows like some primeval Methuselah.

Fran Perette noted that his original accession record suggested that he might have leprosy. This unverified chart note had become Earl's sentence to years of being housed alone for fear he might contaminate some other chimp. It was a great consolation to me years later when I learned that Earl had miraculously been rescued from the research milieu, and ended up living in a garden-like animal sanctuary some-where in the deep South. The only inroads *we* ever made toward elimi-nating his SIB occurred when we gave him a cage-mate named Edith. Edith's sweet and humorous personality was demonstrated during an escape she made from her cage after someone forgot to snap the lock shut. No one noticed she was gone for a couple of hours. She had somehow made her way to the nursery and was sitting outside a cage with little one-year-olds in it, playing with their toes through the mesh. Usually a dart gun would be used in an escape to anesthetize the errant chimp and roll her back to her home cage on a gurney. Edith's care-giver, Minda, instead yelled at Edith, pointing back at her area and tell-ing her to go home. Edith got up yawning and strolled languorously back to her cage.

Edith was an obese and freckly old girl who was being retired from the luxuries of the breeding colony. Her reward for contributing all of her offspring to the noble cause of science would be to go to more restrictive caging and be used in hepatitis research. Fran halted this plan by issuing a directive that Edith was to be paired with Earl for reasons of health. By this simple means she guaranteed an improved quality of life for both chimps. Unfortunately, by the same token, Fran seemed to have guaranteed herself a decreased quality of life, coming to loggerheads over the decision with a meticulous immunologist named Dr. Daven who had wanted to use Edith on an upcoming protocol. Ever afterward, Daven seemed to delight in making a sport out of using his in-house political clout to hound Fran.

Daven was a tall handsome man in his late fifties with a perfectly groomed Van Dyke beard and a full scalp of wavy silver hair. His slim, erect figure was impressive as he strode importantly around the facility. He conducted multiple research projects for corporate clients all over the world and made a lot of money. Beneath his lab coat one could see that the sharply creased trouser legs were cut from high quality fabric. He wore a perfectly knotted bowtie that peeped over the collar of his oddly oversized lab coat, which was the only incongruous part of his wardrobe. One of the secretaries told me that Daven used to be enormously fat and was too cheap to buy a new lab coat. On the rare occasions that I was invited to accompany a group of the intellectual elite to lunch at the local officer's club, I was impressed to see Daven remove his oversized lab coat and reveal a costly tailored vest and trousers. He would don a matching suit jacket, which he kept on a wooden hanger in his office.

I had initially liked Daven. He was affable, but I learned that he was also disingenuous. He had easily agreed to all of my suggestions about enriching the monkey cages where his research was conducted. I methodically installed PVC pipe toys in every cage, and returning to check on them the next week, found them inside a plastic bucket in a storage closet. The care-givers informed me that Daven had ordered the toys removed the day after I installed them. I nervously approached him where he was bent over the read-out from one of the arcane machines situated in his lab. I wanted to discover what was at the root of his change of attitude about the toys. He charmingly disarmed me and elevated me to the status of a peer by offering to conduct a collaborative research project to determine if PVC pipe was poisonous to the monkeys I was attempting to enrich.

"Of course I am very interested in your enrichment work, but when I looked in on the research animals, they were chewing on the little pipes you had installed," Daven explained. "I was concerned it might affect their liver enzymes, and the study I'm conducting in that particular room examines the toxicity of compounds used in children's nightwear. It's very critical we get accurate data."

"Oh, right, I'm so sorry, that is crucial, I didn't know...." I acquiesced as I imagined infants all over America writhing in their cribs, red-faced and gasping because of my inconsideration. "Well," I said feebly, not willing to capitulate entirely, "could we try something else?"

"I've already instructed my staff to place radios in each of the study rooms," he beamed helpfully at me, "but I want to see if you and I can examine this problem of the PVC pipe toys."

"Problem?"

"Are they toxic enough to skew our research results, or even worse, can these enrichment objects you are using actually harm the animals?"

He looked down at me from his lofty male stature, made more authoritative by the pair of half-rimmed reading glasses that perched debonairly on the bridge of his aquiline nose.

"Oh, well, of course, I wouldn't want to hurt anyone," I struggled, clearly outclassed by his research acumen. Now I was imagining primates all over the facility writhing in their berths, red-faced and gasping.

"Here's what I'm willing to propose in order to aid you in your important efforts. We will conduct a study examining the toxic effects of PVC. I can dedicate twelve monkeys for two groups, control and experimental. We can prepare PVC shavings to be fed to one group in increasing amounts for several weeks. Then, when the animals are sacrificed, we will do a complete analysis of the liver, comparing the two groups. And that should settle this problematic question for once and for all." He crossed his arms and peered at me over the rim of his glasses, "Of course," he said in a gracious finale, "I'd be delighted if you would agree to be the study coordinator."

Now I was imagining a cohort of my peers in behavioral science from all over America writhing in their conference audience seats, red-faced and gasping as I explained how I had sacrificed twelve monkeys to further the cause of enrichment. Daven was looking at me intently.

"Uh, well, um, I think the radio is a great idea. I appreciate your offer, I just have so many projects going on...I don't think I'd have time...." I bumbled on inanely.

"Well, just you think about it," he said, patting me on the back as he ushered me out of his lab, "I'm always here if you need help or want to discuss the idea further." Then he turned and strolled majestically down the long corridor toward his office, leaving me feeling as breathless as though I had been sucked out of the window by a tornado.

I sat in the farm kitchen one morning shortly after this exchange with Daven. I felt like he had pulled one over on me and I was trying to express my frustration to Martina in broken Spanish. I didn't think I had really gotten the subtleties of the situation across to this elderly matron from *Durango*. I sighed, lamenting that I couldn't share my dilemma with someone who spoke my own language and understood the complexities of intellectual life. I was remembering a childhood story Martina had told me about washing her family's homemade clothes in a stream, rubbing the stains out with a rock. We'd always had a maid. I was wallowing in my sense of alienation when Martina nodded with complete understanding and spoke.

"*Si, entiendo. El es un Cabron.*"

Daven would consistently create obstacles to my enrichment efforts. He had a talent for ascribing blame to my department for some of the horrific incidents that plagued the facility as the management conditions worsened, especially during the final corporate phase. If a chimpanzee died of hemorrhagic gut because there was a shigella epidemic, it was because I had fed corn with the leaves and silk still intact, thus compromising the digestive process. When twenty beagles on an optical study went blind, crying and biting at each other in their outdoor play yard, it wasn't because they were left outside for hours in the desert sun after being treated with a substance that resulted in severe photosensitivity. It was because I had recommended that they be given an outdoor play yard in addition to their tiny squat kennels inside a modular building. When I insisted that more monkeys be housed together in groups or pairs, Daven surprisingly agreed. He undertook the task himself using his own staff, only to produce evidence a few weeks later supporting his thesis that social living was detrimental to monkeys as shown by the increase in aggression and wounding events.

Primates are social animals. This trait is an evolved and genetically coded adaptation to promote survival. Since almost all of the chimpanzees with severe SIB were housed alone it seemed self-evident that the need for social contact was going unmet. It was very difficult to pair or group-house chimps in the early years when I worked at PRC because there was only antiquated housing, a burgeoning population of chimps, no new money for construction, and the Animal Welfare Act (AWA) had yet to be systematically enforced as law through the regular inspections that were later conducted by the USDA. The implementation of the AWA would forever banish the small, mean cages that had been home to Shiloh and Benjy by specifying a minimum square footage for maintenance of captive non-human primates (with an attached fine for noncompliance). Although desperate conditions did not change overnight with the advent of this legislation, it gave me a powerful new tool in my arsenal of enrichment strategies. I was now in a position to invoke an authority greater than myself when pushing to implement enrichment and socialization. The quarterly visits by the USDA inspector also helped to force many of even the most resistant individuals into accommodating me.

During an administrative upheaval that occurred prior to my return for the third and final time, several million dollars were procured to build spacious new social cages. My first task upon returning to PRC was to identify compatible individuals and introduce them into social groups from their previous solitary existence. This was a huge undertaking that involved a team of professionals from the veterinary and care-giving staff. We created dozens of groups totaling over two hundred chimpanzees in a few short months. We were proud that not one chimpanzee was lost to aggression during these introductions.

In fact, the chimps far exceeded our expectations in the broad range of cooperative social behavior that they enacted. In one group of aged matriarchs a chimp named Robin, who was nearly forty years old, suffered a stroke that left her hemiparetic and crippled on the left side. Another similarly aged member of her group, Elizabeth, took on the role of caring for Robin. Elizabeth helped procure food for her from the feeder box before everyone else ate it. Elizabeth assisted Robin to go outside, and would sit next to her in the warm winter sun. Their squat figures could be seen leaning together as they limped along, Elizabeth's strong arm wrapped firmly around her friend's waist. And thankfully, as a result of the new housing and social configurations, SIB became much less common and easier to address.

The pitiful images of self-inflicted wounding will be branded forever into the matrix of my being. I felt personally responsible for every chimpanzee who exhibited any of these symptoms. I dedicated myself to making every attempt to alleviate the circumstances contributing to self-injurious behavior. I saw an amazing response in decrement of SIB when chimpanzees received even simple environmental enrichment. Providing a toy, a feeding device, or even simply increasing visiting time with a care-giver who could play with or groom the chimpanzee helped decrease SIB. In the best case scenario, where a chimpanzee could have a cage-mate, or even be moved permanently into a social group there would be a decrease and often a cessation of the behavior. I came to believe that there was no clearer measuring stick of the effectiveness of an enrichment program than the incidence rate of SIB in the population. And, no greater evidence of our failure at stewardship than the harm or loss of any single individual due to self-inflicted injuries as a response to intolerable living conditions.

Seven

A Visitation Of Plagues
And The Unhardening
Of Hearts

The inexorable regularity of administrative changes continued to plague PRC as it entered its final incarnation as a private research enterprise. Within a few months of my third reinstallation at PRC, the center was signed over lock, stock and barrel to a private research foundation. The previous management partnership, between a military facility and the local university, had run its course and in general seemed weary of the increasing public scrutiny attached to the use of chimpanzees in research. By the end of my tenure under corporate management I would see many of the gains we had made in husbandry and animal care being eroded. With a priority list typical of a corporate entity, which included acquiring assets (more chimps) and cutting costs (cheap construction, decreased supply lists, and staff reduction) it soon became apparent that my idea of an appropriate standard of practice was being compromised. I realized that the period of my maximum effectiveness for chimpanzee welfare at PRC had passed. With the nostalgia one sometimes feels on the first certain evening of autumn, I recognized that it would soon be time for me to move on to new horizons.

One May morning during the final spring of my tenure at PRC, I found myself sitting across a huge walnut desk from our new CEO, Archibald

Cooperston. He had a fancy for aromatic tobacco and as he talked he periodically sucked on the worn stem of a big meerschaum pipe carved to look like an Arabian sheik. He had made a point of telling me on several occasions about how the pipe had been presented to him by the French consulate in gratitude for something he had once done that involved pesticide and North Africa. The sweet smelling smoke hung in a mephistophelian aureole above his head. When he was finished smoking I knew he would knock the ash out by banging the pipe against the heel of his expensive handmade Italian leather boots. I had been subject to this ritual many times. Later the gardener, Alejandro, would come in with a little dust tray and whiskbroom to sweep the ash out from underneath the big desk.

I had been summoned to wait in court attendance while Cooperston regaled me with stories from his exploits as a war time researcher with the Pentagon. My mandated attendance at these story-telling sessions had become so frequent in the final months of my tenure that I found myself sitting complacently in front of the walnut desk several times each week. I had been surprised to learn that much of Cooperston's research had taken place decades earlier right at PRC, in the now-antiquated buildings. Cooperston's account of the research conducted in that era was uncannily similar to the accounts Festus had provided for me, but a great deal more erudite and harrowing. Cooperston never tired of having an audience, and it gave me an opportunity to develop insights into the complex layers of his genius.

I enjoyed listening to his stories from the viewpoint of historical relativity. It was entirely to his credit that treatments had been developed for illnesses that had plagued mankind since the dawn of our species. His career had spanned some of the most interesting years of scientific investigation beginning in the early 1940's. The changes in bioethics over a short fifty-year period were sociologically interesting, while the changes in the technical aspects of epidemiological research were nothing short of miraculous. The scope of these changes was apparent in the content of Cooperston's anecdotal accounts. I had once sat in horrible fascination as he recounted the use of human subjects that were housed in an insane asylum. The outcome of the story was that a vaccine had been developed for one of the most deadly viruses known to man. Of course, the study subjects had perished.

"They would have perished anyway, progressive brain disease, those were the ones we used. No hope of recovery. They had an opportunity for immortality in benefiting the rest of mankind- their contribution wasn't wasted, either!" He proclaimed emphatically, slapping one hand down on the walnut desk. Cooperston was confounded about the increasingly hostile attacks he and his corporation received in the wider public arena as a changing political and philosophical climate eroded what had once been the sacrosanct halls of science. When an Australian philosopher suggested in the media that apes should be classified as *Homo pan sapiens*, and anyone harming them or killing them be charged with assault or manslaughter in international court, Cooperston stormed in and out of his office for days, banging doors, snapping at anyone who had the temerity to approach him, looking distinctly apoplectic.

The debate over the use of chimpanzees in research had finally garnered a wide public interest, with inflammatory rhetoric pouring in from both extremes of the argument, and endearing images of young chimps being plied against those of the HIV orphans that increasingly peopled underdeveloped nations. It wasn't unusual after the management transition to find various television talk show luminaries setting up their foil canopies and cameras to carry out interviews with Cooperston's corps of intellectual elite, who were mounting a campaign to provide positive media coverage for PRC. The sometimes confusing incongruity of the competing rhetoric was demonstrated to me one day as I pored over an out-of-date Los Angeles paper that I had procured from Cooperston's trash can (probably the only place such a paper might be found in all of Fat Gulch). I ran across a full-page ad produced by a consortium of wealthy patrons, many of whose names were listed in the ad and familiar from movie marquees. Underneath the symbol of a red ribbon, the ad exhorted the government to be more active and provide larger sums of money for HIV/AIDS research. At the bottom of the ad was a heart-breaking list of the names of many talented artists who had died as a result of the disease.

"Rock Hudson," I murmured, incredulous. I had always liked him, especially with Doris Day in *Pillow Talk*.

A few pages later I found another ad. This one had a photo-montage of several different animals, with the face of central interest being a young chimp's. The photo image looked suspiciously like one that had recently appeared on a large billboard that had been constructed in the desert wastelands outside the gate to PRC. It proclaimed in bold red letters four feet tall; *STOP THE SLAUGHTER: PRC KILLS CHIMPANZEES*. Under the montage the ad gave a heart-rending account of the lives of laboratory animals, which prefaced a call for donations. Beneath this riveting presentation was a list of wealthy patrons who endorsed the campaign and whose names were familiar from movie marquees. Some of the names were related to, or actually the same as the names of the supporters I had just read in the ad calling for more research funding.

"Doris Day," I murmured in perplexity. I had always liked her, especially with Rock Hudson in *Pillow Talk*.

I sat uncomfortably in Cooperston's office, since the big swamp cooler had ceased to function a few hours earlier. Although the lack of white noise made it easier to understand his growling intonations, I was having difficulty concentrating. I sat in the intensely warm May sun that came streaming through the windows, trying to politely stifle a yawn by swallowing with my mouth closed. Unfortunately, the combination of heat and sweet tobacco fumes was conspiring to down-regulate my reticular activating system so that every few minutes my head seemed to bob down and jerk up like that of a marionette. I was listening to an oft-repeated and slightly lecherous recounting of two orangutans mating in a Chinese zoo when the phone rang. Dale Murchison, manager of a large animal sanctuary in Texas, was calling to ask Cooperston to donate a chimpanzee. Dale had a famous chimp named Nim Chimpsky residing at the sanctuary. Nim's longtime mate, Sally, had recently died, and Dale thought Nim was very lonely and depressed.

The blood flow through my cerebral cortex seemed to perk up as I casually eavesdropped. By the time Cooperston hung up the phone, I

146

had decided we were going to send a chimp to Dale Murchison's ranch. I started my campaign on the spot, urging him to provide the requested mate. I painted a lavish picture of the fantastic publicity he would garner by enacting this generosity. This was his Achilles heel. Since the billboard pronouncing our sins had appeared outside the gate to PRC, I had noticed that the irritable Cooperston would randomly accost anyone passing his office to offer a searing diatribe against the perpetrators of the animal rights campaign. Just the day before, he had called me into his office and recited the history of vaccines for childhood diseases that he and his research team had developed over the decades. At the emotional climax of the recitation he actually sprang out of his chair, waving the pipe, which overflowed dangerously like Mt. Vesuvius, spewing molten lumps across the desk and floor.

"Why, young lady," he instructed me, "it isn't a case of people *against* animals! Do you realize how many *animals* the world over have benefited from the veterinary treatments my teams developed during the course of our research? Do you realize what the world was like when children still got smallpox? Polio?" he bellowed, slamming his palm down on the burnished walnut desk after each disease pronouncement. "Of course you don't! You're too damned young!" Slam.

I surreptitiously shuffled a glowing ember off the end of my blue rubber shoe while nodding empathetically.

"Ungrateful *bastards*! I gave them an extra twenty-seven-point-five-years of life in order to be able to *protest* animal research by *doing* animal research!! And what have they done with that precious time: *nothing*! They're pig ignorant. Driving around in their cars, using their inks, papers, and computers to repudiate our work! When every *one* of those products was tested on an animal! If they're looking for bloodied hands they can damn well look at their own!" Slam.

Carpe diem, I thought inwardly. I urged Cooperston to take the proffered opportunity to show the world the depth of his compassion for research animals by freeing one to go to the sanctuary. There was a true streak of generosity and altruistic idealism that underlay Cooperston's gruff exterior. I had often reflected that it was this very trait that had initiated his career in epidemiology. He sincerely wanted to cure the ills of humanity. If a bunch of *"damn monkeys"* had to be sacrificed along the way, so be it. In his mind the greater good of all outweighed the suffering of the few.

I had observed that Cooperston was a study in contrasts. By one token, he didn't take my enrichment efforts very seriously.

"A compliance dog-and-pony-show!" He had snapped offensively one day after I had spent hours closeted with the USDA inspector, explaining the enrichment program.

Paradoxically, as he passed by in the hallway on another occasion, he intervened when he overheard an argument I was having with the procurement clerk. He inflated my resource budget by five hundred dollars right on the spot so I could buy Jane Goodall videos to play on closed circuit television for the chimps in the HIV *isolettes*.

"Damn shame not to have something to pass their time with," he growled, as he beetled his shaggy brows at the shrinking violet of a procurement clerk. I stood behind him nodding sagely at the humiliated clerk, my hands stuffed casually into my lab coat pockets. I felt like sticking out my tongue, but refrained.

I was unable to secure a commitment from Cooperston on sending a mate to Nim, but at least he released me from my audience duties. I was hot and drowsy and decided to visit the big metal pole barn in the biocontainment area. It was just after wash down and I knew the evaporating water would make the barn cool compared to the outside blaze of May heat. It was dark and fresh and relaxing to be inside the shadowed reaches of the building with the twelve hepatitis research chimps who resided there, each alone in a boxy stainless steel cage. I left the big roll-back door to the building open, against all rules of the facility in regard to level III containment areas. I thought the dry desert air, the light in a bright sharp rectangle on the wet concrete, and the vista of the remote Noche del Muerto Mountains would be enriching. If anyone complained, I was pretty sure I could wrap myself righteously in the cloak of the AWA. Besides, I had realized by now that no one who normally worked in the animal areas would complain. I was in collusion with all of the care-givers when it came to bending the rules to allow the chimpanzees more freedom and a chance to have a richer life.

This was made apparent to me once again as I left the confines of the barn and rounded the corner of an adjacent outdoor play area and discovered Festus taking a break from his janitorial rounds. He was leaning against the wall in the cool shade next to Dana's cage. His mask was dangling casually around his neck by the elastic band that was designed to keep it tightly affixed over his nose and mouth. Next to him, on her side of the mesh, Dana (an ex-circus performer) was sitting in companionable silence. They were smoking, both taking long lazy drags on their cigarettes and staring contemplatively across the desert to the distant shadowed recesses of the mountains. I took no more notice of their smoking than I would have of Cooperston's pipe, both were a common enough sight. Somehow, though, when Festus and Dana were smoking I found the habit endearing. I had an unexpected and melancholy foreshadowing of imminent change as I joined them in their reverie and a comment made by the Dalai Lama floated through my mind; *"everything that I enjoy will become a memory."*

I continued to carry out my enrichment duties under the new corporate management scheme. While I asked for and received a number of things I had been trying to procure for years, such as beautiful golf course sod in the outdoor play yards, I couldn't help but notice some odd goings-on. For one thing, during the first few months after PRC was relinquished to private corporate interests I noticed that several high echelon military brass seemed to pass with mounting regularity and urgency through the offices of Hilton and Cooperston. Then the two of them made several unexplained trips to Washington D.C. Shortly after all of this socializing among the upper classes had suddenly ceased, a curious house cleaning campaign began.

One morning a giant green trash truck, unmistakably a military vehicle, backed up to the door of the antiquated archives room. Redd appeared, away from his usual in-town site post. With him were two men in military fatigues. They began to dump books, papers, and in-house reports from over 30 years of research into the cavernous bed of the truck. Upon inquiry I learned that it was all to be taken to the military base dump where it was burned the next day. I argued futilely with Redd to allow me to take at least some of the materials to my office in order to preserve the history of the institute, but he was unyielding in carrying out his instructions to the letter. I stood by with a scattering of my colleagues watching powerlessly as the truck drove away across the desert floor followed by a line of dust. The next morning I had a sense of loss and defeat when I spied a column of blue smoke rising distantly from the direction of the dump. Maybe there were *some* stories about Cooperston's war time research for the Pentagon that I *hadn't* heard, I reflected. And now no one would ever hear them, or if they did there would be no evidence to support the allegations.

Then there was the strange incident involving the monkey area util-ity room. There were about fifteen-hundred mixed species of *macaques* at PRC, and I was responsible for their *psychological well-being* as well. The monkey care-givers were not the same people as the chimp care-givers. Different people were used to avoid cross-contamination between the populations of diseases that were species-specific. I wasn't allowed to work in chimp areas on the same day as I worked with mon-keys, and had to utilize separate clothes and shoes for each area. Even my lab had separate refrigerators for monkey and chimp food treats, establishing a kind of research laboratory *kashrut*.

Addressing the needs of so many monkeys was daunting at the very least. Many of the monkeys lived singly-housed in tiny research cages lining the walls of small windowless rooms. There were dozens of these rooms, each containing a different study project, all of them stuffy and bland. The frenetic movements and high pitched chatter of the mon-keys was jarring in contrast to the soothing complacency and focused power of movement apparent in the chimps. Call me a *species-ist*, but I honestly preferred to be among the chimps. I reduced the time and labor involved in enriching monkey areas by enlisting the assistance of interested monkey care-givers to carry out my various schemes.

I received administrative permission to paint one wall in each bleak room a bright color. I believed this added a visual dimensionality that was not achievable when all the walls were white, and thus helped stimulate visual function. I chose blue, yellow, green, pink, and purple for the various room colors. For months afterward, the monkey care-givers complained about the purple, and snarled among themselves about who would be assigned to work in the purple room. Finally I had it repainted a copasetic peach just to relieve my own environmentally induced stress whenever I encountered the monkey crew. Monkeys and keepers both seemed to enjoy another enrichment effort, the little plexiglass feeder boxes that a care-giver named Mitch had helped me design.

Mitch was a quiet-spoken man with three sons who were all in the 4-H club and raised an amazing variety of poultry. We sometimes drove the long distance to PRC together, rising in the pre-dawn darkness to rendezvous at a brightly lit gas station where we procured the acrid, non-fair-trade coffee that enabled us to proceed into the just- awakening desert stretches that led across the missile-testing range to the Center. One year Mitch touchingly presented Nikki with two bronze turkey chicks, which she named Stuffing and Dressing. We didn't have the heart to dispatch the two when Thanksgiving rolled around, so they spent their subsequent life roaming the yard and terrorizing the Basset Hounds that Nikki had decided to raise after tiring of rabbits.

Mitch was at heart an animal lover, like so many of the care-givers, who had taken the hazardous jobs so they could work and play with animals. He was a stalwart supporter of my every enrichment effort, and a constant source of toy inventions of his own. The plexiglass box was one of our joint innovations. It sat atop the monkey's cage and had holes drilled in the bottom where the monkeys could reach their tiny fingers through and attempt to manipulate the peanuts and fruit we placed in the box down into their cages. Once a week we would remove all of the boxes and clean them out in the monkey area utility room, then place them on different cages. We thought this a clever way to maintain the novelty value of the boxes by moving them from place to place.

Sometimes we had to stack the boxes in the poorly-lit corridor outside the utility room because Nancy and Dave would be using it to recalibrate their traps (before their jobs were eliminated to stream-line the budget), or Festus might be cleaning his mops and dumping his buckets out in the huge metal-and-porcelain sink. The tiny con-crete utility room had a huge sink situated under a bare light bulb, and not enough space for more than a few workers. Although sharing the room was sometimes inconvenient, the next closest available plumbed work area was up a flight of stairs, and none of us was inspired to carry our equipment up the stairs. One day, after we had collected twenty of our boxes and pushed the precariously balanced stack of them down the hall on a little cart, we were surprised and disappointed to dis-cover that the metal door to the utility room had been inexplicably welded shut.

I proceeded to the nearest phone and called Greta, the secretary, to inquire if she knew what had happened to lead to this surprising development.

"Oh," she responded, "that might be because of the new safety officer."

"Safety officer?" I inquired, in my by now almost perfect echolalic technique.

"Sure, hon, didn't no one tell you?"

"Uh, no. But I'm all for safety. So, should I call *him*?" I inquired tentatively, thinking that the little over-crowded utility room really could be unsafe. Once we had splashed a lot of soapy water on the floor and I had slipped. If Mitch hadn't caught me by the elbow I am sure I would have split my head on the rounded metal corner of the sink.

"Well, sure hon, I can put you right through." Then she lowered her tone conspiratorially. "They got themselves a safety officer real quiet like after that last USDA visit. I ain't never seen a bunch more secretive than this new group in all my career." The way she said *career* in her charming east Texas accent gave it three syllables.

"Huh, well, okay, I guess you better put me through."

I was connected to an unfamiliar voice that announced itself as Santiago Cordoba, "Office of Occupational Compliance."

"Occupational compliance?" I repeated.

"Yes, how may I help you?" He offered in a helpful and melodic voice.

I introduced myself to him and as we chatted amiably for several minutes I discovered that he was the gardener Alejandro's cousin. The office of occupational compliance had just been instated to ensure compliance with Federal Labor Department safety codes. I was pleased at this improved sense of responsibility the new management team seemed to be exhibiting toward the common worker. As I listened I learned that Santiago was new to the field of occupational compliance codes, having previously been a bank teller at the regional La Plata Savings and Loan Corporation. (La Plata had recently gone belly-up when it was discovered to have been embezzling funds from its senior clients.) Santiago assured me that his extensive experience interpreting State and Federal codes was what suited him so well for his new vocation. When I inquired about the mysteriously welded utility room door, he took on an officious air.

"Please drop by my office to pick up your badge if you are working in that part of the building."

"Badge?"

"Yes, you should have procured one when you were processed through the personnel office."

We had *never* had badges at PRC. When I had been processed through personnel the last time no one had mentioned any kind of a badge, especially not an occupational compliance badge. I imagined it must be something like a union card. I was puzzled, and my silence encouraged Santiago to continue more pedantically.

"Yes, your radioactive register badge. For all employees working in the older part of the building, *or* near the x-ray and ultrasound room, *or* in any of the laboratories, *or* necropsy, *or* storage areas, *or* receiving, *or* biocontainment."

I was waiting for him to put in the next *or*, but apparently he had come to shore.

"You, know, the little red badge. You clip it to your lab coat?" He prompted.

I thought for a moment, well, yes, I *had* seen something like that. It occurred to me. Everyone on Daven's crew had small fat red badges typed with their names adorning their lab coats. I had thought it was a mere affectation. Instead, it seemed to signal my failure to adhere to company policies, along with apparently everyone else I worked with in the older part of the building, *and* near the x-ray and ultrasound room, *and* in the laboratories, *and* in necropsy, *and* in storage areas, *and* in receiving, *and* in biocontainment, *and* in the tiny dark utility room.

"Uh, well, I guess I never got mine," I said, wondering why *I* was feeling guilty. Why *hadn't* personnel given me something that sounded as important as a *radioactive register badge*? "But, you know," I began to protest feebly, "I don't think anyone mentioned it to me, about the badge..."

"Memo dated on the 25th states each employee should have reported to personnel or me directly for their personalized badge. You're required to bring it to me for radiation readings on the 30th of every subsequent month. You should be wearing it daily when you are in the aforementioned areas. To ensure your health." Santiago fired off this offensive in an authoritative staccato that left my head spinning.

"Uh, sure I'll drop by and get it," I agreed, wondering how I had missed that important memo. Then I realized that today's date was only the 26th. As I pondered this information, I realized that I couldn't think of any area that Santiago *hadn't* aforementioned, except administrative offices. I sighed, and decided to return to the topic of the welded door. "What about the utility room?" I persisted.

"Too hot."

"Too hot?"

"Meter readings appear to indicate that the concrete floor is harboring levels too great for general occupational exposure. *You* understand." He coaxed, as if it should be self-evident to someone of my advanced understanding.

"Too hot?" I repeated again, idiotically, thinking about my ovaries.

"Mm-hmmm, that's why you *should* be wearing the badge," he emphasized, as if the badge were an amulet to ward off *mal ojo*. "We'll read the badge every month and be able to track and regulate your incidental exposure levels. Ensure that you're within guidelines. You understand. Please be sure to drop by and visit with me at your earliest convenience. Don't delay any longer!" he reprimanded me in warm, neighborly tones. I could easily imagine my aged landlady Martina handing over her pension check upon hearing the timbre of that rich voice.

"Oh, okay, will do, and, uh, well, thanks for the heads up," I answered, trying unreasonably to be gracious as a sudden unexpected anger began to well its way up from somewhere deep in my viscera. Probably somewhere near my ovaries.

I returned to tell Mitch the bad news. He looked stunned. He didn't have a red badge either.

"Badge?" He repeated, looking vacantly at the welded door. I wondered which vital organ he was thinking about.

We examined the door more closely before hauling our twenty plexiglass boxes up the stairwell. The door was welded on three sides. Since the bottom part of the metal door rested on a concrete jamb it couldn't be welded, so a half-inch gap was left underneath, where one could imagine the bruise-colored fume of radioactivity waiting to wind its way out and up a trouser leg, and then contaminating the myriad cells of the body. Ever-responsive, Festus took my complaints about this irony to heart one day as I was mouthing off in the staff lunch room. The next day I found an old baby blanket with a crocheted rim that Festus had procured from the nursery and stuffed under the door. Oddly, he had also painted the whole door with a remnant of the hated purple paint that I had thought was well-hidden in my lab.

"I knew ye' wouldn't mind if I jest borrowed it t'kinda warn people off." he explained when I quizzed him about it.

Rather than ending with these few incidents, there seemed to be an increase in enigmatic activities being undertaken by the new management. Although I knew many of the researchers, veterinarians, and classified staff, they seemed as clueless as I was about the impetus for these undertakings. Certainly it seemed that there was no dearth of government funds pouring into PRC during this period. I had discovered this by reading through a sheaf of papers Cooperston had shoved into my hands one day in his office. I had been inattentively listening to over thirty minutes worth of research history related to dioxin effects on the Italian population. I may have fallen asleep and dreamed it, but I thought that Cooperston had said that the research concluded that dioxin was not only *not* harmful but might actually be beneficial to the environment if mixed in the right proportions with playground dirt. Probably because of the blank dreamy look on my face after this tutorial, Cooperston had offered to go to the lounge and buy us both cokes. By way of entertaining me in his absence and impressing me with his stature in the world of government, he handed me a report describing the outstanding performance of PRC under his direction as evaluated by a joint committee from the Army and Air Force resource division. The report proposed to give ownership of all remaining military-owned chimpanzees to PRC. As I glanced through the documents I happened to notice that the Air Force was also providing an additional thirty-thousand dollars to *facilitate the management transition.*

A few days afterwards, I was in the pole barn with several chimps peering hopefully at me as I unpacked my enrichment bucket in the gloom. The contrast between the outdoor and indoor light was so dramatic that my vision hadn't adjusted. I pawed vainly through my bucket, seeing only splotches of yellow and green light. I was thinking how much more cheerful, functional and safe the barn would be if they installed skylights. I looked up to the high dark rafters and decided that *facilitating the management transition* might include Air Force funded skylights for the area. I submitted a requisition for the work.

Amazingly, I was approached by the new facilities manager within a few days. He had been directed to install the skylights immediately. This was because Cardenas had decided to expedite my request by complaining to the new safety officer, Santiago, about the dark, dangerous conditions in the barn. Over several years of our companionable work relationship, Cardenas and I had learned how to manipulate the system in our own version of team tag. We were congratulating ourselves on our clever strategy to have the skylights installed after we had seen the maintenance crew diligently dismantling the roof in preparation for the installation. But a few days later we were informed that the work was being abandoned. The official word was that it was just too laborious given the type of building material in the barn.

I simple-mindedly accepted the story, but the savvier Cardenas saw through this transparent ruse. He cornered the facilities manager and reported back to me about the actual events that had occurred. Upon opening the roof, the workers had discovered a layer of rodent droppings and nests almost a foot thick. Alerted by the widely reported and tragic epidemic on a local reservation, the workmen recognized that they were at risk. The dangerous potential for *Hanta* virus exposure resulted in their refusal to do the work, and they decided just to close the roof back up and leave.

"What is Santiago going to do about it?" I asked Cardenas, as an absurd picture of our new safety officer entered my mind, his shovel flashing in the sun as he tried to dig a trench four foot deep and ten foot wide around the pole barn.

"Santiago doesn't know," he replied.

"What! Well we have to tell him. If that stuff is up there it means it's floating down on us every time we go in there, or the wind blows. And what about those chimps?"

"We can't tell him. Administrative directive. Nobody does or says anything until the USDA inspector cites us for it."

"Are you crazy? When is the USDA inspector going to climb up a ladder and cut a hole in the ceiling?" I actually felt my face turning red. I could hear an ocean roaring in my ears.

"I'm as mad at those *chingaderos* as you!" Cardenas exclaimed in a loud and uncharacteristically emotional voice. I pretended not to understand Spanish. "I have thirty-six men working under me, in and out of those areas every day! They all need these jobs. We can't afford to go against the administration!"

"What about their health, and the health of their families, Cardenas?" I snapped back in an uncharacteristically angry voice. For a moment I thought he was going to pretend not to understand English, but with a heart-felt sigh he looked at me from across his desk and answered.

"*Y tu familia, hija?*" he asked, using the familiar address usually reserved for small children.

I actually felt my face turning white. Something frighteningly spasmodic was happening in my T-6 dermatome. I sat down slowly on the edge of an antiquated military chair that was upholstered in cracked green naugahyde. As I gazed at Cardenas I suddenly saw Nikki's face superimposed on his features. Nikki laughing with her wide brown eyes and dimples. Nikki, chasing Stuffing and Dressing around the yard yelling at them to get into their pen. Nikki, holding up her Basset hound puppy to kiss it as it left muddy flowers with its big pancake paws all over the white blouse that Martina had so carefully ironed. Nikki, resignedly lugging her bassoon case across the cotton field to the junior high school with her best friend Yvette Seville, who had more pragmatically chosen to play the piccolo. Nikki, who was now in the glowing, golden health of her blossoming adolescence. I don't know why, because it seemed so obvious at that moment, but I had never considered myself an endangerment to her before.

I looked at Cardenas slumped in his office chair, eyes downcast and now tapping his freshly sharpened pencil on the blotter. I experienced a new comprehension of his dilemma as the *patron,* he was caught in the role of the distressed patriarch. I realized that he had a responsibility to balance the needs of all the people who depended upon him, including me. Many of his crew were poorly educated, even illiterate, all of them with wives and children. There would be no other steady jobs for them in Fat Gulch, and they couldn't afford to create waves against one of the most powerful political forces in the small town by complaining to the local labor board. Cardenas had lived in the valley his entire life and his family had been there for three hundred years before that. He was keenly aware of the regional political power structure.

"Well, what can we do, then?" I offered weakly, trying not to abandon him to sort out the dilemma unaided.

"We're going to supply everyone with higher filtration masks and all areas are going to be shower in and shower out procedures from now on. Increase the bleach dilution in the wash down formula. That's it." He concluded, shrugging his shoulders and with a final wave of his hand indicating that it wasn't open for discussion any longer.

I felt depressed by the incident with the skylights, but I soon turned my attention to other things. Poppy, my assistant, and I were busy characterizing some interesting behavior patterns we had identified in two chimps named Merle and Devon. Merle was a twenty-five-year-old chimpanzee housed in the hepatitis research area. He had a long history of unusual behavior. Devon was three-years-old and had been enacting stereotypic behaviors since birth. Poppy and I sat and watched them by the hour, using a stopwatch to record the frequency and duration of their activities. I believed we could clearly establish that both of them fit all the criteria for autism.

I had first noticed Merle among the hundreds of chimps during my second tour of duty. His behavior was so obviously different from the other chimps that I had remained interested in him over the years. He didn't appear to like to climb or be up off of the floor except on the very infrequent occasions when he was scared. Then he clambered up the cage-side in apparent alarm. His alarm response seemed random, unrelated to any discernibly alarming stimuli such as white-coated strangers or the sight of a gurney. He rarely engaged in interactions with other chimps or objects in the outer world. Poppy and I had started to gather information about Merle hoping we could find ways to help him be more interactive with his social and material environment. As we searched through the literature on stereotypic behavior we became interested in the possibility that chimpanzees could develop autism. We wanted to present our data in a professional forum and perhaps develop a non-human primate model for autism.

I had watched Merle in fascination several times. I was trying to understand what function was served by his apparently carefully choreographed and repetitive series of stereotypic behaviors. He would sit on the floor in front of his mesh caging with both arms extended upwards, his hands gripping the fencing. Then he would begin a smooth regular side-to-side rocking while simultaneously wagging his head in circumduction, his jutted chin scribing a figure eight in space. This self-stimulation would go on for almost an hour. In the next phase of his ritual, Merle would scoot along the fence line, inching his way to a corner. He would face into the corner with one arm extended upward on each of the opposing angles of the caging and re-enact his performance. After rocking rhythmically from side-to-side numerous times he would stand up with his knees bent. He then alternately lifted and stamped his feet as if performing a dance. This one-footed balance routine included a pattern of seven stamps per foot before switching feet, swaying from side-to-side the whole time. After a period of time Merle returned to sitting and rocking. Throughout all of the performance his head kept swaying. His behavior was similar to a record that was stuck in a groove, it was repeated over and over, and continued during all of his waking hours.

As I watched Merle I had an insight that he was providing himself with a carefully modulated series of input. In fact, as I considered his behavior I thought he must be receiving much the same input as a typical chimp might derive from climbing, playing, and social interaction. His head movements had to provide a large surge of vestibular and ocular input to his CNS. Then Merle added a measured series of somatic sensory input by stimulating cutaneous, deep muscle, and proprioceptive receptors during his foot-stomping, swaying, fence-clinging dance. Merle was stimulating and maintaining the input-throughput-output properties of the CNS. Although outwardly his behavior might appear dysfunctional, it must perform a homeostatic function for the CNS.

Other chimps mostly tolerated Merle's eccentricity and had little or no expectations of his behavior. When Merle had been placed in a social group the other chimpanzees did not even try to engage him in dominance politics or social interaction. On the rare occasions that someone attempted to engage Merle, he seemed completely oblivious. He preferred his solitary rocking and scooting routine. Sometimes at seemingly random intervals I watched him engage in interactive chase-play with a cage-mate. His participation was rigid, he used a forward-backward linear movement almost as if he were following lines that were invisibly painted on the floor. It was repetitive and included an unceasing head sway. These play bouts were rare and of short duration, then Merle would return to his self-contained ritual.

I once saw a larger male chimp try to aggress Merle and make a show of his dominance. He ran up to Merle and hit him on the back of his shoulder. Merle began to bare-teeth scream, still in his fence-clinging stance, and directing his protest to empty space. The other chimpanzee stood back in piloerection, waiting for Merle's engagement. When Merle continued to sit vacantly screaming and whimpering the aggressor seemed to understand that it was a futile exercise and relented. Other chimps rarely groomed with Merle. When they did it was a one-way arrangement in which Merle derived the most benefit but failed to return the favor. Merle tolerated grooming by human caregivers if they were familiar, turning his back to the human for a shoulder scratch. When he did accept grooming from other chimps and people it seemed to calm him. His restless and repetitive movement would almost cease during grooming and scratching sessions. He never particularly warmed up to me, but this made it easier for me to simply observe him.

Merle's eating habits were curiously ritualistic. When biscuits were placed in the feeder box, he did not charge over to snatch up as many as he could like any other chimp might. Instead he enacted his ritualistic dance as he slowly made his way to the box, plucked out a few biscuits and placed them between pursed lips. Eventually he'd sit down and eat them, still wagging his head. Merle had a unique habit of collecting and organizing food items. He would take treats, biscuits, and fruit, lining them up in a straight row on the floor between the front of his body and the cage while he continued to rock. Eventually he would eat the treats, but he never seemed in a hurry to devour his food. He never showed the usual gusto for food that the other chimps did. He vocalized in little grunts while he ate, but didn't usually participate in the same long, heart-felt hooting of his comrades. His vocalizations often occurred inappropriately and seemingly independently of typical stimuli like food or strangers.

Curiosity and interactive play with an object weren't part of Merle's repertoire. Merle wasn't interested in my enrichment items. Novel produce like persimmons and pomegranates were treated much the same as the usual apples, oranges, and bananas. Each food item was treated with ritualistic consideration. He wasn't exploratory. Toy objects evoked neither the usual investigative or fear response. A large, hard, blue plastic ball elicited essentially the same response as a yellow ball or a pipe feeder. He would occasionally touch some of the objects I placed in his cage, but the way in which he touched such objects reminded me of a blind person reaching out to define the perimeters of his personal space and accidentally encountering an object. It was ignored or sometimes grasped momentarily and then replaced in its original position.

My assumption until this time had been that all behavior could be modified in some way by environmental manipulations. I remembered how Benjy had shown me that I could not always bring about a permanent change in behavior when I tried to stop his painful habit of self-wounding. But Benjy had at least been interested in, and responded temporarily to environmental changes. Now Merle was teaching me that sometimes I couldn't even *interrupt* dysfunctional behavior for a single moment. Merle didn't appear to be in pain or distress, on the contrary he usually wore a pleased expression and sometimes even laughed out loud. He didn't even appear to be aware of the environment around him. The stimuli he responded to was innate, part of some rich internal landscape I couldn't glimpse- a secret garden to which I had no key and no access. Merle had developed a personal way of relating himself to the larger world through his highly ritualized behavior.

Merle's behavior seemed to fit the descriptions I had read of cases of autism in children. I reviewed all of Merle's records, documenting his childhood health history. His upbringing was unremarkable relative to that of other lab-reared chimps. However, two things stood. One was that he had been enacting stereotypic swaying, rocking, and head shaking behaviors since early infancy. The other was that he had always had hyperactive allergy symptoms and had been treated with various over-the-counter medications almost daily or weekly for the first few years of his life. I was interested these allergy states because I had read similar reports about a large subset of children with autism. Many of these children exhibited sometimes dramatic symptoms of reactivity to various common foods and environmental pollutants.

Three-year-old Devon was similar in many ways to Merle. He had also been plagued with allergy symptoms since early infancy. The nursery crew had nick-named Devon *Mr. No-No* because of stereotypic head wagging he had exhibited from birth. The behavior seemed compulsive and it was not a tremor. It appeared to be intentional. It was obvious that he could stop wagging his head to eat, or if he wanted to look at an object or event in the environment. Devon exhibited self-stimulatory behaviors directed at his face and genital areas, both locations probably provided huge sensory feedback since they were highly innervated with large somatic representation in the sensory cortex. It seemed likely that he was deriving powerful and reliable input by this self-stimulatory behavior. Environmental enrichment didn't alter his behavior noticeably, and I thought it doubtful that merely supplying a toy could interrupt the powerful need for direct somatic input. I sent a videotape of his behavior to a regional pediatric hospital. The therapists who treated autism there suggested that we use a special sensory-integrative therapy technique to help normalize the stereotypies.

It was difficult to integrate Devon into a social group where he might receive grooming and other direct physical input through play and socialization with peers. He broke into screaming fits periodically, clinging fiercely to anything or anyone in the near vicinity. Other little nursery apes avoided him, so that he was a virtual social outcast. Because Devon was still small enough to handle, we often took him out of his cage and used sensory-integrative therapy techniques including joint massage, compression, and swinging motions. As Poppy and I worked with him, we noted that our direct physical contact resulted in decreased stereotypic behaviors for several hours following each session. We were finally successful in pairing Devon with a young chimp named Taylor who was tolerant and even indulgent of Devon's eccentricities. Though they seldom engaged in age-typical juvenile play, Devon seemed calmer with his new companion and his screaming fits decreased in frequency and intensity. The two could be seen sitting and walking in tandem, Devon holding to Taylor like a blind person holds to the harness on his guide dog.

In my own mind I began a process of contrast and compare. I asked myself what made Merle and Devon different from other chimpanzees I treated for dysfunctional behavior. I also more carefully scrutinized the commonalities between the two. One obvious difference from other chimpanzees was that the others all had a demonstrable time period or event from which the onset of behavioral problems could be traced. Events included things like being moved into isolation, being weaned, or undergoing a particularly difficult research project. These events appeared to trigger an initital episode of atypical behavior that was then repeated under stressful conditions. It was almost a profile of post-traumatic stress disease. Merle and Devon, in contrast, had exhibited unusual and repetitive behaviors beginning immediately after birth.

Devon appeared to be more relational and interactive with peers and material objects than Merle was, but it seemed plausible that Merle may have been much like Devon when he was young. The intervening years of isolation and lack of stimulation may have shaped and reinforced his nascent stereotypies into the rigid adult form they now took. I wondered if early therapeutic intervention might have decreased the dysfunctional behaviors he had learned to use to relate to the world. I realized that this all fell into the realm of speculation. Still, I felt it was worth considering the possibility that there was a developmental window during which typical behaviors might be most easily called forth and reinforced. I wanted to support Devon and any other young chimps with a similar constellation of symptoms to develop a greater capacity for functional behavior and social participation than Merle exhibited as an adult.

I didn't believe that postnatal environmental stressors had caused Merle and Devon's unusual behaviors, although they may have enlarged upon an already underlying dysfunction. I was convinced that whatever afflicted them was innate, and had been born into the world with them rather than having been induced postnatally. I thought a clue might be provided by the immune system challenges that Devon and Merle shared. They had both struggled with allergy-like symptoms during infancy. This was not typical of every nursery-reared chimp. I was becoming increasingly interested in the possibility that the maternal or prenatal immune system was somehow implicated in dysfunctional behaviors that were so apparent and continuous from birth.

The larger question of the origins of autism was still unanswered and highly speculative in most of the research I had read. I discovered that some parents and doctors had started to question childhood vaccines as the culprit in causing autistic behaviors. Many children seemed to behave developmentally appropriately until receiving Measles-Mumps-Rubella shots (MMR), after which came an onset of immune system challenges and a cessation of age-appropriate development. Some researchers were trying to implicate the use of mercury-based thimerosol, a binding agent used in childhood vaccines. There was little hard data to verify thimerosol effects. The most convincing data implicating the immune system impacts of thimerosol in the development of autism came a few years after I had left PRC. It was evidenced when the large, rich, and powerful pharmaceutical lobby covertly attached a rider to a congressional bill that exonerated them from financial liability for inducing autism with thimerosol. Merle and Devon differed from the profile of post-vaccine onset autism because they had *always* exhibited unusual behavior. But, I reasoned, if the key was to be found in the immune system, it was plausible that their states were due to prenatal environmental exposures.

My interest in the implications of prenatal immune exposures had been heightened by a strange adventure with Martina that had occurred shortly before Poppy and I had started our project with Merle and Devon. One Saturday morning as we sat in her kitchen drinking our *Sanka con leche* (a sickly sweet brew with evaporated milk that I had found to be a regular feature of most menus in Mexico) the phone rang.

It was one of Martina's fourth or fifth cousins in Juarez. The woman's daughter had given birth to her first-born son during the night. As was not untypical in Juarez, the woman had given birth at home attended by the local *partera,* but something was amiss. My *novella*-based Spanish wasn't acute enough to identify the problem as I eavesdropped on the conversation, but the drama was clearly evident in the tone of voice Martina used and her increasingly frantic gestures as she stood at the phone table in the hallway.

"*Dios mio,*" Martina had said gravely, crossing herself after she hung up the phone and turned to tell me about the baby.

I was puzzled as to why the advent of the baby would be a cause for prayers of lament and protection. Martina seemed somewhat confused about the baby's condition herself but was now insistent that I drive her to Juarez to see the family. I argued against this idea as I thought of the chaotic traffic in the large metropolis of El Paso-Juarez, but soon found myself speeding eastward along the desert freeway toward the border. We compromised about driving in Juarez by parking on the American side and riding the cartoonish and hiccoughing red diesel bus across the border. I watched the dizzy colors and activity of the market strip fade past the windows as we drove further into the true working class *barrios* of the city. It was like watching a film reel unwind back in time. The paved streets declined into patches of asphalt and potholes, and finally became rutted dirt roads. Automobiles decreased in number and soon horse-drawn carts could be seen ambling their way along the dust and debris choked streets. The bus reached the terminus of its route and dropped us among the squat cinderblock houses that were jammed together on the edges of a runneled lane. Even the air was different on this side of the invisible line between countries. It had an acrid, eye-watering quality that most people attributed to the fuming *maquila* factories and the lack of environmental regulatory laws in Mexico.

We trudged our way up into the hills of the barrio. We halted every so often to catch our breath. I turned and looked down on the sprawling city of El Paso-Juarez, divided as it was by the sluggish brown ribbon of the Rio Grande. Martina had recently developed cataracts and

now seemed to have forgotten exactly where her young cousin lived. I
was wondering if we were going to be in Mexico for a long time when
Martina spied the painted turquoise doorway to her cousin's home. We
knocked and were admitted. We had arrived at the same time as a nurse
that the *partera* had called in from a local clinic. With the bureaucratic
seriousness I had noticed demonstrated by most government workers
in Mexico, the nurse was attired in an elaborate uniform. It was an
unblemished white complete with a cap emblazoned with red crosses
and a shoulder full of medals that indicated the extent of the nurse's
qualifications. In America this outfit would have seemed archaic. But
in the stuffy, dim apartment where the young dark eyed-mother wore
a tired, uncomprehending and frightened look on her face, the white
nurse's uniform was a solace.

"*Elle es un medico*," Martina introduced me to the nurse and family.
She had never seemed to grasp the subtle difference between an M.D.
and a Ph.D., and I had long ago given up trying to tutor her regarding
arcane academic categories. As long as no one expected me to produce
a syringe and inoculate somebody it wasn't worth trying to explain the
American educational system in my halting, English-speckled border
Spanish. I sighed and moved closer to the crib where everyone's attention was focused.

I saw a darling, plump baby boy stretching jerkily and yawning. He
blinked his eyes opened. They were the dark, cloudy, and unfocussed
blue of a newborn. The crown of his head had the seemingly typical
bruised and oddly misshapen look of the just-born. He began to cry in
a lethargic and breathy way that resulted in an odd low-pitched keening. The young mother lifted him from the crib and tried to nurse him.
He suckled, but there was an undirected quality to his movements. His
arms jerked about in an almost spasmodic way. The young mother was
speaking rapidly in Spanish and I understood that she was concerned
about who would care for the baby when she had to return to her job
as a *maquiladora* in a week. The nurse responded by encouraging her
to consider sending the baby to the hospital right away for treatment.
An elderly woman in an apron, whom I thought must be the *partera*,

stood nodding in the corner, her arm wrapped around the shoulder of the new and clearly grieving grandmother.

"*Que es la enfermada?*" I inquired.

"*Dolores de la cabeza*," the mother responded, gently touching the bruised and strangely soft-looking crown of the baby's head.

"*Anencephalero*," the nurse enlightened me with a grim sweep of her brown and knowledgeable eyes.

I worked hard to conceal the emotions that wanted to work themselves out on my face as I scrutinized the tiny, almost perfect son. He was beautiful. He had lovely round cheeks and curling dark hair cascading over his forehead in a way that belied the emptiness within. His sweet button nose was nestled against his mother's breast where he was ineffectually suckling. She was gently squeezing his chubby pink arm, stilling it from its frantic dyspraxic gyrations, bending her head forward to press her lips to his fingers. I watched, knowing that she didn't yet understand that he had no future, that if he lived at all, in two, or five, or twenty years he would behave much the same as he did right now. The nurse looked steadily at me and I back at her in a common understanding, no words passed.

My eyes were drawn to a picture on the wall that was overlooking the family drama. It was the Virgin graciously gazing down from the heavens, her heart emblazoned on her blue robes and surrounded by rays of golden light that beckoned the masses into her arms. Underneath her portrait a candle was burning to Santo Nino who sat in effigy with his feet shackled and one hand uplifted toward her. My eyes began to well up and for some reason I couldn't turn my thoughts away from the sluggish brown waters of the Rio Grande, or the Rio Bravo del Norte as the first conquistadors had named it; the brave fierce river of the north. It pulsed its way between the high blue southwestern sky and the dry, hungry earth all the way from the *Sangre de Cristo* Mountains in the north to the litter-choked arroyo below us. It divided our two countries, the laws, and the value systems of cultures. The river was a concrete manifestation of an abstract concept of borders and categories and the way in which the human intellect ordered the world around it.

I had grown up near the headwaters of the Rio Grande where they sprang frothy, cold and blue from the mountains of Colorado. There it was a playground for affluent *Norteamericanos*. We had rafted and fished and swam in it's crystal waters for leisure. From an airplane I had visually traced the way the river bisected New Mexico, moving south like a bulging green artery that fed the agricultural economy of the State. During numerous desert hikes I had taken in Southern New Mexico I had also seen how the foamy, agricultural-chemical imbued runoff from the lush fields drained back into the river. Once after hiking through miles of pecan orchards I emerged from a screen of osage orange trees on the river bank in time to observe a septic company truck covertly dispensing its foul load into the murky water.

By the time the Rio Grande reached Texas and turned left to find the Gulf of Mexico it had been transformed from a velvety green ribbon into something that looked like the forgotten cup of Martina's *Sanka con leche* that I had cleared off my bedside table in disgust when I found a drowned moth in it. The newspaper had regularly reported on water analyses that indicated hepatitis and heavy metals could be found in the river where it divided the countries. Found right here, where people were daily seen cooling themselves, wading and washing themselves and their belongings. Here in this languishing city of poverty-stricken immigrants looking northward with a light of hope in their eyes as they stood on this very earth where the mostly unregulated *maquilas* had often dumped out gallons of mysterious substances. I gazed up at the compassionate Virgin where she leaned toward Santo Nino and remembered recently reading that there had been an epidemic of anencephalic babies born in Mexico along the route of the river. Epidemiological researchers were becoming certain that the distribution of these births was related to environmental toxins associated with the *maquilas*.

That heart-breaking visit to our neighboring country had made me more aware of the various toxins and immunological insults at PRC. Given the almost unlimited opportunities for exposure it was practically inconceivable that there weren't *more* chimpanzees like Merle and Devon. They may well have developed innate CNS processing dysfunction secondary to suffering from environmental toxins and maternal immune insults while inutero. It seemed plausible that pre-natal exposure could alter fetal development, irrevocably distorting the throughput processes of the CNS. Although Devon and Merle weren't related to each other, another possibility that struck me was that the behavioral oddities might be purely genetic, unique family traits like the madness of King George or the Hapsburg lip. Or more probably, the onset of autistic-like behavior was a multifactorial combination of these influences, requiring both a severe immune system challenge and some kind of genetic predisposition.

Having these various trains of thought barreling through my mind left me longing deeply for the intellectual sign posts that my lost *compadre* Bart had once provided. I knew he would have had a dozen pointed, but insightful criticisms of my hypotheses. Especially now that he worked for the Environmental Protection Agency in California, hav-ing moved during my last hiatus. But since his wife had died, Bart had withdrawn from his old relationships and didn't seem to want to keep in touch. I would have to find some other thoughtful sounding board for my ideas about Merle's problems.

As I struggled with how to improve the quality of life for Devon and Merle, and sought to develop a deeper understanding of autism, I ran across a body of work by some autism researchers from San Diego. These experts hypothesized that epigenetic influences beginning early inutero were a probable etiology of autism and explained how the symptoms could be so varied from one individual to the next. I liked the term *epigenetic* because it encompassed the whole of environ-mental influences; the *environment* could be the maternal physiology (immune system deficits) or continual, episodic, or single exposures to influences from the environment in which the mother was living. It had become insistently clear that the world of PRC was rife with oppor-tunities for pregnant chimps, non-pregnant chimps and all varieties of humans to be exposed continually, episodically, or with one good blast by any number of immunologically insulting substances, or epigenetic influences as I now liked to refer to them. It required little stretch of the imagination to hypothesize a correlation between epigenetic effects inutero and the subsequent problems with input-throughput-output functions of the CNS that characterized autism.

The San Diego researchers reasoned that an early embryologic aberration in the development of the CNS would alter cell development in a way that would skew gene-regulatory effects on target cells later in embryologic and postnatal development. A domino effect was set up whereby even a single cellular level aberration effectively scripted successive dysfunctions in the developmental process. One result could be the strange motor behaviors exhibited by persons with autism. These behaviors could be interpreted as the organism's expression of a skewed ability to process and modulate input and throughput due to cellular dysmorphology and related phenomena. This produced dysfunctional output such as the stereotypical motor behaviors associated with autism, hand-flapping for example. Stereotypic behaviors were, in all probability, the individual organism's attempt at organization and homeostasis within a world from which they were receiving unreliable data.

These ideas were similar in basic concept to the conclusions I had drawn about SIB. The expression of dysfunctional behavior in Merle and Devon's cases could be due to distorted CNS output as a result of developmental impacts in the input-throughput processes. I decided to see if I could replace Bart's keen, incisive critiques by using the San Diego researchers as a sounding board for my investigation into Merle and Devon's behaviors. When I contacted them, the researchers were extremely supportive and interested in our findings. They agreed to meet with us in person at an upcoming conference in California for which Poppy and I were preparing a presentation characterizing Devon and Merle's behavior. No one had yet developed an animal model of autism and the San Diego group was intrigued by the potential that cases like Devon's and Merle's might offer to the hundreds of families seeking answers to the mysteries of the condition. I hoped to eventually convince the researchers to come to PRC and initiate a project using our data as a pilot study. Poppy and I began to talk about how wonderfully different it would be to have a true behavioral research team at PRC to counter-balance and collaborate with the immunological, toxicological, and pharmacokinetic research groups. Well, a girl can dream, can't she?

Poppy and I lavished intense imagination on this dream. As it became more and more grandiose we envisioned students streaming in from exotic places like Great Britain or the Ukraine.

"Or even as far away as Saskatchewan!" Poppy exclaimed, almost starry-eyed at the vision of it one day in the lab as we made purple hard-boiled eggs.

We imagined our bright young students eager and ready-handed to solve the mysteries of autism and discover an effective solution. The multinational behavioral research team we envisioned as we patiently made peanut butter roll-ups from butcher paper and filled feeder tubes with squash porridge would eventually feature numerous of the most luminous names in research. Matsuzawa, Povinelli, Gallup, Courchesne, maybe even Jane Goodall all figured importantly in what was becoming our five-year research plan, or else an escapist science fiction fantasy. We made this vision our flagship and I initiated contact with some of the luminaries we wished to attract to PRC. We got an actual commitment from a renowned Japanese behaviorist from Kyoto who promised to come and conduct a six-month long project in the nursery during the upcoming year. He sealed the deal by sending gifts of hand-painted silk with monkey motifs and securing an apartment for his family in Fat Gulch.

This fuelled our enthusiasm and enlarged our dream of a behavioral research center, turning it into a panacea for the wildly pathological institutional politics that were unsettling PRC. It became our antidote for the generalized depression we experienced as a result of the increasingly negative public image PRC was garnering in the national media (or maybe it was a result of the accumulation of radioactive isotopes in our neural substrate). We felt that our work was good and important and widely unacknowledged among our peers in behavior and enrichment throughout the world. Our creative imagining about the glorious future of our department helped us to maintain our motivation. We fantasized endlessly about how someday the world would recognize our deeply important contributions. As it was, not a day went by that we weren't rewarded by noisily grateful recognition from the multitude of our comrades-in-arms, adoring primates who were recipients of our various enrichment strategies.

Our immediate concern related to autism remained the pragmatic one of improving the quality of life for Merle and Devon. I believed that for Merle, increased functionality meant an improved ability for social and object interaction, and decreased stereotypies. For Devon it might mean a decrease in anxiety states, SIB, and stereotypic behaviors as well as improved ability for social interaction. Poppy and I had collected a lot of behavioral data in our little black notebooks and had faithfully entered it into our computer data bank. We reasoned that if we could identify what sensory input they created for themselves by their behavioral routines, we might be able to identify which sensory components of the nervous system weren't functioning normally. We thought we should be able to find some manipulation of sensory stimuli and therefore cortical throughput that would assist them to become more organized and able to respond more functionally within their environment. Poppy and I had usually been able to find some combination of environmental manipulations that impacted dysfunctional behaviors. This situation was more challenging because if Merle and Devon were indeed autistic, our usual solutions wouldn't be effective since their problems were innate and not immediately induced by or responsive to the environment.

Merle was the least interactive of the two apes and his behavioral regimen so rigid and predictable that we could almost literally set our watches by it. I supposed that with twenty-four years of self-reinforcement, from a behavioral standpoint Merle would be a tough nut to crack. I was right. We were never able to reshape his behaviors to any measurable extent, but we eventually settled on a satisfactory social arrangement for him. We pair-housed him with Dean. Dean was a paraplegic who had lived with his pal Clyde in a larger social group. Much like Robin and Elizabeth, Clyde and Dean took care of each other.

Dean had a very normal array of behaviors and an attitude that would have ensured his alpha status if he had been able to use his legs, but he was unable to fend for himself effectively with his disability.

Dean had been living successfully in an all-male social group. His social success may have been due in great part to having a fit ally such as Clyde. Dean was amazingly independent and assertive. Unlike Merle, he was socially intact and quite adept in social interaction and manipulation. He exhibited physical symptoms of a generalized cord injury at the lumbar level. Clearly he didn't have motor control of his lower extremities. He did not seem to be in pain but appeared to register some sensation in his lower limbs. He did not like to sit in water or other unpleasant substances, and groomed his own legs meticulously. He was functionally quite mobile using his strong upper body to swing himself around, dragging his legs along behind him. Clyde always stayed close enough to back him up if he needed it, but he wasn't overweening in his assistance.

I was awestruck the first time I saw Dean enact his impressive aggressive display. He hoisted himself up on the cage fencing using his arms, and then balanced himself upright on his lifeless legs. He clung the cage side using his arms to build up a swaying momentum. When the momentum reached a crescendo, Dean let go of the fence, launching himself into a full bipedal run. He used his legs as fulcrums for his hip flexor and extensor muscles to swing forward, while masterfully keeping the center of gravity in his torso balanced to maintain his momentum. I thought he might be accomplishing this feat by over-using the gluteus maximus, which has a more lateral proximal attachment and biomechanic dynamic in the chimpanzee than in the human. He could run six or seven steps like this, clearly swinging the legs from the level of his pelvis. If you knew nothing of his disability, and were only witness to his full frontal charge you would be convinced of his wholeness and potential to enact great physical harm. But by the sixth or seventh stride I could see muscle fatigue hit and his joints buckle. Dean would crumple slowly to the floor. He reigned in the magnificence of his aggressive display from this seated position, leaning forward on extended arms, resting on his knuckles. His upper body remained tense and erect, his arms sculpted in muscular strength, and the hair on his neck and shoulders curling upward in silvered crests.

Dean's use of complex, intentional, sequenced, motor planning, or praxis, had taken me by surprise. His display required an underlying strength of will and personal volition. His carefully orchestrated and wily social craft would have been hard for even Daven to compete against. Dean was not relying on habituated motor plans or the automatic subcortical motor editing and prediction of the cerebellum to respond to environmental demands. Instead he was using complex and intentional feed-forward motor planning that must have involved a lot of practice to perfect. His measured efforts to organize movement and strategize timing in response to social and environmental conditions spoke of a deep cognitive and sociopolitical acumen. Because his physical energy was limited he had to make decisions that embodied value judgments weighing the importance of making a response to select environmental and social conditions. While he could not procure an alpha position in his group, he could maintain a non-submissive beta status through intelligent use of his physical resources and the strength of his relationship with his *compadre*, Clyde.

The ephemeral nature of chimpanzee social status was sadly demonstrated when one afternoon the caregivers found Dean's friend, Clyde dead on the floor of his enclosure. (It was later discovered that Clyde had suffered a major heart attack.) Dean was seated at some distance from Clyde's body, his face averted. The other males in the group were ignoring the situation altogether. In the ensuing weeks, no one stepped up to take Clyde's role as Dean's ally. Dean was becoming displaced and at risk in his group. He began to lose weight and look nervous. This is when Poppy and I stepped into the fray and suggested pairing Dean and Merle, who was housed alone at the time.

"Like the blind leading the blind," Cardenas grumbled, shaking his head but acquiescing.

When they were introduced, Dean enacted his brave display. Merle kept his back turned the whole time, focused on his repetitive rocking.

Dean seemed a bit puzzled at first, but since he easily secured alpha status, he soon settled into a routine with Merle. The two could be seen sitting together occasionally while Dean groomed Merle. Merle would sit almost still, accepting the attention, his shaggy head weaving to and fro. Merle was not the companionate friend Clyde had been, but he was a warm body. Even with his magnificent physique and apparent health, Merle was incapable of complex praxis. He could not formulate an appropriate motor response to the novel demands of his world. If anything threatening occurred in the environment, such visits by white-coated strangers, Merle would just rock more frantically. Merle's dysfunctional behavior allowed Dean to move easily into the role of dominant troop leader. He would use his social acumen and disingenuousness to rush forward and challenge interlopers that passed through the areas with his improbable but impeccably timed bipedal swagger.

I believed that Dean benefited the most from his relationship with Merle, who remained seemingly oblivious. I could find no way to surmise how much Merle valued Dean's presence within his own private world. But it was clear that Dean valued his role as the alpha male in his partnership with Merle. He no longer had Clyde to back him up, but he had in turn found someone who needed his care and protection, and he addressed his duty with all seriousness. I often thought fondly of the pair in the years after I left PRC, imagining them sitting outside in the winter sun, Merle enacting his dance and Dean carefully patrolling the perimeters of their little territory, striking terror in the heart of the white-coats and the scrawny desert coyotes. Several years later I wept with sadness and shame when I read in a publicly released USDA document that Dean had died. The report described the necropsy results including a systemic infection and the presence of a large abscess wrapped around the ventral and lateral portions of his lumbar cord. The report criticized the institute for not providing adequate veterinary care or performing appropriate histological analyses at necropsy. I felt terrible remorse for not having responded differently to what was clearly a medical crisis for Dean. Maybe I could have convinced someone to give him the medical attention he needed if I had not acquiesced to the generally held assumption that his paralysis was the result of an untreatable and static injury instead of an ongoing and increasingly poisonous condition. My own crippling condition has remained the memory of such sins of omission.

I succeeded in ignoring most of the almost macabre series of events that continued to unfold in the corporate milieu around me. Poppy and I immersed ourselves in our excitement over the potential importance and the far-reaching implications of developing a chimpanzee model for autism. Occasionally something would impinge on my consciousness long enough to make me feel uneasy, but I utilized my advanced human capacity for praxis to respond by digging all the deeper into the autism research project. One evening I stayed late to finish writing our autism project abstract for submission to the conference we hoped to attend, and where we planned to meet the autism researchers from San Diego. I had generally disdained being at PRC after dark since my earlier ugly realization about the nighttime rodent and pestilence conditions. My excitement over the autism project had over-ridden my native caution though, and I found myself conducting several midnight oil burning sessions. I finished up and lugged my briefcase out the back door through the desert darkness to where I had parked my car by the rear loading dock. I was startled to hear Redd's demanding voice assaulting me through the night air.

"What are you doing out here?" he barked at me.

"Oh, you know, some last minute paperwork," I managed, trying to quell the results of the adrenal steroids now racing through my body. With my newly dilated pupils, I was able to observe that Redd was once again accompanied by two men and a green military truck. All three of the men seemed to float like ghosts through the moonless dark in their tyvek suits.

"Well, you're supposed to notify Greta if you're going to be on the premises past six," Redd grumbled.

I watched as his two silent companions efficiently hooked the chemical trailer up to the green truck and then began to pull it gently forward from where it had resided on the rear loading dock. It had

been there for the entire decade I had been at PRC, and looked antiquated enough to have come from the same era as Lucy and Desi Arnaz.
I had been in the trailer several times, both to acquire substances I once
used in a milk lactose assay, and just to keep Dr. McGuiness's lab assistant, Imelda company. Prior to her recent stroke, it had been Imelda's
job to inventory everything in the trailer each month. She had told me
that she thought it was a creepy place, but I had found it fascinating.
It was filled with shelf upon shelf of beautiful colored glass containers
of various sizes and shapes. Some looked like squat crystalline alad-
din's lamps filled with golden liquids, others were like tall blue cider
jugs with dark incomprehensible fluids, yet others hung like tiny bul-
bous test tubes suspended in small metal racks. As I watched the green
truck gently rock the trailer from its stanchions, I wondered how all
that glassware could possibly stay stable and unbroken.

"You better get goin'." Redd admonished. "Can get dangerous out
here at night. All them coyotes."

I silently obeyed.

As my headlights blazed over the dark desert highway on the way
home, I pondered the strange affairs of my workplace. I had begun to
believe there were just as many coyotes inside as there were outside
of the institute. Which ones were more dangerous, I wondered? What
qualities would I have to nurture within myself to avoid both kinds?
Would I remain unchanged by my contact with them, or would behaviors as incomprehensible as Merle's, Benjy's, and Earl's begin to emerge
as I struggled to adapt to the overwhelming conditions of the environment? I crested one of a series of small hills leading over the pass that
would eventually descend toward the homelights of my village. A dark
form dashed across the highway in front of my truck. I stamped hard
on the brakes. The wheels made a skidding, losing-rubber sound as the
vehicle stopped. I could see the disappearing shape of a frightened
coyote with its tail tucked up under its belly. It ran down through a
crown of cactus on the shoulder of the road. I shuddered, wondering
what would scare the usually cunning and fearless coyote into oncom-
ing traffic and through the barbed crown of the opuntia. Just then a

low, broad, and comical form waddling at great speed tore onto the road in hot pursuit of the wild dog.

"What the heck...." I murmured out loud, squinting at the strange, dark animal and simultaneously pressing the high-beam lever. I suddenly realized I was seeing a usually reclusive badger. I recalled the dire warnings of a seasoned and gimpy old field supervisor I had once had during my archaeological excavation days as an anthropology student.

"And don't ever step down a badger hole," he warned us ominously. "When you're out walking your transects a hole's hard to see, but you better watch for 'em. I guarantee you'll never know worse damage than a badger'll do to your leg if you stick it down his hole. There's not a meaner more bad-tempered or sharper-toothed son of a bitch on this planet." Here the sun-wizened field marshal pulled up his denim pant-leg. Visible above the top of his tall, leather, steel-toed boots could be seen dozens of parallel ruts of hardened white scar tissue. "Tear you to bloody ribbons like a hundred razors," he said in the rusty dust-choked voice common to the career archaeologist. He squinted around at us slowly for emphasis as we shuffled uneasily from foot to foot, trying not to stare at his deformed leg. "You'll wish you'd met a rattlesnake instead," he croaked out solemnly.

I almost felt sorry for the loping coyote. But, I reasoned, the bad-tempered badger was, after all, *only* protecting itself. I had to admire its determination and speed, considering that it was really built to dig its way methodically through the complex strata of the earth, not to chase carnivorous scavengers through the open air of the midnight desert. If it took a bite out of the troublesome coyote, I'm sure it was well justified in doing so.

When we weren't working on our autism project, Poppy and I enlarged our scheming and manipulations to send a chimpanzee to the sanctuary. Poppy had started her own campaign to convert Tex Hilton to the cause. She initiated this by suggesting he should establish PRC as a corporate donor to one of the more reputable animal welfare organizations. She weighted the value of her suggestion by simultaneously giving him some Cuban cigars her husband had procured on a recent fishing trip to Mexico. I was pleased that she had paid attention to my lessons in the power of positive reinforcement to affect amygdala responses and limbic state.

One morning when Poppy and I were working in our enrichment lab, Tex actually stopped in to thank Poppy and tell us that the Nuclear Regulatory Commission (NRC) would be sending a couple of field agents from east of the cottonwood clump to retrieve a few radioactive isotopes stored in the room across the hall from our lab.

"Mighty fine cigars, I just want to thank you! I like your idea about a corporate campaign to donate to select animal welfare organizations, too. You're right in guessing that I had a plan like that in mind myself." He smiled disarmingly and went on to explain about the NRC visit with the same casual nonchalance that he might have used to announce that his aunt was coming for a visit.

"Should we be concerned about the radioactive materials, leave the building or anything?" I asked in puzzlement, fiddling with my red badge.

"Oh, hell no, its been sittin' there for years! Typical in these old labs, and it's only four pigs' worth. If it were more'n ten pigs' worth, now *then* you might be worried," Hilton guffawed impatiently, waving us off with the smoking Cuban stogie.

I was afraid to ask exactly what he meant by pigs, as I worked diligently to preserve my façade of intellectual comprehension.

Just drop by my office anytime. You gals know I have an open door policy!" Poppy managed a weak smile as Tex turned to go. He winked and strolled like a smoking locomotive back up the passage toward the administrative offices.

Clearly Tex understood nothing about limbic state. Or, I reflected, if he did, there was something artless but masterful, and pointedly sinister about the response he was trying to evoke. I noticed that Poppy was having an ANS response that had left her looking distinctly pale since the topic of the NRC had entered our conversation. I remembered that she and her husband had been trying unsuccessfully to start a family for the past year, she obviously wasn't comforted by the fat red badge

affixed to her scrub shirt. I wondered if she was thinking about epi-
genesis and her ovaries. I suggested that she might like to take a break,
make an early day of it and go home. This turned out to be a wise suggestion as I am sure the appearance of the NRC field agents would have
produced an uncharacteristic hysteria in Poppy.

The NRC officers wore radioactive-protection suits that looked like
our tyvek suits, only a lot heavier and with a headdress that was reminiscent of a burkha made out of metal and glass. They had a breathing
apparatus akin to scuba tanks affixed to their backs, and they made the
same sound as Darth Vader as they passed through the hall. I stood in
the doorway of my alluringly fragrant lab (courtesy of Poppy's brand
new aromatherapy project) watching them retreat with the object of
their retrieval efforts. I tried to initiate a conversation by waving and
exclaiming "good afternoon" in my cheerful, friendly westerner affect.
They averted their gaze and kept going with their little lead box held
out at arm's length.

It kind of hurt my feelings to be snubbed, and I checked to be
sure that my fly was closed. All I saw were my usual thin turquoise
scrubs with the drawstring waist tied in a neat bow, the fabric clinging
opaquely to my skin. Just the same old scrubs I had been wearing day
in and day out during all of the years that I had padded up and down the
corridors, passing by the room with whatever was now in the little lead
Pandora's box. I wondered distractedly what kind of research *had* been
carried out in the lab across the hall. For that matter, I wondered what
kind of research had been carried out in *my* enrichment lab during the
30 years before I was awarded the abandoned space? Now that I was
thinking about it, it did seem a bit odd that Daven's usually territory-
greedy research team hadn't argued at all when I proposed to occupy
the large, well-equipped space.

All of the strange comings and goings combined with the growing
uneasiness of everyone I worked with only made me more resolute to
exact some small triumph. I developed a badger-like determination to
get Cooperston to agree to send a chimpanzee to the sanctuary. My
repeated audiences with Cooperston over the ensuing days began to

embody my increasingly aggrandized versions of the positive publicity that such an act would undoubtedly engender. I embellished the scenario by introducing descriptions of the by now exceedingly lucrative behavioral research center Poppy and I had imagined. My secret desire to liberate at least a single chimpanzee before my own inevitable exodus became iconic for all of the angst I felt for my chimpanzee friends and found that I had somehow stockpiled in my psyche over the years at PRC. This fueled the passion of my exhortations. I am sure that the arguments I made were as convincing as any civil rights attorney could have made in prosecuting a gross injustice. They were additionally imbued with my shameless attempts to manipulate Cooperston through my feminine wiles and his vanity. However, in the end, the closing argument was not made by my persuasiveness or wiles, nor by the potential for favorable publicity or possible cash flow. It was rather by Cooperston's own often obscure but tender sentimentality that the conclusion I sought was obtained.

Several weeks after Murchison's call I still hadn't received a commitment from Cooperston, and had finally assumed that he had dropped the idea. I had expressed my disappointment to Cardenas and my assistant, Poppy. One morning Poppy and I were preparing diffusers for the biocontainment area aromatherapy program. We were filling the elegant curved glass pipes with a combination of lemongrass and lavender oils, as pensive as acolytes preparing unguents for the temple. Suddenly Cooperston appeared in the doorway to the enrichment lab fiddling self-consciously with his unlit pipe.

"What the hell is that smell?" he barked, shattering the sanctity of our lab, and plunging his pipe into his jacket pocket.

"Lemongrass and lavender," I muttered, feeling a pervasive sense of triviality as I faced this antiquarian genius who had devoted his life to curing children of horrible diseases.

"Lemongrass! Well, hell, that's just a common pesticide. Used that compound in dozens of mixtures over the years." The pipe reappeared as gestural punctuation to his soliloquy.

"Huh, well, actually we use it to enrich the ...." I tried.

"Used all kinds of natural components in my work. Every synthetic compound is derived from something natural. All of this nonsense about chemicals being unnatural, nothing but ignorance. I used to take plant oils and mix perfumes for my wife in the laboratory. She loved them, always wore the ones I made. She said they were far superior to anything commercial." The pipe changed hands and was plunged violently into the other jacket pocket. Cooperston looked suddenly vulnerable and sad.

It was rare that Cooperston referred to Juno, his wife of fifty-two years. The childless couple had traveled the world over and she had often assisted him in his various field research projects. One of the few times I ever saw Cooperston laugh was when he had described a trip they had made to Mongolia to analyze bacterial vectors. Cooperston hired dozens of local herdsman to live-trap the bats that proliferated in the area. It fell to Juno to milk the little things so the fluid could be analyzed for bacterial cells. Cooperston seemed to delight in the image of Juno bent over the table late into the night, milking bats by the light of a kerosene lamp. Juno Cooperston had died the previous winter after a long and terrible battle with pancreatic cancer. Poppy and I stood as immobile as children playing freeze tag, waiting for Cooperston's next proclamation.

"You get started on picking a mate for that Nim Chimpsky. Whole thing's a damned nuisance, and I expect a detailed report. Suitable for the press." Turning on his heel, he stalked down the hall, grumbling as an afterthought, "Damn rotten combination of smells. Poor animals!"

Released from our inertia, Poppy and I grabbed each other and waltzed excitedly around the lab.

"Well, I'll been damned!" Cardenas muttered in wonder, rubbing his chin with a half-smile when Poppy and I raced down to his office to tell him our big news. "I think you just solved the Kitty problem." He said looking from one to the other of us, his half-smile becoming a full-fledged grin.

The Kitty problem had started several weeks earlier after a quarterly blood draw had designated old Kitty as a prime candidate for a pharmacokinetic HIV research project Daven was promoting for some

Korean sponsors. The study was going to be a source of immense income. The whole institute knew Daven needed four *clean* chimps for this project, and had already been promised three from the next shipment of chimpanzees coming from a now defunct lab in New York. He had been waiting like a hungry hawk on a phone line for weeks to find out which PRC chimpanzee he might be able to demand to fill the fourth spot based on the results of the quarterly serum assays from the breeding colony. When we realized that Kitty would win this honor because her liver enzymes had climbed up past the acceptable measure, we had tried to divert Daven's interest by designating her to the foster mother program. Unfortunately, Daven had learned his lesson from the Edith and Earl ploy Fran had used years earlier. Fran wasn't at PRC anymore to use her authoritative demeanor and obscure veterinary arguments to sway the animal care committee to her ends. Cardenas, Poppy, and I lacked the kind of polished political acumen required to emerge victorious from direct confrontations and committee meetings. That was Daven's turf. As primarily non-income producing stewards of animal health and well-being, we had been marginalized to the point that we had to resort to end-runs and tag-team maneuvers to accomplish our benign plots and sense of appropriate husbandry.

"Perfect!" I enthused, picturing the sweetly sad and vulnerable face of my aging friend Kitty. This *was* a perfect opportunity to protect her from ending her science career isolated in a cement block room, and almost more importantly, a chance for us to pull one over on Daven. The implications of this must have begun to percolate in all of our minds simultaneously because we all seemed to be wearing the same cat-who-got-the-canary expressions.

If we were going to succeed in sending Kitty to Dale Murchison's ranch, we decided we were going to have to adopt secret agent personas. As we stood in Cardenas' office discussing our new plan, a giddy sense of elation overtook us. We began to laugh, slowly then boisterously. Long, loud, good laughing that opened our lungs and drove back the dark fumes that had been suffusing PRC and making our hearts as heavy as lead.

Eight

Parting The Seas: A Plan For Kitty's Salvation

I had begun to worry about Kitty after the February blood draws. She was getting old for a breeding colony chimp, thirty-eight. She looked tired as I sat next to her cage grooming her head while she ate a kiwi-and-strawberry salad I had made for her. I was feeling sad and she sensed it, turning every few minutes to look at me. She finally reached a long finger out through the bars and took off my goggles, she laid the back of her soft, fat index finger against the corner of my eye and a big tear welled up and rolled down over it. She pulled her hand into the cage, examined the tear, licked it off her finger, and turned back to her salad. Chimpanzees were ever interested in physiological phenomena, I reflected, but they didn't waste a lot of time on sentimentality.

I was sad because I had met Cardenas in the corridor on my way to see Kitty. He was carrying the sheaf of paper he picked up from the lab every quarter after the breeding colony chimps had their blood work analyzed. This was done to monitor for changes in liver enzymes that might presage the onset of hepatitis. Chimps with increasing enzyme levels would have to be moved out of the breeding colony. They became prime candidates for the most restrictive HIV research protocols because they were *clean*. They hadn't been inoculated with any viral agents, and so made better research models than the many hepatitis-infected chimps. They would leave the least restrictive life possible inside the research setting; the amiable outdoor, multi-age, mixed-gender family group. They would be moved into the harshest possible setting. Alone and isolated from physical contact, fresh air, and natural light, they would languish indefinitely in an HIV research isolette.

My experience with researchers working in the HIV isolette environment was that they resisted any perceived interference in their protocols. Enrichment was generally viewed as an uncontrolled variable, a kind of statistical *demonic intrusion.* As a result my program was severely restricted in what I viewed as this critical-need housing area. The animals who sat alone in their isolated cages day after day frequently had little or no real enrichment. I believed this was a partial explanation for the higher frequency of SIB that was evident in the isolette settings, and I had collected reams of behavioral data to support my hypothesis. Even Bart would be hard put to argue with my conclusions, I reflected. Poppy and I almost exhausted our imaginations inventing what we termed *non-invasive enrichment techniques,* and selling the researchers on their merit. We had installed closed-circuit televisions with Jane Goodall movies, used aromatherapy, painted one wall in each building a bright color (we didn't use purple), and played music on radios or boom-boxes. But these techniques could hardly replace the need for physical contact or real social and object interactions. I had puzzled over why the researchers did not consider the overtly heightened levels of stress with all the concomitant physiological responses as an uncontrolled variable that must impact any research aimed at defining functional aspects of the immune system. My erudite colleagues in the virology and immunology research groups had generally greeted my inquiries along this line with skepticism and condescension.

"Hey, Cardenas, *que paso?*" I had greeted him cheerfully as we met in the corridor.

He looked at me and averted his gaze, crossing his arms and kicking at a dark spot on the shiny gray linoleum. "Kitty's enzymes are up."

"Huh." We stood there silently. I found my own spot to scuff at with the toe of my blue rubber boot. I think we were sharing a similar feeling of dread. I wondered if the spot Cardenas was kicking at looked as much like Daven's aquiline nose as my spot did. It went unspoken that we both knew an HIV isolette would be the death of Kitty. Kitty had been such a kind and playful companion to me when I had been in her area day after day, year after year, that I took a self-assigned role as her advocate and protector. Although it seemed as unreasonable as a parent having a favorite child among their many children, Kitty had somehow become my favorite friend among the many chimps. I wanted what was best for her. I was remembering when I had first recognized that everyone who worked with Kitty loved her.

I think it was when she had had the twins, Rowe and Quist. The littlest one was clearly dying. Kitty sat in her cage hugging both infants to her chest, holding their little heads to her breast. She guided her nipple gently into the little one's mouth. I had attended several dozen human births during my apprenticeship with the *partera*, but I had never observed a scene of such tender maternal solicitude as Kitty portrayed with her weak twinlet. I was conducting round-the-clock observations interspersed with short naps so I could write an article on postpartum behavior toward twins. Cardenas and the other care-givers had been parading by Kitty's cage for days, dropping off various contraband; a dog toy, oranges, a cup of coffee, a pink washcloth that she had decided to sit on. I was thinking of writing a second article on human gift-giving behavior.

When Fran, the veterinarian, arrived Kitty was clearly distressed, gesturing with a dramatic wrist-flicking and bared teeth that she wanted us to leave. She must have feared she would be anesthetized and wake up bereft of her offspring. This had been so usual a routine for most of her incarceration, how could she understand that we were using a different husbandry approach now? We all wanted Kitty to keep her twins.

Kitty had come to PRC over two decades earlier. She was already approximately ten years old then. I had many times attempted to trace Kitty's history, but she was one of the "laundered chimps." Laundered chimps had unknown pasts, they became "laundered" when their owners sold them through a so-called animal broker. The animal broker would eradicate all personal history and present the chimp on the market to any interested buyer, usually a research facility. The broker was always vague and evasive about providing information regarding the animal's origins. Presumably this was to protect the original owner, or quite possibly to disguise the fact that an illegal importation of an endangered species had occurred. Through such brokers, many chimpanzees who were previously pets, entertainers, or illegally imported have been railroaded into research over the years.

My professional guess about Kitty's origins was that she had been raised by humans, quite probably in a home setting. Kitty was exceedingly intelligent, slight of build, and had an odd, light colored hair that seemed tinged with an apricot hue. She was a loving chimpanzee with big funny, velvety ears. She actively sought human interaction. She recognized many household items and became so excited about an old *Farmer's Brothers* coffee can I had one day that I procured a cup of coffee with cream in it for her. She dispatched the coffee with gusto, holding the cup with a practiced finesse.

Kitty had many remarkable children, most of whom were removed at birth thus depriving her of exhibiting her lovely ability to parent. Among her offspring were two full-blooded brothers, Dar and Adam, sons of old Paleface, born several years apart and suffering amazingly contrasting destinies. Adam was a personal friend of mine who was being used on an HIV research project. Dar, who sported Kitty's same droopy ears and Paleface's freckles, lived in a pleasant psychology research center in another state where he ate soup from a bowl with a spoon and talked in sign language.

Fran had to use plenty of bananas and watermelon (Kitty was ever the shrewd economist) to persuade Kitty to finally allow her to place the stethoscope through the bars and onto the tiny baby's chest. After a few minutes Fran stood up shaking her head.

"That one has a severe heart defect, I don't think it could survive even if we pulled it." Fran and Cardenas and I stood shoulder-to-shoulder looking at Kitty with her two infants now swaddled in her groin pocket. She was leisurely eating the watermelon, examining each seed as if it were a jewel.

I was ever playing Ceres to the veterinarian's more medical-model interventionist strategies. Let nature take her course, I exhorted Fran. My feeling was that if the infant couldn't survive, why traumatize Kitty and the healthy baby by anesthetizing her?

"She'll leave the infant when it dies, and we can let her into the next cage over. Then you can get it and take it to necropsy," I morbidly but pragmatically argued.

Fran surprisingly agreed with me. I fully appreciated that it was only her affection for Kitty that would allow her to behave in such a hands-off manner. She was sure to be the target of administrative criticism for not taking heroic medical measures to salvage what would become a high-dollar research animal if it survived. The events unfolded as I predicted. Little Rowe passed away one October night. We found him the next morning tucked into the corner of the cage, Kitty using her body to shield him. When we asked her to vacate the cage into a neighboring enclosure, she lifted the baby's tiny limp arm and let it drop, then without a backward glance she strolled into the next cage and sat calmly nursing the remaining twin. Necropsy confirmed Fran's diagnosis, the heart muscle was severely malformed. The healthy baby grew up into a fine, strong and mischievous youngster, nursed and cared for by Kitty until he was two years old and moved into a juvenile group. It had been Kitty's last pregnancy. I sat beside her now watching her delicately examine and eat the green kiwi slices. The skin on her softly wrinkled face seemed to glow transparently in the late light of day. Evening was coming and it was getting to be time for me to go home.

Prior to Cooperston's change of heart, we had all been wracking our brains for alternative schemes to deprive Daven of Kitty. Daven needed four clean chimps for the HIV contract job he had secured with the Korean scientists. He had already acquired three from a recent bunch of imports from the New York lab that had closed and sold all of its animals to PRC. He had made it clear to the animal care committee that he expected to take the next available chimpanzee from the breeding colony where Kitty was housed. After Cooperston's surprising capitulation to my entreaties to donate a chimp to the Bountiful Harvest Ranch, Poppy, Cardenas, and I had decided that Kitty was going to be salvaged from the nefarious Daven and an unpleasant future in HIV research by this opportunity. Among ourselves we decided to keep the Ranch operation secret and work as quickly as possible so Daven wouldn't get wind of our plot. We all felt sure he would try to derail the plan if he learned of it.

I manipulated Cooperston into silence using a new, exciting, and shamelessly confabulatory facet of my secret agent persona. I convinced him that I was certain that an animal rights activist had somehow infiltrated our ranks and was trying to provoke a crisis from within the institute. Our only hope, as I presented my completely fabricated drama to Cooperston, was to pull off the transfer of Kitty to the Ranch quickly and quietly and then distribute a huge press release.

"Loose lips sink ships," I reminded him, nodding seriously one afternoon in his office after making a show of checking under his desk for a microphone just like I had seen Jim Rockford do on a recent rerun of the *Rockford Files*.

Within our covert operations team, we assigned ourselves tasks for which we would each be responsible. Cardenas would take care of Kitty's health records for transportation across the two State lines that separated her from care-free retirement in a sanctuary. He would also ready and drive the getaway vehicle when the time came. Poppy's job was to spread extravagant rumors about fictional dramas among Daven's crew as a diversionary tactic, while also monitoring all of Daven's moves. I was on an airplane within three days of Cooperston's pronouncement in order to meet with Dale Murchison and Nim.

I had carried some paperwork and research articles to read along with me so I could use my time on the airplane proficiently. Unfortunately I was so restless and excited about my trip I couldn't focus on the content of the articles. My abstract processes would not engage. After the third time I called the stewardess to ask how much longer before we landed, she returned with her arms full of things to amuse me. I seemed to recall a similar scene from my childhood where my exasperated parents pulled over with a screech at a *Stuckey's* restaurant during a cross-country car trek. My father had stormed off to the restaurant while my mom made us exercise in the parking lot. He returned with an armful of puzzle books, coloring books, crayons, and pecan pralines.

"Don't you kids ask me how much longer one more time!!" He fumed as we all piled back in the station wagon and he jammed it into reverse, and then sped out of the lot in a cloud of dust.

"Not much longer," the pleasant lady with the up-do and the stewardess wings pinned to her blouse said in a similar tone as she handed me the dog-eared stack of magazines she had absconded with from the first-class section.

I thumbed through them all with a discontented sigh. I finally settled on re-reading *Autoweek Magazine* several times rather than learning what *Cosmopolitan* had to say about the *dos* and *don'ts* of finding love in the workplace.

Dale picked me up at the airport in a great big red Dodge Ram with a Cummins diesel engine. I felt like Demeter receiving her celestial phaeton to overview the landscape. Climbing into it was like climbing up into a grain combine. Dale was outdoorsy and definitely better looking than the *Marlboro* man. He smelled like fresh-cut hay, which was explained when he later mentioned that he had just finished cutting the hay. I almost wished I had read the *Cosmopolitan* magazine article until I realized I could be conversant about the engine features on his truck only because *AutoWeek* magazine had been more alluring. Since I had re-read it multiple times, I knew all about how the Japanese were trying to buy the patent on the Cummins diesel engine. I think this gave Dale the idea that I really understood trucks and farming, and might be something other than a typical *"egg head"* as he enjoyed referring to the population of over-educated know-it-alls that I did, in all honesty, fit into. In any case it was a great icebreaker. We were soon chatting animatedly while zooming down a labyrinth of backcountry roads past alfalfa fields and the rolling, oak-dotted hills that led from Ft. Worth to the ranch.

We arrived at the ranch and passed under a rainbow-shaped portal of wrought iron that was inscribed with a quote from the famous book *by Anna Sewell*. A white board fence defining the drive was populated with fat gray guineas who made curious mewling noises as we passed. The winding drive led to a ranch style house that was surrounded by an English-style garden. The house was perched on a hill overlooking a pond with an old fat willow that leaned as if it were musing upon its own reflection as it dabbled with its leafy fingers at the water surface. When we stopped I clambered down from the cab and stood looking around the soft green landscape, feeling an immediate sense of relaxation and safety that was now nearly foreign to me. I could smell fragrant jasmine as it wafted in a slow breeze from the trellis it decorated on the northwest side of the house. I instantly wanted to be granted refuge here too.

"Alice! We're back!" Dale called out towards a large barn below the house. A diminutive woman with flaming red hair emerged from the open door of the barn. She held a metal bucket that was obviously full of something in one hand, and a large wooden spoon in the other. She was clothed in overalls, and smiling she raised her hand and spoon to wave at us. She then commenced to bang on the bucket calling *"Baby, baby...."* over and over. Dale looked at me chuckling, "Almost their dinner time! Can you believe that girl is one of the best elephant keepers in the business?"

I noticed then that the pasture attached to the barn had a very tall fence enclosing it that was made of huge steel pipes. As I watched, the bobbing gray heads of three elephants appeared at the crest of an emerald hill at the far end of the pasture, just as if someone had turned to a page in a *Babar the Elephant* book. The two larger ones came swaggering across the field like *Babar* and *Celeste*. As they trundled toward the barn it was evident from their ears that they were different species. One had the characteristic draping ears of the Indian elephant, while the largest one was adorned with ears the very shape of the African continent. The littlest elephant limped along behind the other two, but here the analogy with *Babar's* family went sadly awry. Her lopsided gait caused her drape-like ears to shudder and jolt with each difficult step. Even from our distant over view it was obvious that one of her rear feet was badly deformed.

"That's from a tethering chain," Dale commented as he followed my gaze. "Cut into her leg and she was left untreated for months. We got a court order to remove her from a traveling circus and bring her here. Lucky she can walk at all."

I was amazed by the various animals that Dale introduced me to on the first afternoon of my visit. There were dozens more that I didn't get to meet since the Ranch was large and my time limited to assessing Kitty's transportation, housing, and introduction to Nim. Dale and I walked from pasture to enclosure near the Ranch house followed by a little three-legged dog named *Tug* who was the size of a rat terrier. I watched as a gallant and beautifully proportioned dapple-coated thoroughbred horse hobbled along grazing in the tall spring grass. He had a grotesquely mis-shapen foreleg that was almost completely non-functional. I listened in horror as Dale recounted how the previous drunken owner had abused the beautiful creature using a hoist and a shotgun. There were over forty donkeys that had been airlifted out of the Grand Canyon during a severe drought. There was a tall, old knobby-kneed Morgan horse who looked to be in perfect shape and was a surprising twenty-six years old. He had been a veteran of the New York police department and when he left the service, his human counterparts had all chipped in to transport him to retirement at the Ranch. Every single animal had some deeply moving story of danger, abuse, and rescue. I was on the verge of tears several times during Dale's narration.

As we strolled from enclosure to enclosure in the humid east Texas heat, Dale unbuttoned his shirt cuffs and rolled up his sleeves. His right forearm was criss-crossed with ropy scars like Earl had. I know I stared because Dale explained that a cat had mauled him during a rescue mission. He pointed at a cage that held an irritable looking lynx who was twitching his velvety black nose and watching me like a fell dragon with his slit yellow eyes. The lynx had been rescued from the Big Bend Mountain Range after some teenage boys had finished using it for target practice. Dale described how the rescue scene had turned into a near-fatal encounter for him.

"So, I ended up with half of his upper canine left in my arm bone and three hours of surgery to put it all back together again," he summed up almost jovially.

"Wow. That must be one of the most dangerous animals you have out here." I commented, trying to eradicate the unsavory vision of Dale and the Lynx writhing, locked in combat on the dry, rocky, pine-scattered floor of the Big Bend Mountain range. It was all too easy to imagine them both wounded, flowing blood, the sabre-like canines of the enraged lynx sunk deep in Dale's forearm. Dale broke my morbid reverie with what I thought was a surprisingly benevolent attitude.

"He's not so bad once you get to know him. Now *there's* a damn dangerous animal," Dale pointed across to a nearby pasture.

I followed the line of his arm with my eyes, expecting to see something like the velociraptor from Jurassic park. All I saw was a bucolic pasture scene with African gazelles rescued from a wild animal park and a spotted llama looking like a character from Dr. Doolittle.

"Yep," Dale said, staring darkly at the llama, "Spittn'Sam. He's attacked more people than you can count on two hands."

"You're kidding?" I thought it was a tease, I had already realized that Dale had a sense of humor. But in this case he was quite serious.

"No, I'm not. Don't go in that pasture unless you want to get stamped. Those hooves are like knives. He's jumped and stomped a hell of a lot of unwary visitors."

"Oh." I looked at the cute furry creature with new respect. I was thinking that my experience with animals was, after all, rather limited.

"That's really an instinct gone bad. You see a lot of ranchers using llamas now to keep predators like cat and coyote out of their herds. They have a natural drive to patrol the edge of a herd," Dale continued.

As I watched, it did seem that Spittn' Sam was grazing around the edge of the small cluster of gazelles.

"Spittin' Sam got it in his head that humans are a predator. Soon as you go in there he'll trot up to you. Real pretty sight, too, him lifting his little hooves in a nice trot. But as soon as he comes level to you, he'll spring up about seven feet in the air and come down right on top of you. From there on out it's a fight against hooves and teeth. Better hope someone else is nearby to help you out." Dale and I stood gazing contemplatively at the chubby, spotted animal where it grazed peacefully on the hillside.

In addition to Alice and Dale, the Ranch had a couple of local young men that lived in a bunkhouse on the edge of the property and did a lot of the ranch-hand work. My visit coincided with that of a veterinarian from Glasgow named Seamus McAndrews. He was a quick wit with a leprechaun's personality. When we were introduced I swear I saw a twinkle in his eye. The lulling cadence of his accent was enough to convince me that I had actually entered into a dimension of fairyland. Seamus had traveled all over the world to treat various exotic cases, and had just returned from Thailand where he had operated on an elephant with a foot tumor. Dale explained that Seamus made regular stops at the ranch as he circumnavigated the globe on his animal adventures. He was here now to look at the baby elephant's foot. Seamus was leaving for New York the next day where he had some obligations, but we planned for his return to coordinate with Kitty's arrival in two weeks. I was reassured to learn that he had a long experience with primates of every kind. He had provided services for several ape orphanages in Africa, and had acted in the role of some kind of monitor for animal welfare in a number of research labs on the Eastern seaboard.

"We're going to have a surprise visitor from Oklahoma later tonight," Dale said mysteriously, winking at me over dinner our dinner of green beans, grits, and fried tofu.

"Come now, Dale, don't play cat and mouse with us, who is it now?" Seamus challenged him, obviously enjoying the cat and mouse play.

"Can't say," and he didn't, playing mum until it became a great joke as we ate and made more and more outrageous attempts to find out the identity of the surprise visitor.

"Is it animal or mineral?" Alice queried, taking a bite of the blackberry-apple cobbler she had prepared for dessert.

"Nun or priest?" chimed in Seamus, winking at me.

"With or without a tail?' I ventured, trying to stick with a primate theme. I was grateful to have made it through the fried tofu and was savoring the cobbler and Earl Grey tea that were my evident reward. I wondered if everyone on the Ranch were vegetarians and inveterate winkers, and if I would return to PRC with these habits deeply ingrained.

The long-anticipated visitor arrived later that evening. His name was Augustus Norman. Gus, as we all called him, was one of the people who had helped raise Nim years earlier and taught him sign language. He was a compact middle-aged man with a long salt-and-pepper hair in a neat ponytail. There was an edgy air of contained audacity about him. He entertained us into the small hours of morning with harrowing tales of his recent snowboarding adventures. The thing most remarkable about Gus as far as I was concerned was that he could talk fluently in a human language with another species of animal. He was to be our official chimp translator. Gus had spent years tracking chimpanzees who used sign language and visiting them in their various incarcerations, recording all of their commentary which he was now compiling into a book. I thought about Thelma back home at PRC. She had come to us from a laboratory in New York, but before that she had been trained to use sign language. I remembered her abortive attempts to communicate with the humans in our laboratory setting and how ignorant we had all been. I asked Gus if he knew of Thelma.

"Oh, absolutely. She was an Oklahoma chimpanzee, just like Nim. She went to a lab pretty early on. Nim was one of the only ones from that group to avoid going into research," as he spoke, his earlier jocularity faded.

"I wonder if we could get you to come out to PRC and visit her?" I spoke brightly. Gus looked at me contemplatively and a bit wistfully I thought, puzzling over his extended silence. Finally he spoke.

"I thought about that when I heard she'd gone down there. I tried to get through Cooperston's barriers to access in a lot of ways. Asked him directly, asked cronies at the University and in other research facilities to approach him, basically everything I knew how to try I did. But the response was uniform. No access. Didn't want any unsavory publicity." He gave me another long piercing glance. I felt as though he were measuring me up, and with a sigh prefacing his next remarks he indicated I was to be among the circle of his confidantes.

"When Dale told me Dr. Cooperston had agreed to his suggestion and was sending someone down here to the Ranch to look around and meet Nim," Gus waved his hand vaguely toward a pastel drawing of Nim that hung on the kitchen wall. "I was skeptical. I wondered what kind of a person you would be, another arrogant biomedical prig? I can see I was wrong about that, but my guess is that if Cooperston knew you were sitting here with people like me and Seamus," here he nodded his head at the smirking veterinarian who winked on cue, "he'd call off this whole little project."

"I don't understand."

"Well, if you haven't kept up with animal rights activities you might not."

He was right on the money there. I had tried to do everything I could to ignore the mounting attacks of the outer world upon my admittedly monastic internal existence at PRC. The accusatory billboard by the road to PRC had made me feel angry and guilty by turns until I managed to relegate it to the status of nonessential landscape debris that no longer registered in my consciousness. My sole preoccupation at PRC was to uphold the welfare of the animals. I knew I was more successful at it than most people would have been under the same circumstances.

Most of my enrichment capers were balanced right on the razor's edge of whatever intervention Cooperston, Hilton and especially Daven would tolerate. I had had to enact all kinds of unfamiliar social diplomacy just to implement the programs I *did* have in place. It was all-consuming and stressful because I did not consider myself a social savant. My indulgence of Cooperston's ubiquitous diatribes and monologues was partially historical interest, but probably more a strategy for currying favor so I could continue my enrichment schemes unimpeded.

Years earlier, in my naïve zeal I had approached some renowned animal advocates at a primate conference to ask for any suggestions and their feedback about my enrichment program. When they learned where I worked, rather than greeting me warmly and offering me the whole-hearted support I had fully anticipated, I was snubbed. One gentleman from the Netherlands had actually dramatically knocked over his chair in fleeing from the table where we were both seated. Overly-sensitive by nature, I did not want to open myself to that kind of psychic wounding again. Unfortunately it was frequently unavoidable and I found this ostracism repeated in different dosages and scenarios at the various conferences I attended over the years. While it compounded my sense of isolation at the remote PRC site, it also solidified my identification with the primates entrusted to my care. I knew who my real friends were. They were the raucous, grateful primates who were ensconced at PRC. Apparently we were in the life raft together and could not count on outside help to arrive. We would have to go it alone, the monkeys, the chimps, and I. I made an executive decision to confine myself to *their* feedback and guidance about my enrichment efforts.

Gus explained that he and Dale had actually concocted the whole idea to ask Cooperston for a chimp after Nim's mate, Sally had died, solely for the purpose of trying to get Thelma from PRC to the Ranch. Here was a surprise! I had assumed I was the only one capable of hatching a subterfuge. And now it was revealed to me that the very reason I was seated in the cheery yellow kitchen under Nim's pastel portrait, digesting the hideous tofu was because I had been caught up in someone else's machinations. I began to laugh.

"What's so funny?" Gus asked. Seamus was watching and winking, and I had a feeling that he didn't need a word of explanation. Somehow he had used his leprechaun intuition to understand everything that was passing in my mind.

"Well, Gus, and Dale," I spoke, leaning back in my chair and crossing my arms over my chest. I was intentionally trying to sound offended.

I turned to look at them both. They were squirming in their seats and looking like two boys who got caught with their hands in the cookie jar. "I have to congratulate you on an excellent plot. However, if you only knew all the little manipulations *I've* had to carry out to get myself to the Ranch you'd realize that your sales pitch was less than convincing to Cooperston, and compared to me you are both rank amateurs." I told them about pretending to be Jim Rockford, and by the end we were all howling. Seamus and Alice had tears of laughter rolling down their cheeks.

Before we broke up our convivial party and went to bed, Seamus and Gus quizzed me about Thelma. They still wanted to get her away from the laboratory setting if they could. Gus urged me to do whatever was possible to have Thelma sent instead of Kitty. I was sympathetic because she and Nim had been infants together, and Gus obviously had a deeply affectionate and personal relationship with her.

"I understand your concern and that you want Thelma here," I said. "But I don't think I can convince Cooperston, mainly because Thelma has *hepatitis B* now." This puzzled Gus who wasn't used to the terminology of the biomedical research setting, but Seamus nodded solemnly and with complete comprehension. I continued, "I'm sorry, Gus, but that means she is very contagious, she would be a hazard to Nim. And she is very valuable now as a research animal because of her unusual disease status." Gus excused himself from the table. I noticed he eyes had welled up with tears. When he returned I presented my case for Kitty.

"You would be helping me out a great deal if you took her. She is clean, no diseases, no health threats to Nim. And, you will be literally saving her life." I explained Daven's intent and his need for a fourth chimpanzee to round out the research protocol he had been awarded. Everyone present seemed to know exactly who Daven was and the kind of conditions he would allow animals to endure under the research he conducted. It was unsettling to think people who had been strangers the day before could actually know so much about the intimate life at PRC. But it was also a relief to know that there was a wider public interest in accountability for animal welfare within the laboratory setting, maybe outside help was going to arrive at my little life raft after all. In the end it was Seamus who decided the issue.

"We'll take Kitty now. Her need to be rescued is the greatest, and that is the purpose of the Ranch. We'll see what happens later, Thelma may still come our way." He winked at me and patted Gus on the back.

Gus planned to introduce me to Nim the next day. He would ask me any questions that Nim presented to him. He was going to spend the next two weeks with Nim, preparing him for the arrival of his new mate, Kitty. Gus would help introduce Kitty and Nim by translating Nim's comments to the human audience during the process.

The entire notion of consulting with a chimpanzee about his likes and dislikes, and then following his directions as to how he wanted things ordered in his environment was novel to me. Most of the people I had worked with during my career with chimps wouldn't have liked this new way of thinking. But I took to it immediately. To converse with a chimp, especially after spending so many years trying to intuit their needs and desires, seemed an appealing and straight forward way to conduct business. I wondered if I could teach all of the chimps and caregivers at PRC to interact in this way. I half-jokingly asked Gus about my idea. He seemed to think it would be logistically impossible to train five hundred chimps and thirty-six caregivers in less than a decade.

"People are especially difficult," he commented in all seriousness.

It was still early in the warm, dewy morning when Gus and I walked up the road to the chimpanzee house where he would introduce me to Nim. The house sat against a backdrop of tall trees adjacent to the pond. I could see the top of the outside portion of the enclosure rising up to a height of twenty-five feet and couched against a huge spreading oak. The inside corners of the cage had sitting perches placed at intervals all the way to the top. Nim could climb up and sit in various locations under the enclosing oak arms and have an overview of the Ranch. It created the feeling that he was actually high aloft in a tree. It reminded me of illustrations from one of my favorite childhood tales, the *Swiss*

Family Robinson. At this hour the live oak was filled with rustling song-birds as the golden fume of morning sun began to filter through the branches. Bird song combined with the distant, deep trumpeting of the elephants enjoying their breakfast made me almost believe that we had crossed through a portal into equatorial Africa.

"I'll be using sign language, but I'll also speak so you can understand what I say and what Nim answers," Gus instructed me as we approached the building attached to the outdoor enclosure.

The building we entered was a work area for preparing food for Nim and several adjacent animal enclosures where there were an assortment of wolves, monkeys, and some baby skunks that had been rescued from a large mower at the local golf course. The rooms smelled pleasantly like sweet alfalfa and Alice responded to my inquiry by telling me that baby skunks don't fully develop their scenting skills until they grow older. The work area looked like someone's house, complete with a living room and kitchen. It adjoined Nim's cage and had windows over the kitchen sink that looked directly into his enclosure. It wasn't unusual for Nim to drag his tall bar stool over and sit outside the kitchen window watching Alice work. Alice was busy preparing Nim's breakfast. I was surprised to find that he did not get a pile of monkey chow biscuits. Instead, Alice was placing a yogurt container, a mozzarella cheese stick, an apple, a box of juice with an attached straw, and a honey-nut granola bar into a paper bag.

"Is that his breakfast?" I asked in disbelief.

"Oh, gosh no!" Alice responded, *"That's* his breakfast." She pointed out through a window that looked into the enclosure where Nim was sitting in his cage. "Oatmeal with rasins."

Nim was balancing a bowl on one knee and using a spoon to gently eat the oatmeal. Every so often he took the little carton of milk he held in one foot and poured some of it into the bowl, stirred, and resumed eating.

"This is his mid-morning snack," Alice continued as she folded the top of the lunch sack closed. "As soon as he's done with breakfast, I'll give it to him."

I had been cautioned and chastised so many times at PRC for letting a chimpanzee have anything with a wrapper that I now stood speechless. I thought of all the reprimands I had received with dire warnings about how I would be responsible for untold morbidity and mortality if a chimp was ever to eat a product wrapper. I had always taken the warnings to heart. I had imagined one of my beloved chimps writhing in slow agony and dying in terrible pain, only to find a candy bar wrapper with my name blazoned on it blocking his gut upon necropsy. When I was able to summon my voice I asked in the greatest humility whether the Ranch staff worried about Nim choking or getting sick from eating the product containers.

"Why would he eat the containers?" Alice asked with a wide-eyed guilelessness that combined with the pepper of freckles across her nose made her look like a ten-year-old.

I thought of the chimps at PRC, desperate in their need to have objects to play with, and more and varied foods to eat. They eventually tore and chewed everything I gave them to little pieces that littered the cage floors and often plugged up the facility plumbing. One time the military base sewer plant manager had contacted us in an outrage because some indestructible red rubber toys that I had given to the chimps and had high hopes of distributing widely throughout the facility had been hosed down the pipes during cleaning. They bobbed up incongruously in the dark swirl of the sewer ponds, placing the base water sanitation facility on high alert, at the ready for the possibility of foreign infiltration. Clearly the CIA had missed its opportunity in not recruiting me. Maybe that was the real reason I was limited as to what I was allowed to provide the chimpanzees.

I gazed out through the window at Nim's enclosure. It was spacious. There was a huge natural log bridge suspended by chains between two posts. Underneath it was a pile of interesting toys including a backpack, hats, shoes, pots and pans, and other items that would be strictly taboo at PRC. I watched Nim slowly and deliberately eating his breakfast with a spoon. I sensed no desperation in his languid movements. Here was a chimpanzee who had enough of what he needed and wanted in the world and a deeply felt sense of security. My friends at PRC were like depression-era children I reflected, hoarding and competitive when it came to food and toys; filled with constant anxiety lest there would not be enough to fill their needs. The only thing that Nim was missing was a chimpanzee companion. I almost cried as I envisioned my friend Kitty coming to live here with this quiet comfortable chimpanzee and attended to with such care by the humans.

Gus' voice brought me back from my reverie.

"Whenever you're ready let's go on out. First I'll introduce you and then we'll see what Nim has to say."

"Will he say hello or something?" I wondered out loud.

"Usually he likes to name new people."

"Name?"

"Yeah," Alice spoke up as she handed the lunch bag to Gus. "Give him that." She instructed Gus. "Nim named me *Big Red.*" Alice tousled her beautiful curling red hair with her hands, laughing.

Gus made the signs for *Big Red.* "He uses the letter G for my name," Gus explained as he made the sign for G. "That's how we originally taught him to identify people, with a letter for their name. He invented naming later, but he's being doing it for a number of years now."

I was beginning to feel uncomfortable, as though I was about to have an audience with the queen and had forgotten to brush my hair. Would Nim like me, I wondered? Would he deign to talk to me, and would I get my own name?

We stood on the walkway outside Nim's cage. He pushed his empty bowl through the feeder port, pointed to the lunch sack and signed several gestures in a row. Sure enough, Gus translated everything as Nim signed it.

"Hello. Happy see Gus. What there?"

Gus signed back, still speaking in English for my benefit. "Hello. Happy see Nim. Got food. Here new friend."

Nim glanced up at me briefly and with little interest. He pointed at the lunch sack again and signed. I was hoping it was my name.

"Want that." Translated Gus.

Gus gave Nim the lunch sack. Nim held it in his mouth as he ambled in quadruped over to his pile of toys. He didn't even give me a backward glance. Unaccountably I felt snubbed and my feelings were hurt.

"He didn't give me a name," I said in what I can only imagine must have been a forlorn tone of voice.

Gus tried to comfort me. "Well sometimes he has to get to know a person a little better, it might take a day or two, don't worry. He didn't name Seamus until he'd made a couple of visits."

"What did he name Seamus?" I asked, considerably brightened by this information.

"Laughs-a-lot."

"Oh," actually it was a very descriptive name. Nim seemed to accurately observe both the physical and behavioral characteristics of the people around him.

Gus stood silently as we watched Nim sort through his toy pile. He selected a German felt cap with a spray of boar bristles in the band and perched it on his head. Nim picked up his backpack, opened it, and placed his lunch sack inside. He donned the backpack and then began a rambling knuckle-walk around his enclosure. He eventually climbed up the cage side and sat on a high perch under the branches of the oak. Here he doffed the pack, opened it, rustled around inside it, and eventually withdrew the yogurt carton and a spoon. He opened the carton and began to eat the yogurt, leaning back against the cage in a leisurely way. I was transfixed by this performance. It was like a scene out of the movie *Heidi*. If I had seen Nim in lederhosen climbing the Alps it could hardly have been less astonishing. Nim was not in a hurry to eat his food at all. He actually made it part of an elaborate play sequence he was enacting. He seemed to have an ability to use objects in novel ways to provide his own enrichment.

I began chattering excitedly to Gus about this achievement and how differently the chimpanzees in the laboratory behaved. I had rarely seen a creative play sequence involving multiple steps and objects. Actually, as I chattered on I realized that Kitty was almost the only other chimpanzee whom I *had* seen use multiple objects to carry out a string of related activities. Once I had placed an orange traffic cone in her cage under which was a pile of colored tissue paper. I also placed a large bowl of red chile pistachios in the cage. This was a favorite treat donated to PRC for the chimps in fifty-pound drums on a regular basis by the Fat Gulch pistachio farm. For good measure, I had thrown in a newly emptied molasses jug with the dark dregs of the syrup still clinging to the inside. Kitty had first eaten one of the hot pistachios and then gone to get a drink of water. When she returned, she carefully considered all of the objects before making a plan. Then she filled the molasses jug part way with water, selected a pink piece of tissue paper, made it into a purse that she filled with a few handfuls of pistachios, and climbed up to a perch. Once on the perch she opened her purse and proceeded to eat a few nuts at a time, chasing them down with the sweet molasses water. As I told Gus about Kitty's calculated motor planning I became even more enthusiastic about pairing her with Nim. Clearly these two would be a perfect match. Gus stood nodding and smiling as he indulged my gesticulating monologue about the implications of Kitty and Nim's behavior. I could see that Nim had now finished his yogurt and was watching the interchange between Gus and myself with curiosity.

My three-day visit passed very quickly. Soon it was time to return to PRC. I was very excited about seeing my friends, returning to my projects, and getting Kitty ready to go, but my heart felt leaden as I walked around the Ranch on my last day. I visited Nim for a final time with Gus. I was still feeling slighted because I had not received my sacred chimp name. Nim seemed pleased to see me and presented his shoulder for a groom. He was wearing a red baseball cap and fiddling with a worn leather catcher's mitt. I scratched him and he grunted happily. Alice came out with some bananas and we all stood around handing them through the fence to Nim. He dutifully carried them off to be stored in a box he had in one corner and apparently considered equivalent to a refrigerator. I was talking to Alice about the details of our plan to transport Kitty, and how we would like things to be arranged when she arrived. Nim wandered back from his banana cache and was once again observing my chattering and gesticulations with a curious intent.

Nim turned his attention to Gus and began signing rapidly. Gus watched and then looked puzzled. "Nim say again" he signed and spoke aloud. Again Nim made a rapid series of signs, and then looked directly at me.

"Well what's he saying, Gus?" I asked.

"Um...I think he gave you your name."

"Fantastic!" I exclaimed. "What's my name?" I was imagining something flattering or indicative of my lady bountiful nature, a name like *Tall Girl*, or maybe *Banana Friend*.

"Well, it seems that, uh, well your name is *Woman Who Talks Too Much*," Gus was looking at the toe of his blue tennis shoe where it was digging at a tree root in the dirt.

"Takes one to know one," Alice commented dryly, as she turned and walked back to the chimp kitchen. I was sure I heard her laughing.

I decided that I couldn't really take offense since Nim had actually confirmed my earlier opinion about his astute powers of observation. I gave him a chocolate bar I had been saving for the plane ride home. I left the wrapper on and Nim put it in his backpack for his trip to the ball game.

I hadn't realized how tiring and stressful the environment at PRC had become until I had spent three days on the Ranch and experienced its completely different orientation. The whole organization was designed to support the care and welfare of animals. The milieu of PRC cast me in the role of a pariah because I was employed to support the care and welfare of the chimpanzees as individual beings more than as experimental units. One afternoon at the Ranch we all went out to bale hay in the lower field. Getting the hay in was an achievement of as great a priority on the Ranch as turning in a final research report would have been at PRC. At the Ranch the staff worked uniformly to provide loving, quality care to the animals for the sole reason of keeping them happy and healthy. At PRC my program had a low priority assignment to mop up the psychological and behavioral messes left after the primates were finished with the more important rigors of the research protocols. These contrasts between organizational philosophy and goals were intriguing and motivated me to reassess my own understanding of the larger issues involved in animal husbandry and human stewardship of animals.

In a warm firefly-lit dusk as Dale and the ranch hands lounged on the porch sipping beer we discussed these differences in institutional philosophy and personal motivation.

"Why have you stayed so long at PRC?" Dale queried.

"Mostly the chimps, I guess. I kept thinking if I stayed longer I could do more, get better cages, change husbandry practices, make more toys."

"Not for personal recognition and fame at conferences?" he needled me with a slow smirk.

"Well, it never came. I was mostly ignored by the famous primatologists, or snubbed by the anti-biomedical contingent, but yes, I wanted a paycheck. I have a family to support."

"This is my family," Dale said waving his hand langorously across the fields of the ranch as they faded into the purpling evening, " *'and so I have nothing to fear; and here my story ends'* quote I." Dale finished.

"Quote I from what?"

"That is the last line from the book by *Anna Sewell*, about a horse that was abused and then finally saved and brought home to rest." Dale said, kicking his feet up on the porch rail, and settling deeper into his chair. Some kind of bug was singing from the trees, it sounded like radio static to me. "This place is my home and the end of my story, I will spend out all the days of my life right here taking in the animals my fellow-species has harmed and degraded." He looked over at me in the darkening dusk, but I could still see his blue eyes twinkling mischievously, "What about you, where does your story go from here?"

I shifted uneasily in my chair, I had been asking myself that same question for months. I knew that bringing Kitty to the ranch was some kind of personal summation of my work at PRC. What was I going to do, what was I going to ask Nikki to do? I think it was the first time I actually said it out loud to anyone, up until this point it had only been a persistent echo bouncing around my cranium.

"I'm leaving PRC... I guess."

"What are you going to do, then?"

"I am not sure, really."

"There's a place for you here, it doesn't pay real well, but you got nature, big fields for your girl to play in, and lots of hard work." He crossed and uncrossed his long legs, "We can use another ranch hand and your other skills would be handy for computer work, fund raising, all that sort of thing. You could take that little cottage to live in up on the south road as part of the pay." Dale yawned and stretched, it was fully dark now. "Sleep on it," he said, standing up, "We can talk about it tomorrow."

I tossed and turned all night, the radio static bugs seemed bent on keeping me awake. Did I want to stay at the ranch? It was so idyllic, so lost in time. Of course I wanted to stay, but would my restless soul be satisfied with such a humble and protected existence? Some part of me liked being on the edge between opposing forces, playing the role of mediator and defender. I liked the intellectual hopscotch of research and academia, would simple ranch life and hard work still my mind? Probably not, I reflected. Also, in the back of my brain, growing like a candle flame that finally catches, an idea about my future had been coming to light. It was Devon and Merle who had inspired the thought originally. I wanted to take what the chimpanzees had taught me about their bodies and minds and I wanted to use it to work with children who had autism. I felt deeply that the communication and rapport I had found with chimpanzees could be easily recreated with children who had severe sensorimotor processing challenges. The more I tossed and turned the more certain I felt about it. I had been offered just such an opportunity in a city out on the Pacific coast. By dawn the radio static bugs had given up and the fat red leghorn rooster was screeching like a clarion.

"Dale that is the kindest most flattering offer anyone has ever made to me, really." I said the next morning by way of announcing my rejection of it. We were standing on a knoll above the ponds, the overnight mists still lay like white cotton in the little valleys toward the east, the sun was gilding them before us. Soon they would melt away and another warm east Texas day would be upon us. We were drinking tea, the little colored labels still hung from the strings, waving and fluttering in a small breeze, they reminded me of Buddhist prayer flags.

"*But...*" He prompted as I basked in the perfect beauty of the morning.

"Well, but I want to work with children who have autism. They need a lot of support, and I feel sure that the ideas and methods I have learned with chimpanzees will help make their lives more functional, allow them to express their human potentialities more fully. I know they have important contributions to make to the world and I think I can help make that happen with what I have learned from working with chimps."

"Very noble," Dale said with a sarcasm I thought was uncharacteristic of him "I don't really believe in human goodness or potentiality."

This was a foreign idea to me, I had always believed that all humans were born with infinite possibility, innately good, or at worse capable of redemption. Dale was challenging me with the unfamiliar concept that humans were hardly worth the bread on which we were buttered, a wasted configuration of carbon atoms.

"Look around you," he said, again sweeping his arm over the ranch lands below us, "most of the animals here *are* here as a result of human potential."

Dale's evidence was uncomfortably convincing to his argument against innate good in human beings. The ranch was full of testimonials including abandoned laboratory animals, the horse shot-gunned by his drunken owner, a group of puppies found trussed up in a burlap bag and left in a dumpster.

An elephant trumpeted and snuffled loudly from her pen in hopes of breakfast. "That's Sassy, she's hungry. I had to steal her, you know," he gave me a sidelong look and a crooked grin.

I was wondered how Dale had pulled that off? It was uncanny, not a subtle act.

"She is an example of your human potentiality. Go look at Sassy's leg, she limps because her owner kept her tied to a post with a chain.

As she grew older it just dug in there, no one ever removed it, made it bigger. When we stole her from a circus in New Jersey that chain was deep inside her flesh, chain and bone were fused with infection. Pretty picture, ain't it?" He took a sip from his steamy cup, the lavender tea flag waved gently like a living wing.

"All things human come to naught, you will see that soon if you don't already," he continued, looking at me keenly now, there was a steel in his gaze I'd never seen before. "Helping humans is a vain work. You only unleash more sorrow and pain upon the other living things of the earth. Our species is dead."

I felt ill, ill like I had when Benjy died, when Shiloh had died, when Greta had died. Ill with the truth of what Dale was saying. "My God, Dale," was the only intelligible thing I could manage to say.

"Let's leave God out of it for now, he's too convenient to the purposes of man. I'm here at the ranch because I really believe our species is finished, we'll be damn lucky if we don't do in all the other species on our way out just for spite." He reached over and tousled my hair as if I were a ignorant five-year old. "But, honey, you just go ahead and keep believin', you can come on back when you get tired enough of it. Come on, now, Sassy and the other girls are wanting some hay." Dale turned and crunched off up the gravel pathway, I followed with my head bowed.

I fully understood the importance of biomedical research with primates to the larger dilemma of human health throughout the world. But I was wrestling with a personal dilemma in which I now questioned whether the ends *could* justify the means. Wasn't the merit in preserving human life to be found in our unique capacity for reason? Weren't reason and intelligence only relevant if guided by the human qualities we were supposed to exalt? So many important words used *human* as a root; *humanity, humane.* Didn't furthering the cause of humanity presuppose that we be humane? Wasn't it possible to meet the marks of humane treatment and still conduct biomedical research? Whose definition of humane treatment should we subscribe to? Some internationally recognized ethicists were calling for criminal penalties as a consequence to harming or killing great apes. How could we define the line between ourselves and our cousins? Was it to be by cultural or biological standards? Why weren't these questions discussed at the animal care and use committee meetings? It would be a relief to talk openly about such moral dilemmas. I reflected on what we did talk about in those meetings. Naturally, I talked about toys, diet, and treatment interventions. Often I provided a comic interlude by describing some antic or another of the chimpanzees. Other scientists talked about time lines, funding sources, sponsors, and logistics of protocol. As I mentally reviewed the meetings I couldn't recall a single meeting in which we had gathered as an erudite corps to reason over the bioethics or the social-cultural implications of our work.

There seemed to be an underlying assumption by all of us that the larger work we were doing in human medicine was unquestionably a good and correct objective, one that overrode considerations such as the sense of selfhood innate to a chimpanzee. The assumption seemed to imply that we didn't have to collectively or individually review our bioethical standpoints. There was undeniably a practical material reward resulting from the research enacted around me. I had been around the big money of federally and privately supported laboratories long enough to know that the real impetus to research was not always an altruistic ideal to perpetuate the betterment of humankind. In fact, under the corporate era at PRC I had frequently overheard intimations about research that might support the advantage of certain classes or nations of peoples over others. As I had matured out of my idealistic graduate school student persona into an experienced lab hand, I had come to understand that the profit motive was far greater than altruism.

My trip to the Bountiful Harvest Ranch began to make me question if I could work in a for-profit biomedical research setting. I didn't know if I could support it any longer because the research lacked a succinct philosophical standpoint. Commercial motive had supplanted intellectual zeal and the drive toward enlightenment for enlightenment's sake. It seemed quite plausible that we were degrading our own humanity by the means we had been willing to engage in to achieve questionable material ends. I thought of Africa, a whole continent dying from HIV, and I wondered if what we did in the confines of our lab would translate into salvation for the multitude of orphans there. The longstanding belief that we were ultimately enacting such an altruistic end had given me faith and pride in my work at PRC for a number of years. But recent arguments in the media about the price that should be exacted from African governments for assistance with medications, and the knowledge of the terrible interest rates imposed by international lenders upon these already beleaguered developing nations made me more than skeptical about the material aims of our corporate agenda.

I recalled that I had started my career at PRC because of a need to have a mission and to accomplish something that I felt deeply would benefit someone else. I knew after three days at the Ranch that I no longer felt I was benefiting others by staying in the laboratory setting. At the same time I was pretty sure that I wouldn't feel satisfied to simply take care of animals so they would feel safe and happy as the committed people at the ranch did. I wanted to be part of a larger mission to improve the lives of people and animals all over the world. As nebulous as that seemed as a goal, at least it could be based on a universal tenet to *cause no harm*. I wondered if by staying on at PRC, even if the chimps needed my contribution, I might be colluding with forces that were actually *causing* great harm in the world.

My thoughts turned to Cooperston and the major contributions he had made to improving human health and the quality of life for people throughout the world. He must have started with the same altruistic zealotry I had had as a graduate student. His native humanitarianism, affection, and concern for others were still surprisingly palpable on occasion. The previous Christmas he had thrown a huge dinner party at the NCO club for all of the employees, we all received one-hundred dollar gift certificates to the grocery store tucked inside a beautifully wrapped box of chocolates. Cooperston had wrapped each box himself. I could appreciate that it was Cooperston's own version of humanitarian zeal combined with a sharp intellect that had driven him onto the frontiers of human health sciences for over fifty years.

Yet, now people whose lives he had materially contributed to improving openly ridiculed him. Why? Were his critics enraged simply because his ethics were outdated by our enlarged understanding of the capacity of other animals to have emotional and cognitive qualities similar our own? Or was it that he had developed a sort of scientific arrogance that precluded self-review and assumed a position of unquestionable moral rectitude because it dealt in the kind of arcane knowledge that could mete out the power of life or death? I wondered if I might be prone to a similar arrogance. It was certainly a pitfall if I continued to ensconce myself in the institutional temples where this kind of arcane knowledge was generated and manipulated without the benefit of a guiding philosophy greater than profit motive.

Weighted with these larger insights about my work and myself, I boarded the plane back home. I still felt a badger-like determination to see the Kitty rescue project (as I now referred to it mentally) through to the end. But now I was beginning to formulate a plan of escape for myself as well. I had to rethink my values, skills, and career options. I also had to consider the health and well-being of Nikki; her risk because of my exposure to health-impacting toxins and diseases, her future if something happened to me, and the kind of values and ideals I wanted to model to her as a mommy. I settled into my airplane seat and fell immediately into a deep slumber. I dreamed I was walking through the green hills of the Ranch in the warm field mists of dawn. With the unquestioning logic of dreams, the rolling hills of Texas became the Alps. I was leading a group of children and chimps down the flower-speckled slopes into Switzerland. We were all dressed like the Von Trapp family and singing *The Hills Are Alive With The Sound of Music.*

Cardenas and Poppy had been busy while I was away. Poppy had discovered that Daven was planning on using Kitty as his fourth subject and had set a start date for his project to begin in exactly thirty days. We now had a deadline we had to beat. Cardenas had Kitty's medical records in order to cross the State borders. She met all of the health criteria and wouldn't need any additional inoculations or tests to prove her health status. He had also secured a company credit card and permission to use the animal transport van in written form directly from Cooperston. The only obstacle we had to negotiate was figuring out how to keep Kitty from getting pregnant once she was living on the Ranch. I had promised Dale we would take care of this issue at our end of the transfer since we had better facilities to implement whatever medical procedure might be necessary. At PRC unwanted breeding was never a problem because we kept animals separated by gender when we didn't want offspring. We had several contraceptive options but all of them required the collaboration of a veterinarian.

Normally this wouldn't have been a problem at all, but the continued public pressure and internal politics of PRC had conspired to prevent most veterinarians from considering taking a position with us. The best veterinarians we had were long ago moved on to new positions in less difficult circumstances. A recent series of odd veterinarians had come and gone through the facility, none staying more than a few months and none having had previous experience with primates. In aggravation, Tex Hilton had finally started seeking a human medical doctor to employ instead. In the interim the only veterinarian was the one on Daven's team. He was a burley and disheveled looking man named Dan Mudgood, everyone had always called him *Mud*. He was in his forties and had been a laboratory assistant on Daven's crew for years before Daven had decided to finance his way through veterinary school. It had become kind of an inside joke around the facility to call him *Dr. Mud*. His main role was to ensure or else rubber-stamp appropriate veterinary standards on Daven's research projects. Dr. Mud had been reluctantly coerced into doing general veterinary care throughout the facility as the other veterinarians evaporated. We were temporarily stymied by this problem because any procedure Dr. Mud carried out would certainly be reported to Daven.

It was Poppy who discovered a miraculous solution just a few days later. Cooperston was constantly trying to recruit various graduate students to work as unpaid interns at PRC. We had had a series of interesting young professionals from around the world come and spend weeks at a time with us. They were from various disciplines and usually ended up doing dull and laborious tasks for the other researchers, but it was a great opportunity and experience for them. There was a recent veterinary graduate named Phinneas who was working as an assistant in the histology lab for one month until his job position in California started. He was supposed to have completed a one-month intern at PRC providing veterinary services to the primates. Just days after he arrived and settled himself into a rented condo, the veterinarian Phinneas had been scheduled to work with had resigned. Phinneas declined to be mentored by Dr. Mud, but chose to stay on and learn what he could in the histology laboratory.

"I met him, and he's very nice," Poppy assured us as we pondered this possibility in Cardenas' office.

"I don't think we can risk trying to pull off a surgery," Cardenas commented. "It's too noticeable, we'd have to use general anesthesia, and this guy may not have that kind of experience, hysterectomy or tying tubes. He probably doesn't even have *any* primate experience if he's just graduated."

"You may be right. But I think we can get around the surgery problem. I called Planned Parenthood today," I said brightly.

"Planned Parenthood?" Responded Cardenas quizzically.

"Hyenas," said Poppy.

"Hyenas?" Cardenas and I spoke at once.

"He worked with hyenas, I asked him," Poppy had regained our full attention with this surprising proclamation. "And, get this, he's really bummed out because he wanted to learn to do some procedures on chimpanzees while he was here and all he does now is fix slides in the lab!"

In the ensuing silence I added my revelation. "An implant, that's what I wanted to tell you, we can use a contraceptive implant. Planned Parenthood can sell it to us if we get a veterinary prescription. It lasts five years, is implanted in the arm, and we would only have to use a single Ketamine injection to keep Kitty under for the procedure. They said it takes about five minutes to insert the whole package." I watched as Poppy and Cardenas assimilated this information.

We looked at each other excitedly with a growing conviction that we were going to be able to pull off our plan, after all.

"Do you think that this guy, Phinneas, would he get involved, and could he keep it quiet?" Cardenas quizzed Poppy.

"Well," Poppy considered, "he *is* pretty mad about what he sees as having been duped into coming out to PRC for nothing. He says he wants to go into zoo work or conservation, in fact I think he said his new job is in some wild animal park in San Diego. I don't know for sure, but he's the only chance we have, so..." Poppy let her remark dangle.

We stood around Cardenas' desk silently for a few minutes, until I reassumed my secret agent persona and offered up a strategy that I felt was at least as good as anything scripted for *Mission Impossible*.

"Okay, here it is. We take him out for beer and pizza to the *Fat Gulch Pull'n'Bowl*. We lay our cards on the table and see if we can recruit him to our cause, everything above board. If he's agreeable we'll tell Cooperston what we're planning, I don't know how long Cooperston will keep it to himself though. We *have* to keep Daven's crew out of the loop as long as possible, otherwise, they will for sure put a monkey wrench in the works." Cardenas and Poppy nodded in agreement, and so it was settled.

Poppy asked Phinneas to join us at the *Pull'n'Bowl* the next night. Under the reddish half-light and wafting haze of cigarette smoke, we laid out our project to him. Phinneas listened intently while chomping thoughtfully on a dripping slice of pepperoni pizza with a crust like a cardboard box. We waited almost breathlessly for his response amid the backdrop of clattering bowling pins and an in-house music tape that sounded reminiscent of the *I Dream of Jeannie* theme song. Phinneas boldly swallowed the alleged pizza and then elegantly wiped his mouth on the back of his flannel shirt sleeve like a true desert rat.

"Hell, yes I'm in!" He exclaimed. He was more than enthusiastic, he was practically ecstatic over the opportunity to both perform a procedure on a chimpanzee and to help us pull one over on Daven, whom he found insufferably arrogant.

I regretted not having gotten to know Phinneas earlier as he was clearly a kindred spirit. From my admittedly prejudiced point of view, he would have been a great veterinarian for PRC. As I chewed on my own pizza slice I enjoyed the warm sensation of feeling like everything was lining up quite nicely for Kitty's trip to the Ranch. Help had appeared from unexpected quarters, Daven was none the wiser yet, Cardenas had the credit card already in hand. Taking another slice of the rubbery pizza I looked around the table at my co-conspirators. They were all basking in the glow of happy anticipation.

"I think this might just work," I commented, nodding and speaking with my mouth half-full. Poppy laughed, Cardenas and Phinneas clanged their glasses together in *salud*.

Nine

Kitty's Flight From Bondage

The transport van pulled noisily and laboriously through the clear quiet Sunday morning. We were crossing the pass that led east of the cottonwood clumps and out over the *Noche del Muerto* mountains down into the *llano estacado* of west Texas. The land was desolate here, like the wilderness Sam and Bilbo must have encountered before the gates of Mordor. The earth was lined and gray. It was a landscape empty of towns or signs of human habitation, stretching endlessly and flat away from the rocky, treeless crags of the mountains. As far as one could see the horizon was interrupted only by the sparse bare sticks of now leafless ocotillo which had inspired the first conquistadors to name this land the *staked plain*. As we drove farther east the pungent air began to reek of petroleum and the nodding heads of oil-rigs began to replace the ocotillo. I couldn't waylay the analogy to the fumes of Tolkien's Mt. Doom and the smithies of his dark lord. I didn't know why I felt such a foreboding when all logic argued for elation at our relatively problem free exodus from Fat Gulch and PRC.

We finally stopped for gas in Roswell. It was a town I had been curious about since watching the film *Alien Autopsy*. The station attendant's face and hands looked as lined and gray as the landscape. My chest felt tight and I was having difficulty breathing. I began to wonder if this whole enterprise was a mistake. Maybe we should turn around and flee straight back to Fat Gulch. After all, I considered, even the technologically advanced extra-terrestrials had failed to survive this journey, and the earlier Spanish intruders had sprinkled the geography with picturesque names like *el Jornada del Muerto; the long day's journey of the dead.* I sat on the uncomfortable plastic bench seat of the transport van darkly eyeing the haggard and filthy wildcatter next to us who was filling the tank on his Ford truck while chewing and spitting tobacco. My implacable and less morbidly-inclined *compadre*, Cardenas was cheerfully filling our own tank using the corporate credit card, whistling *exidos*, and looking a lot like Clint Eastwood in his polarized sunglasses. His easy confidence and apparent exuberance at this adventure slowly infiltrated and started to ease my mind. I began to breathe and glanced into the back of the van to see how Kitty was weathering the trip so far.

She was sitting hunched up in one corner of the small metal cage clutching the stuffed, pink rabbit doll that Greta had donated to the cause. Earlier we had had to pull over because Kitty was whimpering in fear. The metal tray under her cage had been rattling as if we were in a tin shack during a hail storm. Cardenas and I had decided to remove the tray and wrap the rattling metal fixture with paper towels and furniture pads that we found in the van. Things thus quieted, we had continued our journey down into the *llano estacado*. Although Kitty still kept a tight grip on the stuffed doll, she otherwise seemed to have relaxed.

Our early morning exodus had upset the usually serene Kitty. Any trip into a transfer cage elicited fear responses in most chimpanzees I had known. Kitty was usually the picture of tranquility even during transfers. But the suppressed excitement of our caregiving crew, the unusually early hour of five a.m., and the fact that we had placed her inside a van had all conspired to leave her almost hysterical. I realized that one of the things that made the captive life of a laboratory chimp more tolerable was the predictability of the various procedures enacted around and toward them. While it was unpleasant to be moved or anesthetized, after a time it became predictable. One knew what to expect. Even the most frightening events in the lab were of a known quantity. Our unusual behavior had unsettled Kitty. Her typical alpha demeanor had diminished until she was sitting curled in the corner of the transport cage, a whimpering study of fear and despair. It made me feel terrible. I worried about her aging heart and whether the stress of the journey would cause her long-term harm. I suddenly realized what the alternative to this journey was, Kitty living out her life in an isolette cage. This thought seemed to renew my will, well, that *and* the possibility that Cardenas could procure some chocolate from the otherwise uninspiring gas station mini-mart. Whatever my misgivings, we were committed to the journey now and I was only struggling with my own fear. I rolled down the window as Cardenas finished gassing the van.

"Hey, mister, why don't you charge us some cokes and chocolate bars. Get Kitty something, too. How 'bout a gummy gas station cinnamon roll?"

Cardenas grinned under the enigmatic polarized glasses. "Sure thing, boss, manna from heaven" he drawled, swaggering into the store. His cinematic persona seemed to be metamorphosing into some kind of a heroic cross between Clint Eastwood and Charlton Heston. His easy confidence made me feel easier, I breathed out in a sigh. Wrestle as I might with my own erratic demons, I had no power whatsoever to dent Cardenas' enthusiastic pragmatism.

It was still early in the day, but the late spring weather was already growing hot. Cardenas returned with a sack full of junk food, soda and *Gatorade*. I crawled in the back and offered Kitty the gummy cinnamon roll. I didn't take the plastic wrapper off of it. I looked at Cardenas challengingly, waiting for him to say something about the wrapper and an obstructed gut. He grinned again and shrugged. Kitty carefully unwrapped the treat, dropping the plastic out between the bars. She began to pull the strands of the sweet-smelling roll apart delicately with her nearly prehensile lower lip. I opened a bottle of greenish original-flavor *Gatorade* and passed it through the feeder port to her. Kitty gently accepted the drink, first turning her head to look into the bottle with her right eye, and then sniffing at it curiously, she extended her lower lip and poured some into her mouth.

"Well, human girl, it's not what we drink down on the farm, but I'll try it." Kitty looked out at me, stretched one hand through the bars and laid the back of her fat gray finger against my left cheek, I looked steadily into the brown pools of her eyes. "And, thanks for the cinnamon roll, I don't know what you're up to, human girl, but I'll play along, I have a feeling its only going to get better from here on out."

She poured another gulp into her lip, savoring it for a long time before swallowing. With signs of approval she collected her midmorning snack, her drink, and her doll and climbed up on the perch, eating and grunting contentedly. As I clambered back into my seat, Cardenas pushed a can of coke into my hands.

"I swear I can almost hear you two talking," he said, turning the key and starting the engine, "Okay boss, let's go."

"Okay *jefe maximo!*" I laughed back. I took a swig of coke and started pawing through the sack, finally deciding on a chocolate covered *payday* bar. I leaned back in the heat of the aging day, closing my eyes as I settled into the vinyl seat. I was thinking about the madcap rush of events that had occurred in the few days preceding our trip. There had been moments when I really thought we wouldn't be here now, on the road, taking Kitty to the sanctuary. I was still relaxing into the reality of it, half-expecting yet another one of Daven's convoluted schemes or a natural disaster of biblical proportions to emerge like a mirage out of the desert and sabotage our mission.

Only one week earlier it had been Cooperston who had let the cat out of the bag, or the chimp in this case. On Monday he had appeared at the animal care meeting to announce to the staff that he was making a gesture of conciliation to animal welfare advocates by sending Kitty to a sanctuary. The local newspaper, *Fat Gulch Examiner*, had sent a photographer and journalist to record the event, probably tipped off by Cooperston himself. Poppy, Cardenas, and myself encouraged the audience by leading a round of applause. Phinneas let out several loud whistles. The only sour face in the meeting was Daven who, due to our skills in subterfuge, hadn't gotten wind of the project at all until the moment of Cooperston's announcement. Daven didn't concede defeat gracefully. We spent the next week practicing a kind of complex aikido as we met his various attempts to derail our project.

Tuesday we had scheduled the surgery room for Kitty's contraceptive implant procedure. She was already anesthetized when Daven's study coordinator appeared and informed us that Daven had an emergency surgery that took precedence. We didn't want Kitty to have another anesthesia before we traveled, and in any case the surgery suite had curiously become completely booked for the rest of the week by Daven's various projects. I stood in the hall outside the suite in my turquoise scrubs feeling anxious and wringing my hands.

"I didn't think anyone actually did that." Phinneas said coolly as he watched me, he remained poised and aloof with the studied detachment of a true surgeon. I knew he was at the beginning of a great veterinary career. I wondered abstractly where he would be in ten years.

"Come on." He waved Cardenas and a second caregiver, Lazaro, to wheel the gurney along the hall after him. He motioned us all into an empty ward-room that was being repainted.

"We'll do it in here, I just need a portable spotlight."

Lazaro disappeared and returned in a few minutes with the light. In the mean time I had taped paper over the ward-room door windows to deflect any spies from Daven's camp. The procedure was very simple. It involved merely a quarter-inch cut and insertion of several little sticks under the flesh of the upper arm. Phinneas worked with deft focus and the whole procedure was done in under ten minutes. As Cardenas and Lazaro wheeled the still sleeping Kitty back to her cage we encountered Daven's study coordinator.

"Tough break about the surgery, sorry. Hope it doesn't hold you up any." I thought he was sneering, but Phinneas told me later that the man might actually have Bell's palsy.

"Yeah, it's really going to slow us up." Phinneas agreed, making a mournful face. The rest of us tried to look irritable and disgruntled. I had to pretend to sneeze as a laugh tried to work its way out my nose. I made several little snorting noises while Cardenas glared at me across Kitty's now wriggling body.

Wednesday was quiet. We had scheduled ourselves to leave on the fourteen-hour odyssey across Texas early Sunday morning, which would put us into the ranch by evening. On Thursday Daven's veterinarian, Dr. Mud, appeared in Cardenas' office where we happened to be getting Kitty's paperwork together.

"So, crossing two State lines?" He queried.

So alike were Cardenas' and my instincts, that I knew the hairs on the nape of his neck were standing up just like mine. If we were chimps we would have been in full piloerection. But since we were human and devious we simply stood looking placidly at our adversary. Dr. Mud was red-faced and miserable, and I had no doubt that whatever scene he was acting out, it hadn't been by his design. I stood silently watching his every movement. Cardenas automatically noted that I had gone into my behavioral observation role and he took over the verbal conversation duties.

"That's right, two States." He crossed his arms in typical Cardenas fashion and waited expectantly for Mud's next pronouncement.

"I was, well I was looking through some medical records, and uh, well by coincidence I saw that fourteen-thirty-six hadn't been TB tested. I think the TB test has to be current within six months to cross State lines." He used Kitty's ISIS number in preference to her name.

I wondered if the use of her species identification number was an attempt to objectify and depersonalize her, like dairy farms do with the ear tags on cows. I realized that he had no idea of the iconic proportions that Kitty had recently attained among the care-giving staff and most of the secretarial pool. That was undoubtedly because he was guilty of the same self-absorption characteristic in everyone on Daven's team. Little gifts had been trickling in for Kitty's trip as soon as Cooperston had made his announcement. The care-givers in her section had compiled a small photo album of themselves to send with her to the ranch. The men in the maintenance department had given me a bag of groceries with many of Kitty's favorite treats, sesame sticks, pancake mix (that was a new one to me, but these guys worked the week-end shift when I was at home), a can of coffee and her own coffee mug. Greta had presented a stuffed pink rabbit with a shiny satin bow to me in the hall one day, for Kitty so she would have something to play with on the car trip.

"I'd hate for that l'il girl to get bored, since you can't go to McDonalds and all." Greta said as she pushed the toy into my hands. *Bored* had the two distinct syllables and an extra *r* typical of east Texas diction; *bor-erd*. I had grown up in Colorado where it only had one of each.

The ordinary workers had felt increasingly disempowered by the many management changes that had escalated as the financial pressures increased at PRC. Financial pressures were being triggered by the mounting media scrutiny that the animal rights movement had brought to bear on us. Many project sponsors had become reluctant to have their product names associated with the controversy surrounding the use of chimpanzees in research. The lowest paid staff members were disproportionately affected by financial losses as their salaries and benefits were reduced and eliminated. Secretarial staff was cut and those who remained were asked to perform the job duties of two or three people, sometimes staying late into the evening to finishing typing and filing. Kitty had somehow become a symbol of transcendence and triumph to the unchampioned staff. She was the living evidence that no matter how impossible one's circumstances appeared, there would always be the possibility of escape, renewal, and the victory of the underdog.

Mud stood in the office with us, unaware of the undercurrent of rebellion moving like a riptide through the staff. It was a tide that I was confident would eventually carry Kitty to shore at the Bountiful Harvest Ranch, in spite of Daven's machinations. But undoubtedly Mud and his cohorts could still enact mean and petty mischief until we were well away from PRC. Mud was an enormously overweight man, his lank hair was now plastered by sweat to his forehead as he presented this latest stumbling block to us. He wiped the back of his hand across his forehead which left his wet bangs in an odd, twisted little peak over the left half of his face. He knew as well as did all of the animal care staff that there was no TB titer to be had. The manufacturer had underestimated demand and supply, and all titer was back-logged by three weeks. Cardenas stood quietly. Mud shifted uncomfortably from foot to foot.

"Dr. Daven wants to help with this sanctuary project." Mud offered incongruously. "So we could let you have some of the titer we still have left."

I was almost snowed by this generosity when I saw something twitch in Cardenas' face that told me that he detected a set-up.

"But, well, since it takes three days to read, it would have to wait until Monday, but then our lab techs could administer it and read it on Wednesday, then you'd be set." Mud finished his offer, a drop of sweat rolling down the side of his nose. We all pretended we didn't see it land in a dark spot on his green scrubs.

We could have the titer, but be delayed by a week. I waited patiently to see what Cardenas would say to this Trojan horse of a gift.

"I'm glad that there is some titer left in the place." Cardenas said thoughtfully looking at Mud. "We appreciate your offer. Sounds like we'd have a bit of a delay ..."

"Only for a week, then you'd be all in compliance, no possibility of problems."

I reflected that the only problems we seemed to have had so far were all generated by Daven's team. I sensed there was a charged undercurrent in the dialogue between Cardenas and Mud but it took me a few minutes to fathom what was really being communicated

"You don't think your lab technician would be too busy to do the titer and reading for us next week, do you?" Cardenas queried.

"Naw, don't think so." Mud answered quickly, wiping the sad little peak of hair to the other side of his forehead, his face reddened.

"You have a pretty big study starting up on Monday, don't you? That four-subject HIV protocol?" Cardenas spoke in a soft voice that belied something as sharp as an obsidian knife beneath.

I was standing frozen to my spot, except for my head, which was bouncing from one speaker to the next as if I were at Wimbledon watching Andre Agassi play Pete Sampras.

"Oh well," here the uncomfortable Mud kicked the insole of his left foot with his right one and looked at the floor, "Well, we're starting the first pair of subjects on Monday, but we should have plenty of time mid-morning if you bring her down to the prep room..."

There was a long pause as Cardenas let the words settle in the air between us. I was imagining Kitty laying prostrate on her gurney in the same room where the two chimps Daven *had* procured for his study were being prepped. What if Kitty were accidentally inoculated by an inattentive technician, it had happened before. One was always reading about hospital botch jobs where someone's left leg was amputated instead the right. And those were trained surgeons, how easy it would be to make a barely literate animal technician the fall guy for a coup in this war over a research subject. It seemed too diabolical of a scheme to be real. Would Daven really stoop to such a devious plot and try to dupe Cooperston out of his media concession to the animal welfare contingent? Even Daven wouldn't go that far, would he? The tension in Cardenas' upper trapezius muscles told me that he would indeed.

"Well, that's real generous, and you certainly have given us something to consider, so let us get back to you about scheduling. And tell Dr. Daven thanks." Cardenas spoke in what I thought was an overly effusive and somewhat naïve tone.

Surely he wasn't going to let our project get derailed so easily and give in to this ridiculous attempt to steal Kitty? My mind was galloping ahead on five different tracks. I was thinking of veterinarians, doctors, and pharmacists in Mexico from whom I might be able to procure a TB titer right now, this very afternoon. I felt flushed and knew my heart rate was climbing. I wanted Mud to leave before I grabbed the stapler off of Cardenas' desk and flung it at his sweaty bulging head. Cardenas looked cool and unperturbed; obviously he didn't realize the gravity of the situation.

Mud looked suddenly relieved.

"Okay then, will do, around ten a.m. Monday would be a great time for our techs, so just let me know and we'll get you scheduled in...." Mud turned to go, and I followed him out, standing in the hall to watch him trundle away still mopping his brow.

I turned on Cardenas to let him have a piece of my mind and was astounded to see him laughing silently and motioning to me to close the office door, which I did.

"What are you laughing about now! We're never going to get Kitty out of this hole at this rate!" I fumed at him, nonplussed.

Shaking his head he responded, with his languid chuckle, "I just bought us three days of peace and quiet until we get out of here on Sunday."

"I just don't see what you mean, Cardenas!" I said impatiently.

"And neither does Mud," he snapped his fingers with a smile when he said Mud's name. "Yeah, we're crossing two State lines, but I've already checked with the USDA, and they're two States that *don't* require TB testing for the transport of exotic animals."

I stared with dawning appreciation for my sly friend. I couldn't keep a big grin from my face. "Nice work, Cardenas." I said with the most complete admiration I think I had every felt for another human being.

We rumbled along through west Texas, leaving Roswell behind but still plagued by the ubiquitous scent of the petroleum industry. I thought about how much I wished we had been able to simply enjoy those three days we had manipulated away from Daven's constant undermining. But then Thursday morning arrived. I stopped by Greta's office to thank her for the stuffed rabbit toy and confide to her our clever manipulation of Daven's team in the latest chapter of our escape drama. Greta wasn't in yet but I found two of her co-workers weeping in each other's arms. There was the unmistakably brutal edge of emotional devastation in the stuffy little office. My back teeth automatically set into a grim clench.

"What?" I said in an aggressive tone as the two women looked at me through their tears and now-flawed make-up.

The pale, chubby woman named Bev finally answered. She was a records clerk who had worked quietly and pretty much unnoticed at PRC for years. She had cropped gray hair and jar ears. She always wore flowered shirts, was wearing one now; green and blue with yellow orchid flowers. Small red birds were perched on little branches in the background of the material, their beaks uplifted gaily. I could still see all the minute detail of the fabric every time I blinked my eyes against the bright desert heat as we lumbered along the road toward sanctuary. Donning my sunglasses couldn't eradicate it. I knew I would remember that print for the rest of my life.

"Greta's dead." Bev had announced to me in her trembling voice.

"What?"

"She died last night."

"What?" I repeated like an idiot as everything in the room seemed to telescope into the distance and a loud ringing began in my ears. I reached abstractedly for a chair and sat down. My vision seemed to be getting darker and darker, I thought I was going to faint so I leaned forward and put my head between my legs. From a distance I could still hear myself repeating again, "What?"

"The train crossing...no gate, it was hot. She must have had the air conditioning up, the radio, she couldn't have heard the train whistle... she was stressed out, I know, she worked late yesterday...five o'clock wasn't her usual time to cross those tracks..." Bev babbled out the disconnected facts until her voice disintegrated into sobs.

Greta was dead. No more Danish. No more stuffed toys for chimps. No more words like *"bor-erd"* served up in two syllables with an extra r courtesy of an upbringing in east Texas. No more Greta. There was no clever scheme I could concoct to alter the outcome. It was too late, had been too late for fourteen hours. I wondered if I was going to vomit.

Friday was terribly somber and uneventful, we almost longed for one of Daven's distractions. Saturday was quiet, I stayed home and made *menudo* with Maria for her son, Pascal's birthday. Nikki and Yvette made unattractive comments about the consistency of tripe, comparing it to something they saw coming out of the nose of the neighbor's sick Angus steer. They pretended that Martina's kitchen was a restaurant. Nikki was the waitress.

"Hello Ma'am, what would you like to eat?" She asked Yvette, who sat at the gingham-covered table looking prim.

"What is your soup of the day, Miss?" Yvette responded.

"Moco de baca caldo!" Cow booger soup. This set them off in to screams of laughter.

Martina sucked her teeth and shook her head, rubbing dry oregano into the bubbling pot.

Sunday finally arrived. I had packed a little suitcase for the trip. I was going to stay at the ranch for a week to oversee the introduction with Nim and help Kitty get settled. Cardenas would drive the van straight back on Monday. There was some small satisfaction in knowing that we would miss our TB appointment with Daven at ten a.m. Monday morning. I was grateful that I would have a week away from what was becoming an increasingly confusing and painful place to work. The past week had eliminated the sense of detached amusement that usually carried me through the challenging aspects of my job with the chimpanzees. The ranch and its exuberant crew were exactly the right medicine for my soul. Thoughts of sanctuary, escape, and survival permeated my mind against a wallpaper of blue and green with yellow orchid flowers. I fell into a hot uncomfortable sleep as Cardenas drove us deeper into the heart of Texas, now humming along to *exidos* being broadcast over the radio from south of the border.

It is a strange thing to the waking mind that there is no time or distance in the psyche. I climbed up a broad twisting tree limb as if it were a long sidewalk, Kitty was right behind me in quadruped. The enclosing canopy was green and blue, yellow orchids trailed over the surrounding trunks. Missy and Jake were there at the top, inviting us into the cool shade that felt like a fresh shower after the hot, humid climb upward. We were sitting in the tree just as if it were a living room when Greta appeared with a tray of coffee and Danish.

"I thought y'all might be hungry after that trip. It tuckered me out, I can tell you!" She somehow contrived to make *you-u* have two syllables, I laughed.

She handed the sweet rolls around and Kitty poured the coffee from a percolator into our Styrofoam cups. I was getting colder and colder and the wind started to blow, rocking the branches disconcertingly.

"I don't want to leave." I told Greta.

"You go on now, girl. Someone's gotta go to the ranch with Kitty."
She was moving away through the trees with Missy and Jake.

I heard a loud hissing as the cold air of an evening storm rushed
against my face. I heard Cardenas talking.

"Well, I'll be darned, that air conditioner does work!" He grinned
over at me from under his dark glasses. "Got your beauty sleep finished? Up ahead is a Denny's and I'm about ready for some lunch, how
about you?"

"Sure." I said stretching, still feeling sleep-drugged. I peered in the
back, half-expecting to see Jake and Missy sitting with Kitty. Kitty just
lifted her chin toward me, she was still clutching Greta's stuffed rabbit,
it was looking bedraggled and well-loved. Its little pink satin ribbon
was untied and straggling along like a tattered streamer.

"I miss Greta." I said.

"Yeah." Cardenas responded.

When we left Denny's half an hour later, Kitty was eating a Caesar
Salad from a take-out box in her cage in the back of the truck. She was
using a fork. She held the utensil with adept skill and grunted in satisfaction with each bite. I looked at Cardenas, he shrugged and looked
back to the road through his mirrored sunglasses. I mused that who
others think we are in life is largely dependent upon context. Like the
research report I had read a few months early that indicated that school
children performed pretty much to the level of expectation placed upon
them by the adults in their environment. Each mile we took Kitty away
from the research institute toward the sanctuary seemed to make her
more human and less chimpish.

"I never knew she could use silverware," I muttered.

"There's a lot we don't know about them," replied Cardenas.

"Like what?"

"Like all circus chimps smoke, all zoo chimps like to escape from
their cages, all home-grown chimps use dishes. Who knows what we
don't know?" Cardenas said enigmatically.

"Who knows what we don't know?" I repeated, and then, "Hey, they
aren't *supposed* to smoke!" I chastised, after a moment's consideration.

231

"Well, whatever. You see them in their cages every day, then one day you bring something new with you, a broom, a coffee cup, cigarettes. Danish," He looked at me for emphasis. "Then suddenly they are telling you somehow that they want it, recognize it. And before you read the rule-book or talk to the Docs, you just find yourself handing it over. They want it, they know how to use it, and you realize how little they have in life. I warn my guys not to do it, and then sometimes without even thinking, I do it myself. I think we all understand that if we were in the joint, we would want someone to pass us a cigarette, too." Cardenas was philosophizing in a new way, a way I had never heard inside the institute, it must have been the sense of freedom that our successful escape and road trip were giving us, he was becoming positively chimpish.

"Yeah," I assented, "you're right, I'd want that too." That was enrichment at its finest, I thought. My *enrichment program* wasn't new on the planet, hadn't I really only raised the art of contraband smuggling to a science? Before science there had been religion, I remembered the Seville's patron Saint, *Santo Nino*. In one hand he carried a basket of fruit, in the other a gourd filled with water. Armed only with the innocence and goodwill of childhood he carried these treasures of sustenance to the ostracized inmates in the prisons of *Atocha*. True camaraderie was built of compassion and the Pan-Human trait of altruistic sharing was a time-honored tradition.

The year I worked in a human prison during a hiatus from PRC, I asked the men what they missed the most from their lives outside. "A car horn honking," said one; "the smell of pizza," said another. I remember being regaled with many small gifts from the inmates when I resigned. Some of the men had unraveled their socks and used the threads to make intricately knotted *objets' d'art*. I received a heart, a cross, a three-dimensional cube. They were icons of self, objects that communicated a uniqueness of spirit and a sense of connectedness with another being. Our chimpanzees didn't even have socks to unravel, personalized coffee cups, or letters from home to alleviate the depersonalization and monotony of life inside. What did they miss and remember?

How could they communicate their own special individuality? What met their need for connection? I knew from long experience with chimpanzees that their drive to be individual and express their personality was as great as our own. The barren sensory-deprived world we imposed on them shoe-horned them into an unnatural environmental homogeneity which we spoke of as *good experimental control conditions,* as if chimps were neat rows of red-bottomed Petri dishes. But in reality these conditions were experimentally poor and completely artificial. The setting failed to control for the unmet biological and behavioral imperatives that drove the physiological systems of our cousins into unnatural endocrine and neurochemical states.

I remembered the time I saw Dana and Festus sharing a cigarette, drawing back into the shadows so they wouldn't see me and be caught out at it. Like two old-timers they lounged in the summer afternoon shade, each puffing contentedly, gazing across the wide desert horizon in a quiet reverie. Pieces of authentic self were what chimpanzees derived from Cardenas' "guys." In those precious moments that crossed the frontier of species, they reclaimed an identity that had been stripped away by incarceration. Removing the roles of jailor and jailed, man and chimpanzee savored these moments free from the stereotypes and polarities imposed by human category. Most of the human narrative surrounding chimpanzees seemed self-serving in the end. The research paradigm favored a patronizing condescension towards chimpanzees as mere *animals,* while many in the animal rights community maintained an unrealistic transference, making an idealized projection of the *noble primitive* archetype onto the chimpanzee. Either they were animals being used in the higher pursuits of science for the greatest good of the human race, or they were primitive wild-children, hostages to be rescued by the hero activists. Every narrative in its own way justified the actions and the pursuit of fame and fortune of many different people. It was dizzying.

One sanctuary activist would later ask me, sensing my reservation about her agenda while standing over a sheaf of plans for millions' of dollars worth of new housing that would involve moving two hundred aging chimpanzees from Fat Gulch to a southeastern State over a thousand miles away; "Well, what do *you* think is best for these chimps?"

"I think their homes should *become* sanctuaries. What right have we got to uproot them from their own world and move them to unfamiliar lands and climates? Why not build your sanctuary in Fat Gulch?"

"These chimpanzees are from equatorial lands," she said defensively.

"Actually most of them are from right here in Fat Gulch, born and raised. A lot of them are actually bilingual, they understand more Spanish than I do! They have friends and relatives that it would be difficult for them to leave, you know, chimpanzees have a deep sense of place and community."

"So, in other words, *you* think they should just stay in research then!" She reinterpreted rather unfairly.

"I think most people want the freedom to simply be themselves; enjoying the things that bring them pleasure as individuals, chimpanzees are no different. They want to stay at home, to know security, be surrounded by family. Each one under his own vine and fig tree."

I wasn't invited to any more of her sanctuary planning meetings, in fact I had developed quite a roster of alienated specialists in every camp, with the exception of the chimp camp. My *Pan* friends still greeted me with enthusiastic accolades every time we met.

Over the years it had often been primarily the relationships that blossomed between caregiver and chimpanzee that gave sustenance to self-expression, identity, a sense of home for both. The social interactions with caregivers, whether affiliative or aggressive, were defining and important in weaving a web of social meaning for captive chimpanzees. As we had improved the housing so groups of chimpanzees could live together instead of in isolation, there developed a lovely sense of interactive community amongst the chimpanzees, but they had continued to include us humans as an integral part of their social and economic world. There was a social interdependency among caregivers and chimpanzees that existed beyond the agenda of the research environment, and beyond the artificially imposed boundary of species, it was based on personal and individual bonds of friendship. It was impossible to understand the social and political underpinnings of the chimpanzee's world in captivity by analyzing only *their* behavior, one had to also carefully consider the comings and goings of the various humans in the environment, each with their own emotional lives, their cigarettes, their sweet rolls, and their rubber snakes.

In our mutual and independent reverie Cardenas and Kitty and I wended our way across Texas. I was lost in contemplation, Cardenas whistling snappy dance tunes, ready to be finished for the day and kick back with an ice-cold *Corona* beer, and Kitty sleeping peacefully with her rabbit doll tucked under her ear. We were crossing borders seen and unseen, while a silent train of events like dominoes was snaking down along behind us in our wake. We knew change was brewing at the PRC, but perhaps we did not know how soon it would be upon us. In our absence, Dr. Cooperston held an all-staff meeting to announce the dissolution of PRC. Dramatic to the end, he stood on the second-floor balcony of the PRC feed warehouse using a bullhorn, arms outstretched, his gaze cast down upon his masses.

"Like Eva Peron, abdicating." Phinneas pantomimed for us later, "we all thought he was going to start singing, *Don't Cry For Me Argentina!*"

Soon after, I surrendered my position, moving to a new career and another State, a thousand miles away. Half of all of the chimpanzees at PRC were later retired. The other half, the valuable HIV and hepatitis-inoculated chimpanzees would be purchased by a private pharmaceutical interest. Cardenas would have to choose between new employers. And Kitty would spend her days watching guinea hens traverse the hills above the ranch ponds, in happy companionship with Nim, hiking the imaginary Alps and eating yogurt with their best tableware. Nikki and I would soon find ourselves residing in a cottage by the sea where a parade of tall boats passed daily, and walks in the woods yielded buckets of blackberries and blueberries as we became dwellers on the fences of yet another international frontier where cool clouds and lush greenery replaced the giant rock and desolate dust stretches we knew. By the summer's end all of us had embarked on our different journeys, our lives altered forever from what they had been before we began our exodus from Fat Gulch; from whatever all of our lives had been in the dim time before fate had joined our destinies with each other in the crossroads of the borderlands.

Ten

Epilogue

I was splitting a pomegranate with Kitty, cutting it into quarters and smashing it through the cage links at the ranch. It was one of the infrequent visits I made to the ranch over an intervening decade. Kitty and I were bent toward each other like two silvered old crones sharing stories from the current context of our lives. I was thinking about Roger, one of the many children I had seen in my therapy practice. I was wondering how to tell Kitty about how much she had helped me to understand him. Kitty was telling me a story about the handsome, lanky cowboy caregiver, Don, who was busy feeding some llamas in the next pasture. Kitty rapped on the cage with the knuckle of one hooked finger.

"I really don't like him." Kitty lifted her chin toward Don quickly, then bent her head to glare at him from under her thunderous brow.

"You don't like him?" I asked. She glanced at me briefly and continued glaring at Don.

"You *are* giving him a really ugly look, Kitty."

"Don't like him one bit," she grunted, motioning for me to cram some more pomegranate through the cage.

"Well, I'd like to know the story behind that!"

"What else do you have in that bag, human girl?" Kitty asked, tossing her head toward my satchel.

"I got you some shoes." I pulled out the red foam gardening clogs that were fashionably appearing on everybody's feet these days. "Look here," I pointed to a design feature on the clog, "this hole is in the perfect place for your thumb."

"Huh," Kitty grunted, poking at the shoe through the cage mesh.

I put the shoes on and ran around on the lawn to demonstrate their utility. "See? Great, aren't they?"

"Okay, human girl, give them here and I'll try them." Kitty knocked on the fence with her knuckle again, and extended two fingers out towards me.

I pushed the foam clogs through the fencing with some difficulty. Kitty held them in her usual near-sighted way close to her face, examining them in minute detail. She placed them on her feet.

"Size ten," I commented.

"Huh," she grunted, "very nice." She nodded her head, removed the shoes, and tucked them up next to her on the straw seat. "Not very practical, though."

"No, I guess not," I agreed.

Kitty's cage-mate Midge sidled over and looked at the shoes. Kitty ignored him. Suddenly, Midge made a grab for the shoes. He managed to get one and went cantering off with a laugh. We watched him toss the shoe in the air, then place it on the ground and turn a summersault over it. Midge sat happily chewing the toe of the clog with one yellowed canine.

"He's not very deep," sighed Kitty.

"Huh," I grunted.

Kitty and I sat companionably through the afternoon, snacking and grooming. When it was time for me to go, Kitty stuck her lower lip through the cage for a kiss. As I drove out the ranch road, I stopped so Don could open the gate.

"Kitty gave you a real dirty look." I told him.

"Oh, well, she don't like me."

"Why not?"

"Oh, well, a few years ago she and the other chimps escaped and I had to chase 'em back into the cage."

"Huh."

"Only it wasn't all that simple - we got into a little tussle, and she nipped me pretty good."

"Wow, scary, sounds like you're the one that should be mad!" I prompted.

"Oh, well, 'course in the end I won and she's kind of held a grudge over it."

"Long time to hold a grudge."

"Yeah."

"You didn't use a rubber snake to chase her with, did you?"

"Oh, no, but I did have to show her my tranquilizer gun to convince her I meant business, and that aggravated her something powerful. Got her back in the cage, though."

"Huh."

"I've tried giving her grapes and fruit and such since, make it up to her, you know? But she just tries to scratch and grab at me. She's never forgiven me for that." He looked kind of sad as he gazed back at the enclosure where Kitty sat pronouncedly turning her back toward him.

"Yeah," I said, commiserating, "that's chimps for you: always remember a kindness, never forget a double-cross. Don't give up, Don. I'll bet you she'll come around if you keep giving her treats."

"Sure hope she doesn't get out again!" He laughed and waved me on.

I watched Kitty in my rearview mirror until I was out of sight of the Ranch. I wished I could tell her about the little boy, Roger, and how she had helped me to understand him and help him emerge from his shell of silence.

Roger was five years old when I met him. He was blonde, and occasionally when his eyes flickered up at me I saw that they were as blue as a summer sky in East Texas. He couldn't sustain eye contact for more than about thirty seconds. Then his eyes shifted downward again and he habitually returned to plucking the hair from a bare spot on the left side of his head. The back of his neck was scabbed from his nervous self-picking and his forearms were bruised from the many places he had bitten himself over time.

I had evaluated Roger in the tract home where he was living with his new foster parents. In my new career I evaluated children for developmental delays day-in and day-out. I had been at it for a decade, ever since I had left PRC and changed species. Mostly I evaluated neurodevelopmental problems, children with genetic diagnoses, and various kinds of sensorimotor dysfunction. Roger was the first child I had met who was suffering almost exclusively from the effects of environmental deprivation. I hadn't even been aware that children in our modern culture could be subject to such severe deprivation. His situation was the result of severe and intentional abuse inflicted by his drug-sick parents.

Every reflex and motor test I had given him was completely normal. Yet here he was, picking, biting, pulling out his hair and completely nonverbal. He used an odd assortment of gestures and gibberish, which I finally concluded was a private language he had created for himself. His foster mother reported that Roger would stand in front of a television for hours, even if it were off, rocking like another youngster I had known, Devon. Roger watched the silent, black screen, disregarding my presence with an intensity I could not disrupt.

Roger had been found in a small trailer on the edge of a tract of rural land in eastern Oregon. He was found accidentally when the local sheriff had made a large drug bust, arresting the child's mother and two other couples who apparently lived in the trailer, and who seemed to be running a methamphetamine lab. There were four children on the premises. Each of the children had been remanded to the State, and all were in very poor condition.

When they were taken into custody, their hair had been matted with a white, sticky dust that was part of the drug components. The doctor's office where the children had been examined had to be closed temporarily and decontaminated by a hazardous waste company. The two youngest, at three and four years of age, still wore diapers and drank from baby bottles. All of the children had bad teeth. None of the children spoke an intelligible dialect. They were bruised and unkempt and had been found locked in a nursery room with pads on the floor for beds and a large screen television as a baby sitter.

When presented with toys they stood in a confused silence, backing away. They did not know what the objects were, or how to play. They reminded me of some of the older chimpanzees I had helped to transition to new housing after they had spent years in solitary confinement. Anything new was suspect and to be feared. All of the children had terrible balance skills, weak muscle strength, extremely poor hand-eye coordination, and an inability or unwillingness to climb, run, jump or laugh. They all had various stereotypies just like Roger's; self-picking, hair pulling, rocking.

As I planned how to help Roger, I thought about what my chimpanzee friends had enjoyed. I remembered how they loved to groom and play, their silly antics, how they wanted to be chased, poked, prodded. Adam would have encouraged me to just sit quietly in my own occupation until he was ready to play. Kitty would have wanted food offerings, or objects to trade. Lennie would have wanted talking, grooming, and company.

One day, as Roger stood in his corner of the room watching the blank television screen, I impulsively galloped over to him in quadruped, making chimp laughter. I fell to the ground at his feet, and rolled over like the boys in Zane and Adam's group had done when they rough-housed. I made buzzing and clicking grooming sounds. I gently butted my head against his shoulder. I carefully groomed through Roger's hair while buzzing, just as I had many times with Kitty. He stood completely still. I galloped away in my chimp persona, jumping onto a pile of cushions on the couch, making soft woo-barks at him. I extended my hand toward him showing the back of my wrist.

I was surprised when Roger turned to watch me. When he saw my extended hand he moved toward me until he was a few feet away and held eye contact with me for over a full minute. I pant-hooted at him and performed more buzzing and clicking. There was a bowl of fruit on the dining room table. I walked over to the table in quadruped and took a sweet, blue plum. I began to eat it noisily, making small pant-grunts. He watched and then reached into the bowl, picked up an apple, smiled and laughed. It was Roger's first laughter since being brought into foster care.

Practically everything I had in my tool-box to help Roger I had learned from Kitty, Lennie, Adam and my other chimpanzee friends. They had been generous and kind in their friendship with me under the most difficult of circumstances for them. I looked at little Roger and smiled a human smile at him, watching his face grow closed again. To reach him I would have to be chimpanzee, not human. What Roger knew of humanity was to be feared. A completely unknown animal was by far safer and more humane, a creature that could be approached, perhaps trusted. By some instinct we both knew, but could not explain in words, Roger and I innately understood the ape language of body movement, gesture, and sound.

The sounds and gestures I used to engage him helped him feel safe. He had an immediate positive response. What we understood of each other moved at a deeper level of knowing than the superficial confines of human intellect could encompass. In the root of our being we possessed a common bond, something more expansive than being human, more primal. This bond was unquenchable, deep and as languorous as the warmth of the equatorial tropics. It beat in unison in our veins; it beat with a rhythm as perfect as the drumming cadence Sampson had practiced for me years before. From it, we recognized each other. I could see from the new animation in his eyes that Roger would make progress from this point onward in his life, and we could thank chimpanzees in biomedical research for it.

The day-to-day camaraderie my chimpanzee friends and I shared inside the concrete and steel world where they had lived was the best tool I had to remediate disabilities in children. Many of the disabilities I worked to ameliorate in children like Roger had been imposed upon them through the misuse of drugs, alcohol, pharmaceuticals, or through environmental toxins. Just as when I had worked with chimpanzees, most of their problems were the result of an environment that had been unjustly forced upon them. The tools I now used successfully as a health practitioner came from contributions that chimpanzees had been coerced into making to science; that much was true. But the tools I used did not come from data collected in the laboratory by inoculations, incisions, injections, and blood-chemistry data. They came wholly from my experience of humanity as it was shown to me by my ape cousins.

30096259R00143

Made in the USA
Charleston, SC
05 June 2014